The Fat

RICHARD GADZ

Deixis Press

Copyright © Richard Gadz 2024
All rights reserved.

The right of Richard Gadz to be identified as the author of this work has been asserted by him in accordance with the Copyright, Designs and Patents Act 1988.

This book is a work of fiction. Names, characters, businesses, and incidents either are products of the author's imagination or are used in a fictitious manner. Any resemblance to actual persons, living or dead, events, or locales is entirely coincidental.

First published in 2024 by Deixis Press
www.deixis.press

ISBN 978-1-917090-02-5 (HB)
ISBN 978-1-917090-03-2 (PB)

Typeset using Sabon LT Std by Palimpsest Book Production Ltd, Falkirk, Stirlingshire

Cover design by Deividas Jablonskis

The Eater of Flies

RICHARD GADZ

THE PLAYERS

ARTHUR FLEMMING ... a clerk, in the employ of Sir Edwin Gull

CAPT. VALENTINE HARKER ... an ex-soldier and widower

RUBY WESTER ... a music hall performer

LILY MURRAY ... a thief, friend of Ruby

CLIPPER ... an underworld associate of Lily's

JACK ... Lily's young son

MRS POTTER ... Lily and Jack's room mate

SIR EDWIN GULL ... MP, financier and landlord

LADY FRANCES GULL ... a philanthropist, wife of Sir Edwin Gull

---

HERBERT MAURICE ... a bookseller

WILLIAM BROWNING ... a journalist, in love with Ruby

JACOB RENFIELD ... a stage magician

DRACUL ... a vampyr

– THE BOX IS UNSEALED –

I

East of Braşov, Transylvania, 21st September 1867

The wedding was a chance for the whole village to put the Outbreak behind them and celebrate. Or so they thought.

The sparse, rural community for miles around Zinavsna had been plagued for months. Now that the horrors they'd faced had finally been driven out, the villagers were happy to seize on a good excuse to eat, drink and be as merry as they could possibly be.

Zinavsna was perched in the foothills of a sharp, gaunt mountain range which dominated the landscape all the way to the far horizon. Dark, jagged peaks formed austere guardians overlooking the village, sheltering it from easterly winds in the winter, breathing a cool breeze in the summer.

Forty or fifty wooden dwellings huddled on the slopes, in a vaguely semi-circular arrangement. Surrounding them were farms and allotments, marked out into crooked shapes by weary fences. Many of the farms raised pigs or goats, which were briskly traded along the dirt track that ran from the centre of the village, through dense woods, to the towns in the lowlands and by the rivers.

Standing a short distance apart from the other houses was the larger home of Radu Grosav, the local magistrate. He was a middle-aged, rosy-cheeked man who'd made his money in cured pork and who had never travelled more than thirty miles from Zinavsna in his entire life. He was loved and respected throughout the area for his fair-minded settling of disputes and for his selfless generosity, particularly during the country's upheavals back in '48. The villagers simply called him Şef, meaning 'boss.'

Although the chill of winter was rapidly approaching, the day of the wedding dawned warm and fine. As sunlight began to filter across the sky, half a dozen young men, one of them brandishing a violin and all of them wearing their best tunics – as freshly clean and white as their mothers could wash them – gathered outside the home of the groom, Cezar, to begin the traditions. They sang and shouted until a shutter was flung open on the upper floor and their friend presented himself with a loud cry of mock surprise. He was promptly pulled back from the window by his sister, who was trying to tug straight his smartly embroidered vest and his dark hat.

As soon as Cezar leaped from his front door, the customary Calling procession began in earnest. With the violin taking the lead, and a heavy flask of wine held aloft, the groom's party progressed in time with the music, laughing together as they took exaggerated, hopping steps.

Smiling faces peeked from nearby windows in

anticipation. Here and there, villagers stood at their doors and clapped along with the songs. Younger children had their ears covered by chuckling parents when the lyrics turned risqué. A couple of matronly ladies, their hearts filled with joy and nostalgia, snuggled together and watched the young men parade.

Cezar and his friends called at every house in turn, knocking theatrically and offering an overflowing cup to every householder while they danced through the downstairs rooms and out again. They were met with cheers and nods and grins, and soon a spirited chorus was snaking its way around the village, everyone dressed for the occasion. Almost the entire population gradually joined the procession, with Cezar towards the front being playfully jostled and plied with wine.

As tradition dictated, the final call was to the home of the bride, Talia. The procession shushed itself and gathered closely as Cezar glanced at his friends with a diffident smile, then rapped softly. The door was opened instantly by Talia's father, his face spread with a broad grin and his eyes recently dried.

"Cezar!" he cried.

There was a moment's silence before Cezar remembered. "Oh! I have come for the hand of my beloved!"

The procession cooed. Talia's father stepped aside to bring forward a figure covered over in a crocheted blanket. "Here she is, my boy! Here she is!"

He whipped the blanket aside to reveal Talia's grandmother, wrinkled and toothless, puckering up her lips with a gleam in her good eye. The procession exploded with laughter. Cezar guffawed and blushed.

"My bride!" he spluttered, trying to contain his mirth. "You've lost weight! Are you eating properly?"

The whole procession laughed again. Giggling, the old woman withdrew to reveal Talia in a new black and white dress, colourful flowers sewn in stripes down the skirt. Her hair was neatly tied and her soft features shone with nervous pride. Everyone applauded.

Cezar stepped inside, faces pressing behind him, necks craning. Talia moved to stand before a tall mirror which had been borrowed from Şef Grosav's house.

Cezar stood behind her and cleared his throat. Now then, three deceptions. As practised, many times. "I am not your Cezar, I am another, in disguise."

Talia flushed a deep pink. "I know you to be Cezar," she said timidly. "You can't fool me."

"You are still asleep, it's weeks until our wedding day!"

"I know I am awake," she smiled. "You can't fool me."

"I love you no longer," he said, placing the back of his hand to his forehead.

"You'd have run away if you weren't my true love. You can't fool me."

The procession was all melted hearts. As Cezar placed a wedding necklace over Talia's head, the oldest villagers whispered cosily to each other about what good deceptions the young man had thought up. The bride gave Cezar the traditional gift of a handkerchief in return, and to renewed cheers the villagers paraded back onto the wide area of open ground which the groom's home overlooked.

And now – tradition be damned! The village had much

more than a wedding to celebrate, with the Outbreak finally defeated! A special event like this demanded special arrangements! Şef Grosav, his elegant daughter-in-law and her baby son, came down the hill to shake the hands of the happy couple and to wish everyone the happiest, and most peaceful, of festivities.

While some stayed back to drag kitchen tables out onto the open ground and light fires to warm the cooking pots, the rest of the wedding party filled the beautifully ornate chapel built onto the side of Şef's house. By the time the ceremony had been completed, chairs had been assembled around the tables and the familiar, meaty aromas of *ardelenească* stew and *sarmale* were drifting in the air.

The sky had become a little overcast, but nothing could dampen the villagers' spirits today. The adults talked and laughed while the children ran around, gleefully chasing a piglet that had become untethered. Cezar and Talia were seated at the biggest table, beside Şef Grosav and his family, but out of nervous deference only spoke to the magistrate when they were spoken to. Grosav joshed them good-naturedly about the nuptials. His daughter-in-law told him not to embarrass the poor things, you dreadful old rogue. Cezar and Talia glanced at each other, delighted to be in such august company, their lips moving as if gently pulled towards their new spouse by magnetism.

Both of them were pretend-dragged from their seats to dance, first separately by their friends, and then together by everyone. Wine and beer were drunk by the bucketful – ah, just one more! there you go! oops, missed the cup! – and as the day wore on, the grass soaked up almost as much as the villagers, and the villagers soaked up their excesses with marbled Cozonac cake.

Fuelled by the warmth of the camaraderie, not to mention the warmth of the wine in their bellies, the revellers barely noticed the chill as the sun dipped to the horizon, flushing the mountains with wildly orange autumnal colours. More fires were lit, and time-honoured songs were roared by swaying voices, while those too drunk to sing clapped in an approximation of the beat.

Whether Cezar and Talia dropped the hint themselves, or whether one of their friends made a joke about wedding nights and thus set elbows twitching, there was a sudden, tumultuous agreement that it was high time the happy couple went off to bed. The drunkest shouted encouragements, the eldest cackled together and the rest of them banged their cups on the tables.

Şef Grosav wobbled to his feet. "Raise a glass to them! And to us! To all of us!" He paused for a moment, to let his mouth catch up with his thoughts. Joy and grief spun his expression from one extreme to another and back again. "To loved ones lost! We drown our sorrows! To survival, oh my dear friends! To the future!" He plonked back onto his seat.

The cheer that thundered forth was the loudest and proudest of the day, every cup held high, every heart swelling. Even in the midst of death, there is life!

Cezar and Talia managed to slip away, almost unnoticed, back to Cezar's family home. Not another soul was indoors tonight, and it would stay that way for hours.

Giggling, they raced up to Cezar's room. His little sister

had placed a posy of wild flowers on the bed, which Talia gently raised to her chest, smelling their sweet scent while Cezar hurriedly turned down the freshly laundered blankets.

The warm glow of the outside fires shone around the edges of the window shutters. The room was bathed in a soft, rosy light that seemed to hug the air. Cezar quickly placed a chair against the door, in case of mischievous kids, and fumbled with the little fasteners at his collar.

Talia smiled at him. "My mother is already talking about grandchildren," she said in a low voice.

"Well, we don't want to disappoint your mother," said Cezar earnestly, kicking away his shoes. He lay down on the white undersheet and began to wriggle out of his breeches. Talia, her gaze fixed on him, slowly untied the cords down her front, one by one, her fingers running to the end of each before letting it go. Outside, another rousing song began, the sound dulled to a bouncing stream of vowels.

Cezar struck up a recumbent pose, grinning at his bride. How beautiful she looked, how glowing and feminine, more vibrant than he'd ever seen her before. There was something different about her entire being today, something shining and alive. So very beautiful. Her eyes, huge and still, laying open his soul.

"What?" he smiled, nervously.

"You," she said softly. She bent slightly, placing a hand on the bedpost. Her body flowed to one side, moving gracefully into a feline crawl towards him.

He giggled. Her eyes, oh her eyes. Her mouth, her lips parting.

Her teeth clacking flatly together. Her jaw working, faster.

Closer to him, her limbs spidering. Closer.

"Your skin is smooth," she whispered. "Such a pretty container. A ripe apple."

Cezar's expression suddenly snapped into shock.

His gut twisted in panic, and his body tried to do the same, but her hand clamped over his mouth. Her legs wrapped tight around his, pinning him down. Her small and even teeth – snap! snap! Then her lips – wider! wider!

She struck, biting deep into the flesh of his upper arm. Pain screamed through him. Blood spilled rapidly. She buried her mouth in his chest, then into his side. From each hideous wound, she drew her husband's blood into herself, gulping, sucking, ripping, her face coated red, the bed splashed and spattered.

The loud partying of the revellers drowned out his agonised screams and her noisy drinking.

His body was found late the next morning, when his mother's gentle taps went unanswered. His body was pale and shrivelled, twisted into soaked blankets. Talia had escaped through the window.

The villagers had been so sure that the Outbreak was contained, but one vampyr was still at large, and it was occupying one of their own. Zinavsna still lay in the shadow of evil.

II

from the journal of Arthur Flemming

10th day of April 1868

The journey into Brașov was extremely uncomfortable, and the foul-smelling mud of the road has all but ruined the lower parts of my trousers. I had to contend with the violent jolting of the coach (<u>why</u> are rocks <u>so</u> liberally scattered on the Continental highways?) and also with the endless chatterings of a young woman and her chaperone as she variously: read aloud from a volume of travellers' reminiscences; remarked to her companion upon the sweetness of the lambs in the fields; remarked to her companion upon the stark grandeur of the Carpathians; asked me if I was intending to visit the Gothic Biserica Neagră, so named (how <u>fascinating</u>) because of the blackening it suffered in a fire?

I replied, politely, in the negative. By the time we arrived in Brașov I was burdened with an aching head and a frayed temper as well as an inconvenient laundry bill.

My accommodation is at an inn overlooking the Piața Sfatului, a broad, wedge-shaped market square out of which rises the town hall, with its tall, square clock tower pleasantly dinging the quarter-hours. After I'd changed clothes and eaten, and once I'd left my trousers with the genially nodding innkeeper to see what his wife could salvage of them, I felt considerably better.

It was too late in the day to travel any further, so I took a walk around the town, strolling at random among the narrow streets and passages. A number of the buildings have frontages painted in a variety of colours, while every steep and spiky roof is laid with identical red tiles. The overall effect is both quaint and picturesque, in charming contrast to the austere character of the surrounding country. The town is dominated by the heavily wooded mountain that curves in a shallow arch-shape behind it, and at the town's extremities I walked along several stretches of pock-marked medieval fortifications which speak of Transylvania's turbulent past.

I passed a busy array of shops, seemingly unmarked as such but with their wares visible through open doorways. At regular intervals I skirted jolly cafés, into which the locals appeared to have been herded in much the same way as the two flocks of sheep I encountered – for which I had to step aside – being driven along the streets!

With the air turning chilly, and being without my overcoat, I turned back in the direction of the inn. No sooner had I done so than I was accosted with a cheery wave by the young woman from the coach, and her chaperone, who were engaged in a short stroll similar to my own. Was I not impressed by the White Tower and the Black, both built in the fifteenth century? (Indeed!) Was I planning to take the excursion south-west to Bran Castle, haunt of the notorious Vlad III, the Impaler? (Perhaps, time permitting.) Had I noticed an eatery of sufficiently clean appearance? (Regretfully not.)

11th day of April 1868

I slept surprisingly well and presented myself at eight o'clock for breakfast, which turned out to be ham and eggs. I asked the innkeeper about transport to Zinavsna, trying to make it clear that I required a large cart or similar, for collecting goods.

However, as soon as the name of my destination was mentioned, the innkeeper's wife – who has worked miracles with my trousers, I'm relieved to say – visibly blenched and retreated to her kitchen, leaving her husband to twist a tea-towel in his hands and attempt to convey the local community's opinion on the subject of Zinavsna. Through his fractured and stumbling English, clarified a little by mime and hand movements, I managed to gather that the village suffered some sort of dreadful trouble a few months ago. At first, I thought the man was warning me that the place was plagued with a deadly disease, and I was thoroughly alarmed as a consequence! However, what I eventually gleaned from his wide eyes and fluttering fingers was that there had in fact been a spate of violence, but that now – after a second wave (or brief rekindling) of the problem

– Zinavsna had become both peaceful and (I think) 'unhappy.'

I thanked him heartily for his alert. What he was attempting to convey, I concluded, was that Zinavsna has fallen victim to one or two of the bands of armed militia, loyal to the old regime, which are widely reported to have incommoded the countryside of late, intent on stirring unrest. Naturally, he wasn't aware that my entire journey has only become possible now that the military dictatorship of Transylvania is ending. Thankfully, with Franz Joseph returning to the throne under the old Hungarian constitution, my employer can finally press his claim, hence my presence. It seems I was wise to take advice and bring a cosh.

Still evincing a peculiar reluctance to see me complete my task, the innkeeper obtained a stoutly built cart for me to hire, complete with a driver whose odorous attire was entirely in keeping with his sour expression and darkly greased hair. The innkeeper gave him his instructions and the man glanced at me dubiously before taking his seat behind a pair of thin, elderly-looking horses.

We travelled for a little over three hours, up overgrown tracks and through narrow passes where jagged rock-faces rose high to left and right. There is something bleak and forbidding about this landscape, as if the land and the mountains were resentful of occupation, as if they harboured a grudge against the human race. Despite the brightness of the daylight, the sky felt low and oppressive. I pulled my coat around my shoulders. At last we reached:

Zinavsna

What a god-forsaken place! The cart, having passed a series of unkempt and overgrown enclosures, pulled to a halt in what I took to be the centre of the village, an open area surrounded by simple wooden huts and buildings. I clambered down onto the rutted grass while the driver untied the horses and let them drink from a nearby trough.

With my briefcase clutched under my arm, I surveyed the scene with a certain despondency. All these dwellings were rustic, time-worn and functional, none of them a likely home for the man I'd come to see. A dog wandered around and in between the houses, sniffing at corners, its head keeping low to the ground. Somewhere a child cried. The only villagers visible were a handful of labourers, scattered among open doorways, each of whom stood still and silent, watching me with undisguised suspicion.

The very air itself seemed heavy with – how best can I describe it? – a sense of <u>sorrow</u>, of something irretrievably absent. I had an impression, gleaned from closed shutters and cleared-out herb planters, that some of the houses were uninhabited. I have never found myself in a location so hushed and so profoundly ill at ease, so strangely lonely.

The effect was unnerving in the extreme, even macabre. I could only surmise that the military brigands who had passed this way were responsible for <u>many deaths</u> and that consequently the villagers were deeply distrustful of strangers. I shuddered inwardly.

It was with trepidation that I raised a hand in greeting. After observing me for a few moments more, one of the labourers slowly approached with a farm implement swinging from one hand.

"Good day to you," I said, in as friendly a manner as my apprehension would allow. "My name is Flemming."

The labourer glanced over to the driver of the cart, who simply sniffed and inclined his head as if to say 'this is <u>his</u> business, and none of mine.' The labourer gazed warily at me.

I cleared my throat. "I'm here to meet with Radu Grosav."

"Grosav? Şef Grosav?" he said suddenly.

I took some of the papers from my briefcase and consulted them. "No, the name is definitely Radu. Would this Şef be a relative?"

The man's eyes filled with tears. "El este mort," he said, his voice cracking.

Even I could tell what that meant. My heart sunk and my eyes closed for a second. "Of all the damned luck," I muttered to myself.

The man said something softly and patted at my shoulder. I couldn't begin to work out why.

"This other Grosav," I said. "Is he here? How does the late Mr Grosav's estate currently stand?"

The man looked blank and I repeated myself, a little louder, trying to copy the way the innkeeper down in Braşov had illustrated his words through play-acting. However, I must confess that the news of Grosav's demise set my mood darkening and my mind whirling, imagining all manner of tortuous legal obstacles that might now be flung in my way.

Fortunately, via both of us acting the mummer, I was able to ascertain that Grosav's residence was a short distance up the hill and that one member of the family – a daughter or daughter-in-law, I could not work out which – was still living there. With a smile and a nod, I bid the man show me the way, and without further comment he led me out of the village, the scattered handful of his fellow labourers watching me intently and continuously.

My nerves settled once I was out from under their magnifying glass. Behind a shield of trees, and situated in a clearing at the end of a winding footpath, there was a generously proportioned two-storey mansion. It was in exactly the same plain-fronted, red-tiled form as the buildings in Braşov, in all respects but one: at its right-hand end was a wide, rounded extension which, from the coloured glass in its arched windows, I took to be a chapel or chantry.

The labourer left me in the hands of an ancient servant, of melancholy countenance, who conducted me to a sitting room in which I was silently directed to wait. In appraising the mansion, I noted the simple whitewash of the walls, the heavily trafficked flagstone floorings, the high wooden beams. The room in which I sat, although not particularly large, was cold and echoing. Of furnishings, there were many. Hefty wooden sideboards and bookshelves dominated each side of a tall, empty fireplace, and an equally weighty table was placed beneath the window, the daylight from which was filtered and dampened by the proximity of the trees outside.

Across the table were spread a great number of papers and ledgers, arranged haphazardly as if someone had been poring over them with no real idea of their contents or significance. An impressive pair of candlesticks had been drawn aside to accommodate the heaped documents. Throughout the rest of the room, barely a flat surface was free of copious ornaments and *objects d'art*. I concluded, as my gaze roved around, that Radu Grosav must have been a collector of taste. In several places there were grouped porcelain figurines which, to my admittedly inexpert eye, might have been by Bustelli or possibly Kändler.

Upon turning to look at whatever might be positioned behind me, I saw a large painting that immediately excited my interest: a woodland scene in which human figures, intent upon each other's company, were framed by Classical statues around which fluttered nymphs and cherubs chased by horrible, ghostly forms. At first glance I took the scene as belonging to the Baroque school, but from its curves and colours I realised it was more likely late Rococo – or rather *Rocaille* – in style. I felt sure it was by Jean-Honoré Fragonard!

At that moment, the gloomy servant returned with a woman to whom I shall refer simply as Miss Grosav, since embarrassment prevented me from asking her to repeat her Christian name a third time. She sat opposite me while the servant remained by the door, watching me in as hawk-like a manner as the villagers.

Miss Grosav was beautiful, rather statuesque, with bronzed skin and dark, fluid eyes. Her fair hair was firmly tied back and the simple white dress she wore was both practical and uncluttered. From her general appearance, I judged her age to be perhaps no more than five-and-twenty. Although she was friendly and welcoming towards me, offering me refreshment and smiling as she indicated for me to retake my seat, her demeanour was unmistakably wan and troubled. She had a weight upon her shoulders that went beyond mere <u>bereavement,</u> a terrible burden of – fear? guilt? – that seemed to engulf and oppress her. Clearly, her relationship with the deceased must have been a particularly close one and it struck me that, to judge from her manner and the atmosphere of the village, the recent ransacking by loyalist militia must have been brutal.

I marvelled that the mansion itself appeared undamaged and had obviously escaped attack by the looters, no doubt due to its more isolated position. I remarked upon this fact, but it was quickly evident that the lady spoke no English either, and nor did her valet. However, she was fluent in French and as my command of that language is serviceable, we were able to conduct a rather halting dialogue.

Once I had introduced myself, I found I lacked the precise vocabulary needed in order to express my distress at the news of her recent troubles, although my admiring comments relating to the artworks around us did communicate themselves to her. I gathered from her that the collection, which was housed in this room and two others, had been assembled by earlier generations of the Grosav family, at a time when the family's fortunes were considerably greater than their current state. She said that – I think it was her husband's(?) grandfather, or great-grandfather? – had travelled widely in Europe. He'd had artistic sensibilities which, it seems, baffled and amused later generations. However, the collection now evoked only sad memories for her. The woodland scene behind me, she found positively distasteful!

(At this point, I took a moment's opportunity to have a closer look at the painting, casually. <u>Indeed</u> – by Fragonard!)

With admirably providential timing, she dispensed with this pleasant chit-chat and asked me what had brought me all the way from London. Was I a partner in one of Radu's commercial interests? Was I offering to buy up the mercantile firm he had owned?

I took a handful of the official papers from my briefcase and, resting them across my knees, passed some of them over for her perusal as I explained the situation. I said it was my sad duty to inform her that the late Mr Grosav's business interests consisted of nothing but debts; I was given to understand that Mr Grosav's considerable assets in local land had been sold off some years ago and that at the time of his death his income relied solely on overseas investments.

The lady's cheeks paled slightly and, glancing over at the untidily laden table, she told me that the family's finances were dealt with through Bancă Tovărăşesc in Budapest. She added something to the effect that the sale of land had enabled financial aid to be given to Zinavsna and other villages, but as her voice was very low at that moment, I had difficulty distinguishing her words and it seems somewhat absurd that this was what she actually meant.

I said that a number of loans had been arranged by Mr Grosav through Bancă Tovărăşesc and that upon default these had been sold on to Crédit Métropole in Paris, who in turn had passed them to the London consortium which I was hereby representing. The sum owed, taking into account the interest and fees due, now totalled £511, 9s and 2d. A very considerable sum, unfortunately, hence my attending to the matter in person rather than via an intermediary. I passed her the document I had obtained through the relevant embassy in London which set out, in both Hungarian and Romanian, my authority to remove goods from the possession of Radu Grosav to the value of the above sum, their value to be calculated at my discretion.

I sat quietly while she read through the document, a shaking finger scanning the lines methodically. At last, after sitting silently for a moment or two, she folded the paper up and slipped it into a skirt pocket. She stood and, with a shrug and a huffing breath, swept a hand to encompass all the room's minor treasures.

"Prenez ce que vous voulez – *have what you want*," she said quickly, her eyes taking in everything around her except me. Her expression became impassive and her voice chilled. "*It is yours. My father*[-in-law?] *would not want his* [foreign?] *debts to go unpaid.*"

I gave a single nod and thanked her for her understanding and her generosity. I obtained her signature on a copy of the document while she asked that my activities be confined to the ground floor and not include the private apartments on the upper storey. I replied that I would be most happy to oblige, provided my valuations allowed this to be possible.

With that, Miss Grosav drew herself up to her full height, swatted briefly at her cheeks as she bid me good-day, and quietly withdrew. Her gloomy servant, having not understood our transactions, was left in a quandary as to whether to follow his mistress or attend to my request to summon the cart from the village. I assumed I would see no more of the lady, but I was wrong.

An Ornate House of Prayer

In keeping with the policy of my employer – indeed, with his <u>express</u> instructions before I left London – I assessed the monetary value of each item I examined with a sceptical and rigorous frugality, keeping a detailed written record as I proceeded. The cart I had hired was well stocked with sacking, so pieces such as the figurines and the Fragonard painting from the sitting room could be safely wrapped for the return journey to town prior to their being properly boxed for shipping.

I was left very much to my own devices, with Miss Grosav's valet making occasional appearances to check on my progress. Now and again he stalked distantly through whichever chamber I happened to be in, ineffectively pretending to be merely about his duties or passing from A to B.

The three rooms in which the objects on display made

up the Grosav ancestor's collection were a treasury of interesting artefacts. There were further paintings, including portraits in the Venetian school by Tiepolo, Guardi (a fine regatta scene) and Piazzetta; there were metal plates and dishes of Greek design; there were Oriental boxes and teapots, with tiny handles fashioned in the shape of fish or dragons.

I had collated a total of nearly £475 when my wanderings took me through an arched opening set back from a hallway. A short passage suddenly turned to the right and I found myself in the built-on chapel that I had observed to one side when approaching the house.

It was surprisingly large, consisting of one very tall open space, glitteringly decorated in the ornate Eastern Orthodox style. Dusty shafts of many-coloured light, dulled by outside foliage like the light through the sitting room window, rolled around its cavernous interior.

It was also surprisingly cold. No church of my experience has ever been deserving of the word 'cosy' yet this one was chilling in the extreme. My breath ghosted as I stepped among the ranks of short wooden benches which occupied much of the bright, mosaic floor. Oval incense burners hung on long chains from beams high above, and the broad altar that I now faced was overlaid with colourful cloth and festooned with assorted bowls, chalices and icons.

My footsteps echoed in the stillness. As I approached the altar, I shuddered from a sensation which ran deeper in my veins than the chill of the air. I felt a strange and inauspicious sense of unease, as if some form of supernatural emanation, invisible and intangible, was sitting upon my very shoulder and eyeing me with curiosity.

I spun on my heels, thinking myself observed, but there was no sign of the lugubrious valet. I quickly pulled myself together, reasoning that I was letting myself be influenced by the mansion's mournful ambiance, by the inhospitable nature of the landscape and the villagers, and by exotic superstitions relating to holy sites.

My fears were cast aside entirely when I stood beside the altar and saw, upon lifting one of the chalices, that these objects were made of <u>gold</u>, and that half a dozen of them would readily furnish the remainder of the debt owed to my employer. Consequently, I set aside the most antique pieces, added them to my written notes, and was about to conclude my business for the day when I thought to myself: if valuables, independent of the *objects d'art* in the rest of the house, are placed in plain sight upon the altar, then perhaps—?

I looked around the chapel, along the stone walls and into alcoves and niches, intrigued by the possibility of further finds. However, there appeared to be none. Once again, I prepared to depart, when a peculiar <u>intuition</u> – I can scarcely account for it, otherwise – gripped me and I was drawn back to the altar. For a few moments, my fingers ran along the coarse fibres of its colourful covering and an icy sentiment nipped at my nerves.

Slowly, I tipped myself to one side, to look at the narrow gap between the rear of the altar and the stone wall. There, as clear as day, was a sizeable <u>hole</u> where the material had been cut open. I leaned closer and saw, slid into a recess, what I immediately suspected to be the most precious thing I had yet found. Eagerly, I reached down and placed my hand on its surface – and the moment I did so, a thrill ran through me which I might ordinarily have claimed to be terror but which in this instance was surely nothing more than the excitement of discovery.

It was a box, evidently Oriental in origin, roughly two feet in length, one foot in width and one in height, raised on black, wooden wedge-shapes at each corner. Its sides and lid were overlaid with the most exquisitely beautiful *cloisonné* enamel I had ever seen, the metal lines delicately worked into intricate curling patterns, and the inlay rendered in many shades of blue, a technique I believe the Chinese call *jingtailan*.

I wedged myself deeper into the dusty gap in order to take a proper hold of it. The thing was <u>immensely</u> heavy! It was only with great strain to my lower back that I managed to haul it free of its hiding place and set it down upon the altar. The box was certainly of significant age, possibly hundreds of years old.

Judging by its great weight, I reasoned that it contained more gold – possibly a great deal more – and judging by the lack of dust on its surfaces, which showed that it had only recently been concealed, I reasoned that this concealment of gold must have been undertaken for the very purpose of <u>evading</u> Mr Grosav's creditors!

It was only when I had dabbed the sweat from my brow with my handkerchief that I saw the thing had been deliberately vandalised. In the chapel's half-light I hadn't noticed that the flat lid, which was inlaid into the upper surface rather than forming the topmost part of the box itself, had been sealed shut. Looking closer, I could see that all four sides of the lid had been crudely fused with a thick and continuous band of molten lead. Into the cooled metal had been scratched a long line of words in what I took to be one of the Transylvanian dialects.

Once I had huffed and tutted and overcome my annoyance at such an outrageous act, I wondered what the devil had been its purpose? I reassured myself that, with great care, the seal could most probably be removed and the box restored. Whatever was inside must be of <u>such value</u> that it was worth the damage caused and the trouble taken to shut it away like this.

Frowning in curiosity, I heaved at one end of the box and raised it. Something shifted inside! A weight slid from the upper end to the lower.

There was now no question but that this elegant piece should join the others I had acquired. With some awkwardness, I scooped the box up in my arms and carried it through the mansion, feeling the flush of effort on my face and in the strain on my knees.

As I stepped out into the open air, I was overtaken by the valet, who must have been lurking somewhere along my path. He began to speak in a manner far more animated than hitherto, continuously pointing at the box and expressing himself in urgent and pleading tones. I had the notion that perhaps he had been charged with its concealment and was much concerned that he would now be in trouble with his mistress.

His voice became more strident as I hauled the box onto the rear of the hired cart, although at no point did he attempt to take it from me, or even to touch it, apparently afraid to do so. As I covered it with the last of the sacking, he disappeared back into the house, calling wildly.

The cart was quite heavily laden, with wrapped items secured by a series of thick cords tied in a lop-sided web. Knowing that there would be little-or-no chance of the driver going easy on the return journey, I climbed into the rear of the cart myself, to keep the cargo steady, despite the discomfort this would inevitably cause. The driver gathered the reins and turned to give me a look that was simultaneously disinterested and disdainful.

The moment the cart was set in motion, I heard a loud clatter from above. Looking up, I saw Miss Grosav leaning far out of a high window, calling loudly in her native tongue. She pointed towards the chapel end of the house, her face awash with what I took to be anger – the distance, and her agitation, denied me a clear view of her features – her voice becoming ever more shrill and her gesticulations ever more wild.

The driver glanced at me and I nodded him onward. With the cart picking up a little more speed, the valet came running out and <u>gave chase</u>, if you please, shouting lamentations with arms extended! I motioned for the driver to chivvy the horses along.

The valet was still at our heels when we drove back through the village. He began to address his cries to the other villagers as well as to me, and a number of them quickly joined him. For some moments I was fearful that this rabble might bring the cart to a halt, or drag me down from it, and my stomach suddenly rolled in horror, but I soon saw that their attack was to be a verbal one only. They had ample opportunities to grab hold of the cart's sides, or to run ahead and block the way, but they took none. They held back, their faces fearful and wide-eyed, as if their strong emotions were not strong enough to overcome some peculiar reluctance they had to take action. Their objections and exhortations seemed perfectly sincere, yet there was some dreadful, over-riding consideration which prevented their interference.

I expect the truth is that they saw their only sensible course of action was to allow me to carry out my duties unhindered. They must have been cognisant of the simple fact that to delay my work – or to frustrate it entirely – would cause significant <u>financial</u> and <u>legal</u> repercussions.

The journey back into town was a worrying one. Any time I did not spend watching the road behind for signs of ill-advised pursuit, I spent attempting to steady everything around me against the violent rocking of the cart.

I was most relieved to arrive at the inn and I immediately made arrangements to get all the items properly crated for shipping. I am happy to report that there were no breakages.

III

from the journal of Arthur Flemming

<u>26th day of May 1868</u>

It was only after considerable delay and paperwork that I was finally able to book passage for myself (and over a dozen packing crates of assorted sizes) aboard a Russian schooner, *Demeter*, which weighed anchor at Varna on the 11th May. I was unable to secure sufficient space on an earlier vessel, and so was forced to take a berth on a ship that would not dock in London. The *Demeter* was inconveniently bound for Whitby, far to the north. However, as my trip had already taken rather longer than anticipated, I judged that a further day or two travelling south would not make matters too much the worse.

I left my (at last!) final stopping point of the journey, a coach house inn not far from St Albans, before sunrise this morning, since the day was promised to be a very warm one (although, as it has turned out, it has not been) and since I wanted to be back in my lodgings before noon. My transport, a sturdy goods delivery vehicle for rent via the coach house, was far superior to that in Transylvania and its owner, a Mr Birch of Walthamstow, seemed competent and to know his place – at first!

We gained sight of London just after dawn, having traversed a small wooded area and begun a gentle descent down a long hill lined with new houses built for the artisan class. Already, the air was taking on a yellowish tint, the heaving pall of sulphurous soot and steam which speaks so clearly of the city's mighty engines of commercial industry. Every time I return from a business trip, I find I must re-acclimatise to the city's atmosphere and odour. As the cart descended the hill, the southerly breeze brought the familiar, seething reek of massed humanity but, as ever, in writing these words some hours later I cannot detect it at all.

Glimpsing the London vista from that high hill, it was possible to perceive the capital's scrapbook nature, as perhaps only an outside observer can – this vast web of villages and districts, stitched together over centuries to create the growing, beating heart of the world. A living thing, expanding and pulsing, the sight of which is surely the pride of any Englishman.

I Am Witness to a Vile Scene

I was unaware that Mr Birch of Walthamstow had deliberately deviated from the most direct route to our destination until it was <u>too late</u>! It was only when we had driven down the Goswell Road and circled around the meat market that I knew we had travelled too far east. I challenged Mr Birch of Walthamstow in reference to our location and he feigned ignorance, claiming that this was his habitual way of progress towards the river.

His true purpose soon became clear. We passed St Bartholomew's and entered (I think) Giltspur Street, at which point I could both hear and see the <u>immense</u> crowd that had gathered along Old Bailey, blocking off the streets to the north entirely, and concentrating tightly into the open area beside the Newgate prison.

He wanted to see the execution of the Irishman, Barrett! The cart was soon jammed into the general mêlée and then: dear me, sir, says Mr Birch of Walthamstow, how <u>unfortunate</u> and <u>unforeseen</u>, sir, we are <u>stuck</u> here for the time being, sir, says he, and <u>oh</u>, with an excellent view of proceedings, by the way.

Of course, I initially knew neither the name nor nationality of the person condemned, but once we were stationary, Mr Birch of Walthamstow – with repugnant salaciousness – most kindly furnished me with the full history of the miscreant, his crimes, his trial and his imminent consignment into the flames of Hell itself, as related to Mr Birch the previous evening, in Walthamstow, at the Cross Keys public house.

Outside the hulking, block-like edifice of the prison itself, a hefty platform, some ten feet above the street, had been built for the occasion. It was made from wood which had been stained black, as was the high rectangular frame of the gallows which rose up from it. From the centre of the uppermost horizontal beam hung the rope, already noosed, the instrument of execution. A barrier, manned by police, kept the pressing sightseers back from the temporary construction.

The crowd – men, women and children, many hundreds in number – seemed to ebb and flow like the muddy shores of the river, by turns sombre and jubilant. There was laughter, there were shouts, there was the singing of popular songs from a myriad throats at a time, as the masses swayed and surged. Some made isolated and inaudible speeches, some danced, some circulated to sell pies or penny pamphlets. A girl who fainted was lifted up and borne away aloft on many hands, accompanied by jeers and hoots. More than once a violent scuffle broke out, raising further commotion. A ragged-looking man broke off from the edge of the crowd and staggered out of sight, his nose badly bloodied.

I don't believe I have ever seen so large a gathering, most certainly not at such an early hour of the day. Those in the tightest press of bodies, closest to the scaffold, must surely have secured their places in the dead of night!

I have always had a nervous dread of crowds. The feeling of <u>enclosure</u> and <u>entrapment</u>. They have a suffocating life of their own, like some hideous wriggling beast with a thousand legs. There is much to be said for a little solitude.

A few minutes before sentence was due to be carried out, a dog-cart inched its way to the door of one of the buildings opposite the prison, flanked by policemen who battered at the crowd with sticks in order to let the vehicle through. The well-to-do lady and two gentlemen who were perched on the cart quite rightly paid no attention to the loud and baying disrespect of the rabble, and alighted to enter the building with the casual air of a stroll in the park. Catcalls and waved fists continued until the lady appeared at one of the upper windows. She flung a handful of coins over their heads, and they overlooked their animosity as they scrambled and scratched among themselves.

At that moment, there came the distant ringing of a bell and the condemned man appeared from inside the prison. An almighty cheer rang out, a tumultuous and horrible yell that was in equal parts vengeful anger and raucous amusement. He stepped onto the high platform ahead of several police and a priest, who read aloud from a Bible, addressing himself only to the prisoner.

"Fenian devil," muttered Mr Birch of Walthamstow.

Devil or not, I thought he cut a surprisingly dignified figure, dressed in a short, plum-coloured coat and striped trousers. He did not, to me, appear like one who would stoop to murder any individual, let alone explode a bomb in Clerkenwell and kill many.

I felt my heart beating in my chest. The nauseous grotesquerie of such a scene! The cackling <u>screech</u> of the mob! It seemed as if directly opposing forces were welling up amongst them, a sneering hatred of this man on the one hand, a chuckling indifference to his fate on the other. I was sickened by it all. It is irresponsible and dangerous to stir aggressive passions in the masses. <u>Thank goodness</u> these judicial dispatches are soon to be handled <u>inside</u> prison walls, and will no longer be the subject of entertainment for roughs and idlers!

The condemned stood his ground, making no acknowledgement of the noise around him, listening only to the words of his priest. Without warning, the hangman stepped forward and placed a hood over the prisoner's head.

For the first and only time, the sound of the crowd flickered out, like the extinguishing of a flame. There was absolute silence. I'm sure I could hear the harsh rubbing of rope as the noose was pulled about the prisoner's neck, and the sound of his boots as he was placed atop the trapdoor.

The crack of the bolt being pulled aside echoed up the street.

The prisoner dropped! – and was still. His neck must have snapped instantly.

An enthusiastic whoop of pleasure surged forth from the mob. I was left feeling jittery and miserable. The crowd began to disperse at once, all except for a small, perverse minority who were staying to see the dead man cut down.

After a few minutes, our cart was able to be on its way. Mr Birch of Walthamstow seemed pleased with himself, but said nothing more. I tried to overcome my shuddering disgust by turning my thoughts to matters in hand and my schedule for the day.

I deposited the crates from Transylvania as instructed, and at long last returned to my rooms. I have bathed and dined and next I shall call upon my aunt whose delicate health, I expect to learn, has become upset while I have been away. Then, I must find my employer and relay to him the good news about my voyage.

IV

As the long shadows of the evening stretched hazily across London, the dome of St Paul's peered down into the oily air of the streets. To its west was the broad, continuous thoroughfare leading from Ludgate Hill, through the slow curve of Fleet Street, to the Strand, then on to Charing Cross and the grandeur of Northumberland House. Halfway, the spires of St Clement Danes and St Mary's pierced up past their surroundings, each church on its own island in the road, like two giant ducklings swimming madly upstream to reach their cathedral mother.

All along this thoroughfare, an unending teem of people, transactions, endeavours. Day and night, babbling in flows and tides past the ducklings, down the maze of squeezing side streets and alleyways, posh hotels and infested slums, the moneyed and the penniless, the lost and the pleasure-seeker, the boozer, the leech, the criminal, the banker.

West through Fleet Street, past pubs, shops, and newspaper offices; under the ornate arched bulk of Temple Bar and then, immediately on the right, a wide area of cleared and levelled earth, between the top of the Strand

and Carey Street, a phoenix-to-be in the municipal urge to rebuild and modernise; past the lights of King's College and Somerset House, and on down the Strand, its theatres and private clubs of every type and reputation.

In a well-lit street, not far from the Lyceum and the Covent Garden market, stood Holmwood's Music Hall, its name proclaimed in brightly coloured lettering from which only one of the *o*'s was missing. Patrons filed into the front of the building, while two young women lifted their skirts to hop-and-step down the muddy side alley that led to the artistes' entrance.

One of the women was a performer. Ruby Wester skipped ahead, her dark hair boldly loose, her lips boldly rouged and her red-and-black dress bold all over. Lively and gregarious, she was the sort of person to whom all eyes would dart when she entered a room.

Hired as a singer, she was nine weeks into a six-month engagement at Holmwood's. She also acted in some of the nightly melodramas, if any of the bit-players didn't turn up, and was on-stage assistant to the hall's current illusion act: Renfield! Sensational Swami of the Stage!

The fact that she was the discreet mistress of an unnamed wealthy West End habitué was an open secret. The fact that she'd already blackmailed three wealthy West End habitués – and intended to blackmail this one too when a convenient opportunity arose – was a secret she kept to herself.

Her companion that evening, Lily Murray, lived in one of the nearby tenements with her eight-year-old son. She was a year or so younger than Ruby but the two of them had been friends since childhood when their mothers, both long since dead, had worked at the same tannery south of the river.

Lily was fair and waif-like, with pale eyes and a delicately rounded face, smog-sanded from a lifetime in the city. She dressed as well as her wafer-thin income would allow, and behind her deceptively gauche manner she was watchful, thoughtful, her heart sewn firmly to her sleeve. Her nimble mind and ingenuity might have taken her far, had circumstances been different, but like Ruby she'd grown up inside the web of the city's intricate underclass, the parallel economy which sustained and ensnared the majority of the local population. At one time she'd been tempted to follow her friend onto the stage, but she didn't share Ruby's flair for performance or her need for applause.

The two of them breezed into the music hall's backstage labyrinth, Ruby's heavily heeled shoes clattering on the wooden boards. As they made their way to the curtained-off dressing areas they hallo-ed and y'allright-ed any familiar faces who crossed their path in costume or out, the air heavy with the smells of pale ale and human activity.

Close to Ruby's dressing table, beneath a gas mantle sputtering its warm glow, a boy was dipping a cloth into a cup of warm water and vinegar. In front of him, up on end, was a hefty and expensive-looking coffin with its attached lid opened wide. The coffin's exterior was colourfully decorated with mystic symbols copied from an old book, while its interior had been stripped out and painted black. The boy swung down a hinged sheet of glass that ran from top to bottom inside. It clicked into place at a steep angle, then he vigorously began to rub the cloth over it.

Beside him, Jacob Renfield sat scowling. "Have a care, boy! That's my mystical spirit cabinet you're washing, not some tart's knickers! You break it and that's a pretty penny you'll owe me!" He was a thin, bony old man, with a heavily lined face and wattled neck. His white hair was flattened back by its own natural grease rather than with any fancy pomade. His once-smart stage outfit had changed very little in the forty-eight years of his career, but in recent months he'd added a navy blue cloak to it, to give himself a more dashing air of mystery.

He glanced up at Ruby. "You're late. Where have you been?"

"I do beg your pardon," smiled Ruby, her stage voice moulded into the crystal tones of a seasoned entertainer. "I was waylaid by Viking bandits on the Northumberland road and it took me half! an! hour! to slice them all up and escape on horseback."

Renfield's lips wrinkled as if he'd tasted something nasty. His eyes narrowed at Lily. "And who are you?"

"This is Miss Murray, a lady of refinement," said Ruby, "who's just downed two whole meat pies from Fishwick's in the two minutes my back was turned!"

Lily swiped her on the arm. "I was hungry. And now I'm off."

Ruby kissed her on the cheek. "Not staying for the show?"

"My Jack's been with Mrs Potter all day. She gets tired, bless her."

Renfield tapped her arm and wagged a hand at the

glass screen inside his mystical spirit cabinet. "You haven't seen this, girl. Don't you give my secrets away."

"What, these secrets?" cut in Ruby. "The ones you nicked from the show at the Royal Polytechnic?"

"And I'll have more respect from the likes of you, thank you very much!" He folded his gnarled hands around each other, muttering cheerlessly. "I was the marvel of City Road. I packed them in at the Eagle and the Green Gate."

Lily weaved her way through the crossover and around dangling ropes and pulleys. She excused herself past a barely contained argument over a gambling debt and gave a wide berth to Mr Holmwood, the chairman himself, who was vowing to skin these ruddy performing dogs alive if they dropped their guts here on his stage just one more time, so help him God. She flickered around the edge of a tall red curtain and emerged into the rush of sound and light that filled the vastness of the crowded music hall. With only a few minutes to go before the evening's performance, the place bounced with a rowdy atmosphere of good-natured anticipation. It was a gorgeous palace of excess, a haven of beauty and opulence where patrons could escape the harsh and stifling greyness of a meagre life, and all for sixpence. Or, devoted patrons, why not splash out another 9d for a seat upstairs?

The apron of the stage jutted out far enough to accommodate the resident musicians, three violins and a piano, tucked tightly together to one side. Above, rose a magnificent proscenium arch, curved and curling like a fever dream of ancient Greece. From the high, symmetrically decorated ceiling hung a series of gasoliers festooned with rows of glowing glass orbs. Below, five long lines of dining tables radiated out from close to the stage, filled with people eating stew or sandwiches, knocking back porter and ale: couples young and old, families from baby to grandmother, groups of workers from the offices in Fleet Street or the basement meat market further down the Strand. Other customers packed the walkways and the wide standing area at the back, engaging in animated conversation or striking up little entertainments of their own, telling dirty jokes or roaring a chorus or two from a well-known song.

Light glittered along the Classical designs of the immense upper balcony which glided lithely around three sides of the auditorium. Up here, where reputable ladies never set foot, men of all kinds smoked and drank in anonymous, informal female company. Arms lounged on balustrades and girls leaned into each other and smiled.

Back down near the stage, Lily spotted someone she needed to speak to. Sitting at a nearby table, where those arriving alone had drifted together like scraps in a sieve, was a portly gentleman with a jowly face. His tiny spectacles would have been barely visible against his eyes if not for the long cords of metal that tied them to his fleshy ears.

". . . I'm afraid not, sir," he said to a younger man across the table, inclining his potato head and smiling with pursed lips. "Although I do know the person to whom you refer, since Mr Whittlecome collects rents on a number of local properties near my own establishment. You're seeking new lodgings?"

"I am," said the young man, whose trimmed moustache

and cherry complexion were topped with an unruly drift of sand dunes, "and I must be moved within a fortnight."

The portly gentleman nodded sagely at the young man's ink-stained fingers. "You keep ledgers of account?"

"I'm a reporter."

"Ah, then the dissemination of knowledge is our common goal, sir."

They exchanged cards, Mr Herbert Maurice, Purveyor of New & Divers Books, Frye Court, London and Mr William Browning, *London Daily Examiner*, Fleet Street. Then Lily's pointed expression drew Mr Maurice away from the table.

"H'lo, Bert."

"Herbert."

"We on for tomorrow?"

"Come to the shop at five. Mrs Maurice will be out."

> "Ladies and gentlemen! Appearing for
> the first time before a London audience!
> The talk of the European continent!
> Les D'Argents Volants!"

The acrobats leaped over each other and formed a pyramid, the audience hooting and *aah*-ing for all they were worth. Lily exchanged waves with a couple of girls she knew, pickpockets out to dip a few shillings from the crowd, then hurried out into the lofty foyer. With her thoughts elsewhere, she didn't notice a well-dressed man tottering down the wide, curling staircase that descended from the gallery, and collided with him as she passed close to the bottom step.

He grabbed her arm and swung her to face him. "Agnes!" he drawled, breathing brandy over her. "I thought it was you. How lovely!"

Lily's cheeks flushed, half in anger and half in embarrassment. "G'd'evening, Mr Webb, I'm afraid I'm—"

"'Mr Webb'? Aren't I your Teddy any more? It's only been a year or two . . ."

"Let me go." She wriggled to worm out of his grip. "I don't do that now. I haven't for a long time."

"Soiled doves don't clean themselves," he muttered, tilting close to her face. "Be a sport, Aggie. I'll give you an extra shilling."

"You want a scene? Let me go," she hissed.

His grip tightened. "You want it rough?"

Suddenly, he floundered in confusion as a hand landed on his collar and pulled him back sharply. "Did this lady's struggles not convey her meaning to you, sir?" said a hard, guttural voice.

The newcomer was of average height and build but had a bearing which made him appear broader, from white neckerchief to tall boots. Curling hair flopped above a harshly melancholy, clean-shaven face.

"Who the devil are you? 'S none of your business!" slurred Webb.

"And you are none of hers." He glared humourlessly at Webb's indignant huffing for a second or two before shoving the drunkard on his way.

"I trust you're unhurt, Miss?"

Lily thought his demeanour seemed both brusque and sad. "Yes. Thank you."

He glanced down at the pocket on the front of her

dress, where a stain was beginning to spread at the corner. She opened it to find that the two meat pies she'd hidden away at Fishwick's had been squashed and were leaking their contents.

The man gave a curt nod, as if to draw a line under the incident, and headed upstairs to the gallery. Lily hurried home, to the two-mattress room she shared with Mrs Potter, and made eight-year-old Jack's meal for the day into a fun game called Pocket of Pie.

> *"And now! Direct from the headlines to this very stage! A scene depicting the frightful fall of a Fenian fiend! The Holmwood company of players are proud to present* The Trial of Michael Barrett*!"*

At the top of the staircase, the brusque-and-sad man headed to the bar before looking around for the person he was here to meet. Glass in hand, he ignored the smiles of a trio of women seated along a chaise that was partly masked by a triptych screen. At last, he spotted Arthur Flemming beckoning from lounge seats which directly overlooked one side of the stage below.

"Enjoying the show, Flemming?"

Flemming would have poured disdain on the show and everyone involved in it, but stayed silent because his employer hadn't yet expressed any thoughts on the subject. His employer was sitting beside him, watching his surroundings like a python watching a rabbit.

"Sir Edwin," said Flemming, jutting his beaky nose forward and indicating the new arrival with a florid gesture, "may I introduce you to the old acquaintance I mentioned earlier? Captain Valentine Harker. Harker, this is Sir Edwin Gull, MP."

Harker raised an eyebrow slightly. "I see," he said flatly, politely concealing his discomfort. "I've read about Sir Edwin's speeches and business dealings many times in the papers."

Gull made a smiling acknowledgement. He was a bloated, reptilian beast, with an oddly barrel-shaped body and disproportionate legs and feet. The bald pate of his overlarge head was mottled with middle age and the pink shine of his skin looked slippery to the touch. He habitually wore his black surtout buttoned up to the neck, whatever the weather, and he spoke with an exaggerated movement of the lips which generally repulsed anyone who stood too close.

"Captain?" he growled. "You're a – do sit down – you're a military man?"

"At one time," said Harker. "I work at the War Office now, have done for some years."

"He served with the 70th in Peshawar," said Flemming, "during the Sepoy mutiny in '57, and fought with the 51st in China eight years ago."

Gull was impressed. "The Indian insurrection, mm? Showed the Bengalis who's in charge."

Harker quietly flared into a scowl. "Preserving the peace was my personal concern."

From the stage came a sudden flash and a bang. From the audience came a fearful *woooh*. Barrett, that fiendish Fenian of Fermanagh, had brought the blood and brutality of a bomb blast to the Clerkenwell jail! The actor dressed as the prime minister jumped up and down shouting "I told you so! I told you so!" to howls of laughter. To a doom-laden march on the piano, a wigged judge and a wooden cut-out of a gallows appeared from the wings.

"Perfectly dreadful," muttered Flemming, before he could stop himself. He glanced nervously at his employer, but Gull's narrow eyes were busy taking in the hall's luxurious sparkle with obvious disdain.

Flemming paddled an ornamental hand at the goings-on below. "I was unfortunate enough to witness the fellow's actual execution this morning. I've never seen such a frightening display of public bloodlust. And now they make a tawdry amusement of it!"

"If you don't like the music hall, Flemming, why ask me to meet you here?" said Harker.

"Because I was to report in person to Sir Edwin, following my return to London today, and when that time came, I learned that Sir Edwin was on his way to inspect Holmwood's. He's just purchased this building and several others, as part of local redevelopment plans."

> "Back by popular demand! You'll be delighted!
> You'll be entranced! By the comical antics of
> Mr Albert Hayes and his Dancing Dogs!"

"You're to rebuild these streets?" said Harker.

"No," said Flemming, "Sir Edwin's consortium intends to win the imminent contract for the construction of the new law courts—" he pointed vaguely eastward "—on that large, cleared site at the top of the Strand, by Temple

Bar, do you know it? Yes, and also for the laying of additional roads along the new Embankment."

"The Metropolitan Board of Works has made itself a far harder nut to crack than the parish governors," said Gull, "but I'll find a way." He chuckled heartily at the dogs leaping over the top of each other on the stage, and joined in the applause.

"But do you intend to close this place?" said Harker.

"Certainly not," muttered Gull, "it's highly profitable." His gaze ran over the intricate plasterwork on the ceiling above him. "Even so, I do not approve of cheap access to surroundings like these. As other public figures have noted, it is a disincentive for the working classes to better themselves. Holmwood should raise the admission charges."

Flemming nodded heavily in agreement.

"Ladies and gentlemen! Holmwood's is proud and privileged to present to you, our very own Starling of Song! Miss! Ruby! Wester!"

"Your note said you needed my opinion on something, Flemming," said Harker. "I know nothing whatsoever about construction or contracts."

"My apologies," said Flemming, hands pressed together in supplication, "I've been dashing from one thing to another all day. My aunt in Chiswick is unwell again . . ."

On stage, to hoots of delight, Ruby tippy-toed along in a bird costume, flapping her wings to the music. She sung at the top of her lungs, so that her well-enunciated words would reach the back of the hall, over the whistles of her admirers and the clinking of knives and forks.

". . . I'd like you," said Flemming, "to cast your eye over one or two of the items I've brought back from my business trip abroad . . ."

Ruby's song tonight was a bawdy satire inspired by Disraeli's recent comment about having climbed the greasy pole of politics. In it, a sparrow flew through the Houses of Parliament passing comment on members.

". . . in particular a very fine box which I believe to be Oriental, although I recovered it in Transylvania, of all places . . ."

> ". . . *the government's minority*
> *is quite hard to sustain, dear me,*
> *a minister's authority*
> *depends upon his height, you see . . ."*

"I'm not exactly an expert in antiques either," said Harker.

"You're the only person I know who's been to that part of the world," said Flemming. "You may be able to tell us if it's genuinely Chinese or a reproduction."

Gull watched Ruby's every skip and twinkle, his expression becoming more thunderous.

> ". . . *Hunt and Lord Stanley*
> *are men who stand tall,*
> *but Gull, Cairns and Northcote*
> *are awfully small . . ."*

"Very well," sighed Harker. "Where is this box?"

"Under lock and key, across the road. Seward Walk, number 19."

Gull glowered down at the stage. As Ruby skipped close to the tables, he recognised the bookseller Herbert Maurice in the audience, bright red with laughter. Gull glowered down at him instead.

The reporter William Browning, still sitting opposite Maurice, was oblivious to everything except the singer and her voice. He loved Ruby Wester with all his heart and soul, but he'd heard about her unnamed rich lover, and thus, he'd already resigned himself to the intense pain of a love unrequited. He came to Holmwood's every night to see her perform, and every night his heart broke.

*". . . Sir John and Sir Edwin
have gold by the bar,
but in height, in the Cabinet,
are shortest by far . . ."*

Sir Edwin Gull heaved himself to his feet, mumbling about overdue legislation. "I've had quite enough of the vulgar hoi polloi for one evening. Captain Harker, do excuse me, we'll conclude our business at five o'clock tomorrow, at the address Flemming has arranged."

With a mixture of amusement and annoyance, Harker watched Gull imperiously stalking towards the stairs, with Flemming scuttling along beside him like a tugboat fussing around a steamship. The lowering storm on Gull's face made the smiling women who approached him swerve aside at the last moment.

"This place is a mutton walk," he growled. "I want something done about it."

"I'll see Mr Whittlecome," said Flemming, "first thing in the morning."

"Mr Whittlecome has been dismissed," said Gull. "I'll be collecting local rents myself for a day or two. Other matters are in your hands."

"Yes, sir."

"Your friend back there, is he one of these reformist Robert Owen types?"

"I'm afraid he is a supporter of Mr Beesly, sir, yes. He's much changed from the lad I grew up with. He eventually recovered from war in the Far East, but was then terribly affected by the deaths of his wife and child two years ago, in the cholera epidemic, the same week you earned that large sum from the crash of Overend & Gurney."

"Poor fellow. Mm. I'll eat at Hamilton's and overnight at the Clanborough. I am not to be disturbed."

"No, sir."

> *"Ladies and gentlemen, there are forces of darkness in this world which are beyond human understanding! Forces which can be controlled by only one man! Prepare yourselves for a journey into the realm of the dead! Prepare to witness. . . Renfield! The Sensational Swami of the Supernatural!"*

Harker fetched himself another brandy and water, and leaned on the balustrade to soak up the weeping violins and the decorated coffin which was being carefully wheeled into an upright position on the stage. Ruby appeared again, this time in a slim costume cut low at the front, her arms held out this way and that to present Jacob Renfield, swooshing his cloak to suggest that the forces of darkness were at his very heels and had better watch out for themselves. His quavering voice might have been lost if the audience hadn't hushed themselves in eager anticipation.

> "What lies beyond death, my friends? Can we visit the spirit realm? Can the souls of the departed speak to us? Peer into my mystical Portal of the Undead, and find the answers . . ."

He flung open the lid to reveal the coffin's dark and empty interior. Nervous surprise surged across the hall. The violins wailed softly while Ruby, after striking a grand pose, stepped into the coffin and assumed a death-like stance with eyes closed and forearms crossed over her chest. Renfield closed the lid with a flourish. A slight rumble and bump could be heard, which might have been a roll of distant thunder from beyond the grave, but which was Ruby pulling forward the top of the hinged glass panel behind her and dropping down beneath the stage through a trapdoor. Renfield raised his hands to the heavens.

> "O spirits! Call this humble soul into your care!
> Let her walk among you for a while!
> O spirits, I command thee!"

Renfield, his eyes held wide, swam his hands around the lid. He wrote mystic symbols in the air, glancing into the wings until someone signalled him the all-clear. When the coffin was reopened, the audience gasped loudly. Two of them, including Herbert Maurice, fainted in shock. Mutterings rippled across the tables and around the gallery.

Ruby had vanished. Inside the coffin there suddenly appeared a pale figure, floating and transparent. Ruby's ghost! A spectre shimmering in the celestial ether!

Out of sight, in the confined space below the open trapdoor, Ruby swayed. The movement helped keep her shielded from the hot hiss and pop of the limelights that threw her reflection up to the coffin's angled sheet of glass. The ghost spoke!

> *"O Swami Renfield, I make utterance from the land of the dead! I have messages from the recently deceased! Here, in this place, tonight, is one who grieves for a loved one and. . . yes, I hear you, O spirits!. . . one whose name begins with a W. . . or an M . . ."*

"My sister, Maude!" cried a woman half way down the hall. She clutched her hands to her face. The murmur of the audience rose into consternation and amazement, drowning out those who were wrinkling their noses and smelling a rat.

> *"She is happy and at peace. . . but she says there were troubles which beset her in life. . . troubles*

*unresolved, concerning. . . money. . .
or a personal matter . . ."*

The woman thought for a moment "Her leg!" she cried tearfully. "Her leg pained her for years!"

"Her leg is cured. . . all troubles are gone and forgotten in the seas of time. . . From her tranquil repose in Heaven, Maude bids you a loving farewell. . . Now what say you, O spirits?. . . A new message, from a man. . . a kindly and generous man. . . who left to someone. . . a pocket watch . . ."

A family group, occupying a whole table near the stage, began to chatter at each other. A pocket watch was thrust into the air and shown for all to see. Uncle Charles, it was declared, had been buried just last week! The audience reeled in astonishment and Herbert Maurice fainted again. The family puzzled over this description of Uncle Charles as kindly and generous, but it was eventually accounted for by his being with the angels now.

Renfield read the mood of the room and closed the lid. He sensed a little discontent among the rat-smellers and didn't want some unappreciative philistine's dinner ending up on his cloak. Not after the last time.

"I conjure thee, forces of the night! Return my disciple to her living form! Return! Return!"

• • •

Moments later, Ruby stepped out of the coffin to rapturous applause. Renfield walked downstage and bowed low as cheers filled the room.

Captain Harker clapped along, smiling and shaking his head, then downed the last of his fifth drink and left to go home. He walked through the strident night crowd who sloshed along the Strand, weaving his way around the hawkers, the revellers, the moochers kicking through street detritus for discarded fag ends to remake.

He paused briefly at the western end of Fleet Street, looking out across the dark expanse of dug ground he now knew to be earmarked for the new law courts that Flemming's employer intended to build. The homeless scavengers who peppered it would soon be moved on.

He walked to his lodgings not far from St Paul's, the harmless fakery of Renfield's act swirling through his thoughts, into which were then stirred all the unwelcome memories Flemming's talk of Oriental boxes had uncorked. That night, he dreamed of events in 1859, in the war-ravaged landscape to the north of Pekin.

V

from the private papers of Captain Valentine Harker

entry dated 18th November 1861

It is over a year now since I returned from the war in China, but I cannot say I have had one day's peace in all that time. My mood has grown more morose and more dour with each passing day. This lowness of spirit has been suffered with great patience by my dear wife Violet, and not even the joyfully flourishing first months of our infant daughter have lifted the darkness that clings fast to my soul.

Violet has asked me, on more than one occasion, and with that gentle insistence which is so endearing, to tell her about the experiences which have caused such a regrettable change in my character. But I have no right to burden her with my private troubles, and I will not do so.

Instead, I propose to embark on a programme of research in order to better understand the events of that day in Zhili Province, and thereby perhaps ease the burden upon my mind and thence upon my family. What form this research will take, and how protracted and esoteric a study it may prove, I cannot yet say. However, I propose to begin by herewith setting down the events of late June '59. This is entirely separate to the official report I made at the time, which of necessity omitted a number of facts.

No, that is not true. I have a duty to record the truth.

The official report need not have omitted any facts whatsoever. But I was persuaded, much against my will, that portions of my testimony be amended or deleted entirely, to remove the supernatural aspects of the narrative and avoid what my commanding officer termed "suppositions and speculations."

MY NARRATIVE

The events of our latest military intervention in China were stretched across the four years up to 1860. Like Lord Elgin and Mr Gladstone, I now consider our nation's actions during that time to be a scandalous disgrace, although in this opinion I remain at odds with the public mood. Throughout this time, China was also in the grip of a viciously bloody civil war fought between imperial troops of the Qing Emperor Xianfeng and Taiping rebels under the command of the so-called Heavenly King, Hong Xiuquan. That war still rages, even though the Emperor fled the capital last year and is now reported to be dead.

A year after our capture of the Taku Forts near Tian-Jin

in May of '58, I was assigned to the naval convoy that left Shanghai under Admiral Hope. Twenty-one ships, carrying over two thousand English and French troops, sailed north as far as the mouth of the Hai River. We had British and French ambassadors on board, and Hope's orders were to see them safely installed in their respective embassies in Pekin, by force if necessary.

With the fleet waiting offshore, Hope's negotiators deliberately stirred up a fuss with Sengge Rinchen, the great Borjigin warlord appointed as imperial commissioner. Hope demanded free passage along the river, while Rinchen insisted our ships move further up the coast to Bei-Tang. The ruse was sufficiently distracting to allow three small landing parties to reach the shore. One was to head west, one north and one south. All were to scout the land and report on any troop movement encountered, either the armies of the Emperor, or the considerably less organised forces of the Taiping.

I was placed in command of the group going south. We were to skirt around Tian-Jin, then go across country, even as far as Pekin if it was possible, anticipating a round trip of about two weeks. We numbered twenty English soldiers, dressed in mufti, and half a dozen Chinese. We landed under cover of darkness and were almost three miles away by daybreak.

It was hard going for the first day and a half. Heavy rain blotted out our view of anything distant, and the ground dissolved into grey mud through which our boots could only move with great effort. I was tempted to order a portion of our arms left behind, to ease the weight on all our shoulders, but my inexperience of the land ahead quickly changed my mind. As it turned out, it would not have mattered in either case.

Early on the third day, we crossed a shallow valley through which meandered a bubbling stream swollen by the downpours. While we paused on the far side to check our bearings by map and compass, my second-in-command, Sgt Higgs, discovered a broad line of freshly made footprints nearby. From their size and spacing, and from their consistency of outline, it was clear that a small group of uniformed men had come past this point at great speed and were heading in the same general direction as ourselves. Our Chinese translator, Yu-Chin, was certain that the marks matched the boots of imperial soldiers. Their limited numbers suggested a scouting party similar to our own, but their rapid movement suggested some other deployment altogether.

As the officer in charge, I pocketed my nervous misgivings about what might lie ahead and ordered a cautious advance. Our maps showed a walled town about a mile to the south-west, and the running footprints led us directly to the tall wooden gates at its entrance. That the gates were barred, and that no locals were in evidence, struck me as odd. The imperial troops we were following were far too few in number to present a danger to the town. Indeed, they had evidently been welcomed inside it, since their tracks vanished under the gates in an uninterrupted line.

I suggested to my men that we present ourselves as mercenaries seeking food and shelter. There were plenty of army deserters and foreign adventurers in the country at that time, either seeking fortunes or escaping punishments, and I anticipated little resistance to such a disguise.

I pounded heavily on the gates with my fist. Over the preceding weeks, I had tried to absorb as many Chinese words and phrases as I could, and I called out a friendly greeting. This was answered by a sharp voice from immediately behind the gates, which conveyed sentiments decidedly less than friendly.

However, no sooner had Yu-Chin explained our presence as soldiers of fortune than the gates were unlocked and partially opened. We were told that we'd be welcomed inside provided we would offer our services as protection for the town overnight. I was reluctant to agree to these terms, since my orders didn't cover such arrangements, but it seemed likely that we'd be able to gain valuable information from the soldiers we'd been following.

A few minutes later, those soldiers turned out to be the most bedraggled and terrified wretches I had ever seen. There were seven of them, each one as ragged and dirty as the next, only recognisable as imperial troops by the mud-smeared remnants of their blue uniforms and the way their hair was cut in the characteristically severe cue of the Qing. They cowered and trembled in a way that elicited my most heartfelt sympathy, and also caused me considerable disquiet about what could possibly have reduced them to such a state.

While they sipped at steaming bowls of soup, they spoke haltingly to Yu-Chin and to the old lady who presided over the open-air eatery at which we were gathered. We learned that they'd reached the town only a few hours before our arrival, and had spent at least two days fleeing the scene of a battle between the Emperor's forces and a division of Taiping rebels. This battle had been long and brutal, ending in an almost complete massacre of the imperial troops despite their vastly superior numbers and capabilities.

At this point, I happened to remark that the Taiping were well known for undisciplined ferocity. No sooner had I done so than the poor soldiers began to mutter darkly and angrily at me. They had already sworn, amongst themselves, that their days of fighting for Xianfeng's Hunan Army were over, but they were emphatic that this had nothing to do with the bitter divisions which usually drove ethnic Chinese to scorn military service for the hated Manchu elites. It was purely out of fear.

I shall never forget the look on one soldier's mud-smeared face as he muttered the same phrase under his breath, over and over again, the half empty bowl shivering in his hands. "Yǐn xiě zhě . . . Yǐn xiě zhě . . . Yǐn xiě zhě . . ."

The old woman clutched nervously at her smock and busied herself with ordering her young cook about. Yu-Chin glanced at me, licking at his wind-dry lips and apparently reluctant to speak.

"What's on his mind?" I said.

"It means 'the drinkers of blood,'" he said.

"Jiāngshī," trembled another of the soldiers. "Dí yǐ gōng xià jiǔ jiāngshī." He quickly dipped his head to his soup bowl, as if uttering these words was the most terrible of blasphemies. Yu-Chin was visibly alarmed and for several minutes talked in low tones to all the soldiers, with the old woman chipping in quietly here and there, nodding as if to confirm the worst.

Sgt Higgs nudged my arm and leaned close. "What's lit their fireworks, sir?" he whispered.

I had no answer. The obvious distress that clouded the faces around us was becoming infectious, and my earlier disquiet steadily increased as I awaited the outcome of their conversation. When at last it came, my blood ran cold. I might have rejected what they told me as superstitious nonsense, were it not for their absolute and sincere earnestness.

Hong Xiuquan, the Taiping's self-appointed Heavenly King, had always been widely reported as a leader of eccentric and capricious habits, but it seemed that his devotion to religion had lately broadened into an obsession with the occult and that he had effectively become a recluse, leaving day-to-day command of the Taiping to his cousin Hong Rengan. It was on Xiuquan's orders that teams of academics were sent out to remote parts of Mongolia, Tibet and India, even into Turkestan, for the express purpose of finding dragons or similar monstrous beasts to aid in the struggle to overthrow the Emperor.

News of these expeditions was spread by amused whispers throughout the country and, until a few weeks earlier, treated as no more than silly gossip, a sign of the Taiping's haphazard organisation. However, at around the time Admiral Hope's fleet was assembling in Shanghai, very different stories began to circulate. These made the incredible claim that the Taiping had succeeded in capturing creatures who were already cutting a swathe of death across Szchuen and Hupeh provinces, en route for Pekin.

These creatures were said to be a group of nine 'jiāngshī,' described as supernatural beings which consume human blood. A jiāngshī, I was told, is an 'undead' evil spirit, a form of wraith or *huó yān*, literally meaning 'living smoke,' which occupies a human host and drives its victim to unspeakable acts of murder in its pursuit of sustenance. It can animate a human body even after death, until it finds a fresh host and begins anew.

Where these horrors had been found, and how they had been brought to heel, none could say. The trembling soldiers in front of us all claimed that they'd seen the jiāngshī with their own eyes and that only by abandoning their comrades and turning tail had they avoided a grisly fate.

Their arrival here had confirmed frightening rumours picked up by the town's tradesmen. This is what had caused the people to retreat inside the walls and bar the gates.

I couldn't help but be chilled to the bone by what I'd heard. Nevertheless, as willing as I was to help these people and repay their hospitality, I had my orders and the lives of the men under my command to consider.

"We'll form a town guard until tomorrow, as agreed," I told Sgt Higgs, "then we'll move on. We still have a large area to survey and all intelligence needs to be relayed to the fleet."

"You think there's something in these fairy tales of theirs, sir?"

"I'm not sure what to think. But this place is barely a dot on the map and unlikely to be of strategic value. Let's hope it's beneath the Taiping's interest."

I hoped in vain. The attack came an hour before sundown, with the sky streaked in bright and fiery colours.

Warning cries came from the men I'd posted on the western wall. There was a hubbub of fright among the locals, a rapid scattering of feet and a scooping up of children. I clambered up to the nearest lookout and took a spyglass to scan the wide, grassy plain that stretched from the nearby river to the south-westerly horizon. What I saw set my stomach contorting in knots.

The approaching force was fronted with around five hundred infantry and at least one hundred cavalry. At first, they moved at a loose marching step, but as they reached a point approximately half a mile from the town they began to quicken their pace. Tall banners, emblazoned with Chinese characters, fluttered high up at each flank. I could soon make out the yellow uniforms and trailing red bandanas of the riders. Mud was kicked into shallow storms by feet and hooves.

I ordered my men into sniper positions and shouted down to shore up the gates with whatever bulk was available. Much would depend on how long they held. Some of the locals armed themselves with bows and gathered around a brazier ready to fire flaming arrows.

The Taiping increased their speed into a steady charge. The sound of a massed and continuous howling war cry reached us on the wind, and I fought back the draining sensations that were creeping through my limbs.

"Fight proud, lads!" I yelled. "For we are men of the 51st! Take aim!"

A few yards to my left, Sgt Higgs wiped the sweat

from his eyes. I glanced over my shoulder at the solid stockade of carts and furniture that was rising quickly at the gates.

A split formed in the middle of the oncoming Taiping line. A long wooden wagon, pulled by a team of horses and shaped like an elongated rectangle with flat top and sides, appeared though the gap and moved ahead of the troops. It wasn't quite tall enough to be a siege engine, and at first I thought it might either house a formidable canon, or be used as some form of battering ram.

Through my boots, I could feel the shuddering thunder of the enemy's approach. The very air seemed to vibrate.

"Fire at will!" The hammering of rifle shots burst forth.

The split in the Taiping line widened and it was apparent that they were manoeuvring to surround the town rather than concentrate the greater part of their attack on gaining entry via the gates. This appeared a strange tactic, until the true nature of the peculiar wagon became clear.

It was aimed squarely at the wall beneath my feet, careering headlong, its horses strained and frothing. Some forty or fifty yards from us, it suddenly veered aside, its driver steering it out and around in a sharp turn of ninety degrees, to bring it in close parallel to the wall. It clattered and jerked to a halt directly below.

As soon as it stopped, a series of broad hatches in the top of the wagon sprung open. These were slatted so that, once flipped up and in contact with the wall, each formed a short, rudimentary ladder. There were nine of them, atop nine compartments of the wagon.

Out of these compartments they leapt. The jiāngshī.

They bounded up the ladders and were over the wall in seconds. They were ordinary men and women, dressed in simple peasant garb, but their faces were alight with a gleeful lust. Each wore an iron collar, from the back of which snaked an endless metal chain.

One of them collided with Higgs before the sergeant could draw his revolver. The attacker seized him by the head and bit deep into his neck! I was so shocked and appalled that it took me a moment to come to my senses and put three bullets through the murderer's chest. The man reeled in pain, but instead of dropping dead upon the spot he continued to drink the blood that fountained from my second-in-command. He suddenly flashed his shining face at me, his teeth and lips dripping, then jumped from the wall onto the roof of one of the town's modest dwellings, chain rattling as it unspooled behind him.

There was chaos. Those of my men who were stationed at defensive positions were among the first to die. The jiāngshī rampaged through the little town's handful of streets, killing indiscriminately and flushing people out of their hiding places. The courageous citizens who'd prepared lighted arrows were quickly overwhelmed. Two scored hits before they fell, but flames were no more effective than bullets. Some of the townspeople desperately clawed at the barricade thrown up against the gates. I had ordered that barricade to be built, and now it had trapped us all, like rats in a barrel!

Blood soaked the muddy ground, and the screams of the dying filled the air. The jiāngshī were no mindless monsters, they were cunning and systematic, each keeping to their own territory and often flicking their chains to prevent entanglements. Anyone brave enough to pull at their leashes was instantly set upon. They carried swords, which they used to slash open their prey before bathing themselves in blood. Many of the dead were left grey and shrivelled, as if the supernatural evil of the jiāngshī had drained the very life essence from their bones. Those who escaped slaughter and jumped in panic from the walls were cut down by the Taiping troops waiting outside.

To both my personal and professional shame, I must report that I was paralysed with fear. My lack of action was tantamount to cowardice. I became unworthy of my rank and uniform.

I emptied my revolver and my rifle, but didn't bother to reload either one, since the effort was obviously futile. I was no stranger to the tragedy and savagery of military conflict, and have seen active service in India and elsewhere, but this hideous onslaught was a nightmare of brutality and horror beyond anything I could have imagined. My mind struggled, in vain, to devise either a useful weapon or a practical defence against these rabid killers. They moved with swift efficiency through the town's small population, sometimes running with sword wielded, sometimes scuttling into windows or under trader's stalls almost like a crab or a beetle. The stench of death clung to everything.

Those who were labouring to remove obstructions at the gates managed to clear one side. They hastily removed the planks that kept it closed, only to be confronted outside by a line of troops with blades drawn. Several begged to be taken prisoner but were run through without mercy.

I was endeavouring to gather together whatever strays might cross my path. I hurriedly ushered a couple of mothers with children, and a handful of others, into the dark and narrow space behind the re-opened half of the gate. Among them, by some miracle, was one of my men, a young private named Sullivan. He was badly injured, with bites torn into his side and much blood drunk from them, but he was able to walk.

The cries of the wounded and the desolate began to subside as the numbers left alive dwindled. Through slim cracks in the planking of the gate, I saw the long chains attached to the jiāngshī being wound in, tugging them bit by bit back into the wagon, all of them heavily stained in red. They put up no resistance and returned to their 'homes' with all the self-satisfied swagger of generals retiring to smoke and swill port after a regimental dinner.

By now, night was falling. The Taiping troops were busy looting the town of food and useful items. In the few moments between the setting of the sun and the lighting of lanterns, we ragtag survivors managed to slip away and head across country.

Our hair-raising journey to safety isn't a necessary part of this account, so I shall omit it entirely except to record that poor Sullivan succumbed to disease within a week. In all, it took more than a month for me to regain contact with the fleet, by which time events had moved on considerably. My report on the jiāngshī attack was, as I have already stated, forced into substantial alterations.

I returned to England aboard the *Earl of Liverpool*,

but not before hearing of Lord Elgin's infamous order to burn down the Summer Palace at Pekin. This shocking act was ostensibly in reprisal for the deaths of prominent prisoners at the hands of the Chinese authorities. However, it is so at odds with Elgin's usual attitude to the Empire's business in China that I can easily give credence to the alarming stories, whispered in the ranks, that the Summer Palace had been over-run by violent monomaniacs and that its destruction was a regrettable but condign action to wipe out these deadly individuals.

Here I end the narrative of my experiences in China. I intend it to form the cornerstone of my researches and investigations. I have already unearthed accounts from European folklore concerning creatures called 'vampyrs' which are directly related to the jiāngshī phenomenon. How extensive these researches will need to be I cannot guess as yet, but through them I aim to understand the true nature of what I witnessed, and to understand the fear that has weighed so heavily upon my nerves and upon my conscience, like an incumbent nightmare, ever since.

VI

Seward Walk was a short gloomy backstreet where upper floors jutted out ahead of lower ones, giving most passers-by an uneasy sensation of tottering imbalance. Number 19 was an abandoned shop. Damp-softened wooden shutters covered its windows, and the jaunty wording above them, "Lee & Shelley – The Noted Confectioners," had worn away into an almost illegible series of grey and brown shapes.

Captain Harker hesitated outside for a moment but, no, this was definitely the address Flemming had given him at the music hall. Tapping the muck of his short journey off his boots, he went inside. The place was thick with the smell of mildew and he could hear the stealthy scampering of vermin.

The creaking of the shop's door summoned Arthur Flemming, who appeared from a passageway holding up an oil lamp in the gloom. "Ah! Harker, come on in." The glow of the lamp revealed decaying floorboards and high wainscotting where little strips of bright blue paint still clung, here and there, splinters of a happier past.

"Well, this is an odd idea of a store room," said Harker.

"It certainly is," huffed Sir Edwin Gull, arriving behind

him from the street at a marching pace, his heavy tread sending the floor into groans and screeches.

Flemming bowed to his employer. "Follow me, gentlemen, all will be clear. I think you'll find – be careful of the sharp hole in the wall there – you'll find, Sir Edwin, that this old shop is unique in your portfolio of property."

"In odour, most certainly," sneered Gull. "Why is it empty? Why has it no tenant?"

"I have kept it in reserve for just such a contingency as we now have, sir," said Flemming, a note of smugness in his voice. "It's ideal for the safekeeping of, er, certain types of goods."

The narrow passageway opened out into a room which was in a slightly less dilapidated state. Apart from years of slowly accumulated grime and mold, it was completely empty. In the centre of one wall was a flat, regularly sized door made of tarnished copper which had been engraved to give an old-fashioned panelled effect.

Flemming held out his lamp in triumph. "It has a strongroom."

He hung the lamp on a high hook and took a long key from inside his coat. The thin but sturdy door opened with a series of squeaks to reveal a chamber roughly six feet square. Its floor, walls and ceiling were made from the same metal as the door, and the room was piled high with the crates Flemming had brought back with him from Transylvania.

"Astonishing!" declared Harker with a laugh. "Was this shop once a bank?"

"According to the freehold, a jeweller's," said Flemming, "and before that a pawnbroker's. If you look on the uppermost metal plate of the door there is a date of 1790, which coincides with the building of the whole street. Here we have what amounts to an all-but-impregnable little vault, tucked away from even the most prying eyes, unknown to anyone but ourselves."

"Mm. Good," said Gull. "These recoveries cover the full sum?"

"They do, sir," said Flemming, pride making him simper contentedly to himself. "I await your instruction as to whether they are to be retained as capital?"

"If that would be to greater advantage . . ." muttered Gull, running a large, knuckley hand along the nearest crate.

"Ah! This is where we need your help, Valentine," said Flemming. "In relation to just one item, as I think I mentioned last night." He busied himself among the crates for a few moments, placing the lamp on the biggest of the packing cases, inside which were paintings sturdily wrapped in sacking. "Yes, here it is. I've already opened the crate it travelled in, it's such an exquisite piece I simply had to see it again."

He reached down, heaved out the ornate box he'd taken from behind the altar in Radu Grosav's chapel, and set it beside the oil lamp. Yellowish light glowed warmly against it surfaces.

"It's beautifully made," said Harker. "That coloured enamel work all around the sides was on many items I saw in Pekin."

"The only point which makes me question its provenance," said Flemming, "is the lid. It's inlaid into the top of the box, in a way I've never seen before on genuine

Oriental items. If you happened to have come across something similar, then I'd be happy to accept your assurances, but if—"

Harker silenced him with a raised hand. He took a step forward and stooped close to the box, his breath quickening and his expression slowly changing into horrified curiosity.

"Flemming, where exactly did you get this?"

"Ah, you've seen one like it before?" said Flemming.

"No. But it reminds me of something I read about, in my researches." His voice dropped to a whisper. "I never in all my life expected to see a real one."

"It is valuable then?" smiled Flemming.

"If it's what I suspect it might be. . . might! be. . . then it should never have been brought here."

"It is lawful repayment of debt," scoffed Gull.

Harker ignored him. "It's this crude seal that alarms me, around the lid. Is it lead?"

"Done by some bungling hand," tutted Flemming. "It alarmed me also! Dreadfully poor work, carried out, I've no doubt, in a laughable attempt to conceal the contents."

"Then you know there's something inside it?" gasped Harker.

"Oh yes," said Flemming. Before Harker could stop him, he lifted one end of the box and from inside came the sound of an object sliding. "Something of greater value than anything else here, I suspect, and hidden from creditors in a panic, otherwise why so ridiculously ineffective a hiding place?"

Harker's shaking fingers hovered over the wayward, encircling seal. "There are words scratched into it. Yes, all the way around. Flemming, hold the lamp up, will you? Hungarian, I assume. Do you know what it means?"

"I'm afraid I have no idea," shrugged Flemming.

Without taking his eyes off the box, Harker searched his pockets for a notebook and pencil. He began to copy down the scratched words in meticulous detail. The nervous misgivings he'd been feeling were rising into outright fear.

"Surely," harrumphed Gull, "the more pressing question is whether the box will be damaged when the seal is broken?"

"There *will* inevitably be a little damage, sir." Flemming pointed along the outline of the lead, by way of reassurance. "But such hasty work won't be difficult to dislodge. I have a small hammer and chisel with me, which I used to open the crate. I'm sure a few taps—"

"No!" cried Harker with sudden vehemence. "Do not *touch* it!"

"I beg your pardon?" said Gull slowly.

Harker looked through what he'd written. "I'll get these words translated, with great urgency. In the meantime, you must set this box aside and leave it absolutely *undisturbed*. Both of you. Is that clear? It may be extremely dangerous."

"Dangerous?" stammered Flemming, his hands pulling up to his chest. "In what way? It can't be explosive, or it would have detonated on its bumpy journey. It can't possibly harbour a living breathing animal, and what's inside isn't liquid, some form of *aqua regia*—"

"If you won't take my warning seriously," said Harker, his voice rising, "then I'll keep the box with me!"

"You'll do no such thing," said Gull.

Flemming was politely confused. "Can't you tell us the nature of this danger?"

Harker let out a sharp breath and forced himself to speak calmly. "I swear to you, Arthur, on whichever holy book you may choose, that I do not know exactly what's beneath that lid. But I have the most terrible suspicions. If they're proven to be wrong, and that is my fervent hope, then no harm has been done by complying with them."

"If you won't voice these peculiar suspicions, Captain," said Gull, "then why the devil *should* anyone comply with them?"

"Perhaps a little more information might be persuasive, Valentine?" said Flemming softly, with a forced smile.

Harker's calm was beginning to fray at the edges. "Very well." He took a breath. "I think this box has been used to trap a supernatural being, a vampyr. One of the *uk'vdavi*, or *nosferatu*, the so-called undead, as they're referred to in those parts of Eastern Europe where you found it. Break the seal, and you will release the creature. And I promise you, you'll wish you had not. Leave it untouched!"

With that, he stalked off, the notebook clutched tightly in his hand. Flemming adjusted his waistcoat and quietly cleared his throat. Gull spoke once Harker was well out of earshot.

"Open it."

"I thought, possibly, in view of what Mr Harker said. . .?"

"A monster?" snorted Gull. "Must be rather a small

one, don't you think? Your unfortunate friend mistakes me for a superstitious peasant. Mm. You said the box is full of valuables?"

"I do have reason to believe the object or objects inside are gold, sir, but perhaps. . .?"

"Then open it. It's my property and if I want it open, it'll be opened."

Flemming gathered up his hammer and chisel from where he'd left them on the floor. Adjusting the lamp to make sure it gave him a bright view of the box's lid, he started to cautiously tap at the lead seal.

A small section broke off almost at once. He held it up to the light, turning it over between finger and thumb, squinting at the flakes of enamel that were embedded in it. "As I said, some impairment is unavoidable, alas."

With Gull looming over him, he tap, tap, tapped along the lid. Another section was knocked loose, and another. After a few breathless minutes, almost all the lead had been chipped off. Flemming delicately plucked each broken piece free.

The only sound in the small vault was the breathing of the two men. Flemming poised his hands over the box in various positions until he'd decided on the best way to raise the inlaid section of the lid. He tried to lift it out, but it wouldn't budge. Grasping it from a slightly different angle made no difference.

"Oh dear, it may be glued," he muttered. He glanced up at Gull. "Levering might split it."

Gull nodded a reluctant 'carry-on,' and Flemming, wincing, slid the sharp end of the chisel into the lid's edge. He paused for a moment, in a squirm of hesitation, then pressed down hard and pulled the chisel back. For a couple of seconds, his hands quivered with effort, then the entire lid suddenly popped up and off with a sharp, splintering crack.

Instantly, the stench of rotting flesh filled the air. Flemming dropped the chisel and clapped his hands to his face with a gasp. Gull stepped back, the sleeve of his coat pressed tight over his nose and mouth.

Something more than foulness was also in the air. A cold, penetrating sensation of death that was even more horrible than the stark shock of what was under the lid. Inside the box was a tiny human corpse, wrapped in a Christening robe.

Both men saw – were sure they saw – the shadows in the vault move. They had a terrifying, momentary impression of a shape which had no shape, dark and curling, like blown smoke, rearing up from the dead body like a cobra. Flemming cried out, a long and trembling wail of fright. Then the shadow was gone and, for the time being at least, they could pretend they were mistaken.

Gull, his face boiling back and forth between disgust and fury, seized the box and hurled it into the far corner of the vault. It shattered noisily in the darkness beyond the lamplight.

They hurried along the passageway and into the comparatively fresh air of the shop. Neither of them spoke for a while, Flemming dabbing at his cheeks with a handkerchief and Gull staring angrily at the street outside, through the gaps in the shutters.

"'Undead'?" he spat at last. "Damn him." He flung the shop door open and stood blocking it, his hands battling each other behind his back. He spun on his heels. "That man's got us jumping at our own shadows, damn him!"

"I a-agree, sir, I agree, we have fallen victim to credulity."

"Then get that abomination off my premises! You brought it here, Flemming, it's your responsibility! Yours! Yours alone!"

Both of them had a crawling feeling of dread, but neither were aware of the dark form, which had no form, drifting in the extremities of the room. It surged like an incoming tide, disoriented from months of imprisonment, hungry and searching.

Gull barked a single loud cough and snuffled. To business, moving on. He consulted the pocketbook he'd brought with him, angrily flipping pages, savagely eyeing columns of numbers.

"You have an inventory of what else is in that vault?" he snarled, without looking up.

"Yes, sir." Flemming veered between nausea and tearfulness. He wanted to lie down.

"Might any more items prove problematic?"

"Absolutely not, sir," said Flemming quickly.

"Then present your inventory, minus the one item, to Lady Gull at my home. I have no interest in artworks and curios. If she wishes to retain anything, so be it, the rest you may sell at the earliest convenience."

The vampyr sighed a meandering route out through the open door of the shop, hugging the warm ground, a mist that was not a mist, a gossamer wraith which burned with the need to find human flesh in which to live.

Gull didn't wait for Flemming's answer. He slammed the door behind him and marched away up the street.

He paused at the corner, breathing heavily and gathering his thoughts. From where he stood, half of Holmwood's facade was visible in the blotchy sunlight of late afternoon. Without its illuminations, and without patrons tumbling in and out of it, the place seemed to lie in a peaceful slumber, undisturbed by shouts or hooves or the other noises of the street.

The air was oppressive and muggy, and Gull could feel sweat on his shoulders. He touched his top button to make sure it was fastened, then switched direction and headed deeper into the backstreets.

Fifty footsteps away, a spindly woman was tramping home. The pain in her hip and the emptiness in her stomach showed themselves in the sour pull of her wrinkled face. As she reached the door of the tenement in which she lived, she suddenly baulked at the sight of a bald, thick-set man walking purposefully towards her from the opposite direction. Although Sir Edwin Gull cast a familiar shadow from Drury Lane to St Martin's and the Haymarket, it was a shadow normally cast by gaslight.

She hurried inside, her heart trembling, congratulating herself on narrowly avoiding an awkward encounter with that crabby old twister. A moment later, the door opened and he was standing behind her in the dim hallway, his pocketbook poised.

"Are you a tenant here, madam?"

"Mr Gull, sir, an unexpected pleasure."

"Are you a tenant?"

"Yes, Mr Gull. I'm Mrs Potter." Her finger wavered in mid-air for a moment, half-pointing up the stairs towards the room she shared with Lily and young Jack.

Gull consulted his notes. "Potter, Potter. . . Mrs E Potter, five pounds, nineteen shillings and sevenpence in arrears."

"I pays Mr Whittlecome, on a Thursday."

"But not, apparently, on any recent Thursday."

"I allus pays me nethers, Mr Gull, allus. Ask Mr Whittlecome."

"Mr Whittlecome has left my employ. I am notifying his addresses of revised arrangements. All rents currently owed are to be paid in full by the last date of this month. From the first date of next month, each week's rent to be paid in full on the specified collection day."

"What? Why?"

"Why?" spat Gull, the stink of the derelict shop lingering in his nostrils. "Mrs Potter, each and every citizen of this borough benefits from the new underground drainage system, the railway network expansion, the clearance of unsanitary slums in Newcastle Court and Wych Street. Do they not? These things cost money. All that is required of you, Mrs Potter, is to meet your obligation to your landlord."

"I pay every penny I can, Mr Gull. I'm sixty-eight years of age, I'm a widow and I has to beg down at the market."

"Fortunately, in the enlightened market economy, even a sixty-eight-year-old widow is entirely at liberty to find work. The aforementioned improvements alone provide employment for thousands."

"I can't, not with me hip."

"Have you not hands?"

"I can't pay money I ain't got, Mr Gull."

"Then reduce your expenditure, Mrs Potter. Buy fewer luxuries. The principle is a very simple one."

"I eat off the scraps buyers as it is! I has nothing left!"

"Then find cheaper accommodation."

"I had cheaper in Wych Street. It's *these* rents is too much, I'll be out on me ear."

"Where, thanks to Parliament's concern for your welfare, there is shelter at the recently modernised workhouses."

He flipped a page in his pocketbook. "I trust you will convey the new arrangements to. . . Miss L Murray, three pounds and fifteen shillings. . . Mr and Mrs F Dobbs, one pound, nine shillings and tuppence. . . Mr B J Childers. . . and the other two, three, four, five rent payers here?"

Then he was gone, all thoughts of the shop chased from his mind, to call at the other houses in the street. Mrs Potter stood scowling for a minute or more, dust dancing in the ghostly beam from the grimy transom over the door. She spat hard on the floor. "Bastard! Bastard!"

– THE FIRST HOST –

VII

An hour earlier, at the exact moment when Captain Valentine Harker was first entering the derelict premises in Seward Walk, Lily Murray was entering the bookshop owned by Herbert Maurice, three streets away. She was accompanied by one of her occasional colleagues, a weaselly, oval-faced man with a permanent sniff, known in the underworld only as Clipper. His beady eyes bobbed. His clean and fashionable clothes were completely at odds with his stubbled chin and the dirt ingrained into every fold of his hands.

Maurice was behind the counter, setting down a saucer of milk for the hedgehog he kept to control the beetles which lived beneath the floorboards. Hearing the bell over the entrance, he stood up and, without a word, motioned his visitors past the dark, heavily laden bookshelves which reached from floor to high ceiling, and led them through to the rooms at the back.

"Why's it so cold in here today, Bert?" said Lily.

"Herbert," said Maurice, pulling back the thick curtain at the entrance to his photographic studio. "It *is* chilly all of a sudden, isn't it," he muttered.

The vampyr unwound itself from Lily's ankle and slunk

into the shadows. Not this female. Unsuitable host. Poor physical condition. The smell of recent disease too strong on her skin. Nor the younger of the males. An ulceration. The stink of growths. Likely to die.

"Make yourself comfortable," said Maurice.

"You've got a new seat," said Lily brightly, patting the upper curves of a worn, purple chaise which sat between two tall and bushy house plants on stands.

"I purchased it a couple of weeks ago," said Maurice, busying himself with bottles of solvent and silver nitrate. "It used to be in the lobby of one of the hotels off Trafalgar Square."

"Fancy," said Lily, shimmying her fingers to indicate just how fancy it was.

Maurice's studio was a large room, whitewashed throughout, which had once been a yard at the rear of the building. An angular glass roof had been built over it, and now a flood of natural light rolled and reflected inside. A table of chemicals, trays and other photographic equipment stood close to the curtain, along with an old roll-top desk and some wooden racking. A tall box camera, on a sturdy tripod, stood in the centre of the room, pointing to the chaise at the far end.

"Got my fakements?" sniffed Clipper.

"Yes, the whole dozen," said Maurice, going over to the desk. "I've varied the writer's circumstances a little more this time, in case regular marks start noticing similarities." He handed Clipper a small stack of letters, all written in beautifully regular copperplate handwriting on expensive paper. "I've kept to 'Dear Sir' or 'Dear Lady' for the sake of simplicity. The signatures are more or less at random."

Clipper skipped through the first few, his lower lip moving as he followed the lines. "Abandoned wives, evil uncles. . . please help us. . . only your kindness can grant our father's dying wish. . . implore you to act in haste. Yeh," he nodded. "Quality."

"I'm much obliged," grinned Maurice with a nod. "Any likely recipients?"

"I got a couple o' really fresh tips yesterday, so we should beat the rush to 'em. One's inherited three thousand in March, and apparently, he's soft as shite. You can take the chink for these out of what you owe me. I owe you some too, since yesterday."

Maurice looked over the top of his spectacles. "The governess paid?"

"More gulpy than we thought, eh?"

"Can we get on with it?" said Lily. "I'm half frozen."

She stood naked by the chaise, her clothes dropped in a heap next to the camera. Maurice bustled around the equipment table, unfurling the tall, black fitted hood he used as a darkroom for preparing and processing glass plates.

"I'm still getting used to this collodion process," he said as he worked, his voice muffled by the hood. "It's so fiddly, and I've got to do everything in one go. I'm starting to miss the old daguerreotypes." He emerged with a tightly shut wooden frame which he clipped to the back of the camera. His eyes kept flickering at the floor. "And it drips."

"I'll drip you in a minute, Bert," said Lily.

"Herbert."

She adopted a standing pose in front of the chaise,

with one foot trailing, her hands held out like those on a marble statue, and a look of wistful innocence directed slightly to one side. Maurice cupped two fingers around the camera's lens cap.

"And . . ." He removed the cap for a few seconds, while Lily stood motionless. "Done." He unclipped the exposed plate, returned to his hood, and called from underneath it after a couple of minutes' work. "A rear view next?"

Lily suddenly had a strong inclination to be elsewhere. Since before even entering the shop, she'd felt an unsettling whisper of threat, like a deer sensing hunters in the wood. The whisper had been getting louder, and now it was nagging her to leave. She started gathering her clothes off the floor. "No, sorry, Bert, I've just remembered I got to be somewhere."

"Herbert. But I thought. . .?" tutted Maurice, his annoyance conveyed in shifting shapes under the hood.

"Be where?" mumbled Clipper. "Waste of time coming, if you're only doing the one."

Lily, pulling on her chemise and petticoat, flung a finger at the chaise. "You do a few, then. That'll give us a good laugh, in this cold."

"I do wish you'd –" Maurice's grumbling was cut off by the sound of the shop bell. He extricated himself from his darkroom, smoothed himself down and went to attend to his customer. Lily peeped around the side of the curtain to see Sir Edwin Gull, direct from his meeting with Mrs Potter, browsing along the shelved volumes.

"Good afternoon, Sir Edwin," said Maurice. "How many I be of service?"

"I happened to be nearby on business. I thought I'd call to collect my order."

"Of course. One moment." Maurice crossed the bookshop and unlocked a small fastener on the wall panelling behind the sales counter. He slid out a section on wheels to reveal a rack of photographs, books and illustrated pamphlets. He picked through a selection of small parcels, each one firmly tied with string.

Gull searched for something to say, something about the previous night at Holmwood's Music Hall, something about Maurice's laughter at Ruby Wester's song, something which would embarrass the bookseller, but he searched in vain. Instead, he merely watched the man's every move with scorn.

"Here we are," said Maurice, pulling out a slim package. "You'll notice an improvement in detail and clarity. Also, these new images are now reproducible, should you wish to obtain copies at a future date. Marvellous what the latest innovations can do these days."

Gull grunted. He took the package and slipped it between the pages of his pocketbook.

"While you're here, perhaps something warmer as an accompaniment, Sir Edwin?" said Maurice, gliding a hand over the rows of loose photographs. "Pictures for the new stereoscope?"

"No thank you."

"I have the current Gentleman's Guide, available bound into either a wallet or a cigar case."

"I'm sure you do. I don't want one. Good day to you, Mr Maurice." He clapped a handful of coins onto the counter and stalked out in a cloud of loathing.

Maurice glanced at his pocket watch. Mrs Maurice would be back shortly. He could tell her the good news about the governess over supper. He slid his range of special purchases out of sight and returned to the studio. Lily and Clipper had already left via the back gate.

He took a cloth and began to wipe the thin nitrate deposits from the inside of his camera. Let's see, if materials were now a little cheaper, and with copies possible. . . add in the costs per print, minus the girls' percentage. . . business was looking up. Worth the update after all. He might consider raising the fee per sitting, to encourage spicier poses, and might even—

He suddenly turned, folding up his cloth. "Hello?" He thought he'd heard movement. The bell was silent. "Anyone there?"

He shrugged and carried on tidying up, but he couldn't shake a distinct feeling that he was being watched. In the end, he shuffled out into the shop – nobody here – then leaned out over the staircase that led up to his living rooms – nothing there – then looked up through the studio's glass roof in case someone was clambering about outside. Nothing and nobody.

Unseen, a ghostly presence flowed silently into the space beneath the equipment table. The vampyr needed safety, craved a new host, was hungry for blood. This human was older and fatter than it usually preferred, but otherwise seemed sound.

Maurice fetched a cup of water to feed the leafy plants beside the chaise and checked over the developed glass negative of his latest photograph. Tut tut, a spot, and he'd washed the whole plate so thoroughly beforehand!

Never mind, it barely touched Lily's figure and shouldn't affect the price.

He felt a peculiar tickle curl along his arm. He carefully put the plate down and scratched, but the sensation seemed to be rippling under his waistcoat. No, under his shirt, up his chest.

For the blink of an eye he had an impression of – was it a trick of the light? – something dark and distorted, rearing up in front of his face. Before he could react, it vanished.

A searing pain suddenly flashed across the inside of his nose and sliced into the back of his throat. It spread like a raging fire, through his neck, up behind his eyes.

He screeched in pain, falling to his knees with his hands clamped to the sides of his head. His eyes bulged and his face reddened. He squirmed from side to side as if trying to throw something off himself. His whole body trembled and twitched.

And then he was still. It had a firm hold on him.

Maurice-vampyr took a deep breath and got to his feet, smiling. A fresh host, at long last.

He held his hands up in front of his new face and wiggled his new fingers. He felt the beat of his new heart, the flexing of his new limbs, the push and pull of air in his new lungs. "Sight, and sound, and voice once more," he said quietly to himself, relishing the cadences of a language that was new to him.

He was getting hungry. His tongue darted, in and out between shining lips, and he clacked his teeth together. Very hungry.

He strode to the tiny kitchen under the stairs. A knife

would be useful. He had little energy left for a fight or a struggle. A knife would be quicker.

The shop bell rang. "Only me, Herbert!" called out Mrs Maurice.

VIII

Backstage at Holmwood's Music Hall, Renfield the magician dragged at a long, thin pipe, puffing the smoke in curly clouds. "I miss those days. It's not the same now. It's all hurry, hurry, hurry, on to the next act, do your turn, off again. He was a sly old goat, was Renton Nicholson, but he could put on a show. His *tableau vivants* and his Lord Baron acts. All the best ones were his. Or copies of his. Real theatre."

"Real theatre?" snorted Ruby, stepping into the skirts of a brightly striped dress. "You've never played a real theatre in your life."

"I'm talking about theatrical traditions," grumbled Renfield, "the real traditions of theatre, handed down through generations of players. Have I told you I once met Joseph Grimaldi himself, when I was a lad?"

"Often," said Ruby flatly, fluffing her hair in an age-spotted mirror.

"He wasn't a well man. You could see it in his face. He'd given his life to his public. As have I. The penny gaffs I played were rough and ready, yes, that's true, there's no denying that, but they brought the old traditions to everyday people. We'd dramatise important issues of the day, like murders and famous personalities." He waved a finger in the direction of the Strand. "An evening at the Coal Hole down in Fountain Court, or the Cyder Cellars, gave you entertainment *and* education."

"And bare bums."

"And a bit of innocent saucy fun, *sometimes*."

"Bare bums."

"I'll have you know, girl, I saw W. G. Ross perform *Sam Hall* at the Cyder Cellars. Must be twenty years ago now. Marvellous he was, he really made your flesh creep. You could have heard the drop of a pin in that pub."

"And the drop of a jaw when he got his bum out," said Ruby, lacing her shoes.

"Watch your lip! There's no discipline these days. Nothing's innocent any more, it's all got to be crude and flaunted in your face. Don't you get snooty about real theatre, young lady, not when that Finette and her hoofers are doing the cancan at the Lyceum – the *Lyceum*! And I bet *you're* singing something dirty again tonight."

"My Buckingham Palace banquet song," grinned Ruby. "By popular demand."

"It's disrespectful."

"You may be interested to hear that my current gentleman friend has *been* to a banquet at Buck House. There's no disrespect in singing about miserable Mrs Victoria Brown shovelling it down her throat when that's exactly what happens. People cheer."

"I don't believe you've got a current gentleman friend. I notice he won't show his face around here, will he? And you don't seem to be getting much out of the arrangement."

Ruby pursed her lips and Renfield knew he'd touched a sore spot. "Yes, well," said Ruby, "that will be changing very soon, I can promise you that."

> "Welcome, one and all, to Holmwood's! Our first act of the evening, ladies and gentlemen, is that peerless pickle of posh personality, The Tottering Toff!"

Up in the gallery, Captain Harker threw back his third drink as the violins began to hiccup a wobbly tune. The audience hooted at the arrival on stage of a slenderly built man in a battered top hat, who staggered and tumbled acrobatically while lamenting, in song, his dreadful bad luck at gambling – oh no, what a loopy Lord, he's lost all his money *again*!

Knives and forks were tapped against tables in time with the music. Sitting in his usual spot close to the stage, William Browning, journalist on the London Daily Examiner, joined in cheerfully while he waited for tonight's performance by his unrequited love, Ruby Wester.

Harker was waiting for someone too, and kept glancing over at the top of the stairs. The Tottering Toff was launching himself into a series of flips and rolls when, to Harker's surprise, Arthur Flemming appeared and scuttled over.

"My dear Harker, I didn't realise you frequent this place."

"I don't, I'm expecting a messenger any moment, this is a convenient point of delivery. Are you racing at the heels of your master again tonight?"

Flemming had no ear for sarcasm. "Indeed I am, indeed I am. I've spent half the day attending Lady Gull. She's a most gracious woman, of course, descended from a noble family, but she cannot make a decision should her life depend upon it! How her household avoid hurling themselves from the Tarpeian Rock in absolute frustration, I have no idea!"

"It may be fortunate you're here," said Harker, craning his neck in search of the expected message. "I trust you and Sir Edwin did as I asked?"

"Good heavens, what outrageous behaviour!" Flemming cocked his head to get a better view of two well-dressed men who were dangling over the balcony further along. One was holding onto the legs of the other, who was in mid-air trying to light his cigar on a low hanging gas lamp. Several women formed a squealing group behind them in the gallery, some scared and some giggling. A couple of bread rolls were flung at the lower man from the tables underneath, accompanied by cheers.

"Not altogether sensible," muttered Harker. At that moment, his messenger arrived. He quickly paid the uniformed boy and tore open the letter. It contained the translation he'd requested, of the words carved into the box's seal.

"A pair of common roughnecks!" said Flemming. "I've a mind to remind Sir Edwin about doubling the prices here, and keeping out the— How did he put it?—"

Harker suddenly grasped Flemming's arm and swung him around sharply. "You did as I asked, yes? Tell me you did exactly as I asked!"

"Asked about what?"

"The box, man! The sealed box!"

"Ah. I'm afraid I have something of a confession to make—"

"You opened it?" gasped Harker. His face became a thunderstorm of fear and anger. He brandished the letter in his fist. "You bloody fools! Where was the seal broken?"

"At the empty shop, in Seward Walk."

"My god!" spat Harker, looking around as if he might glimpse the vampyr at any moment. "Then it's in this very district! It could be hiding inside someone right here!"

Flemming raised his hands for calm. "I sincerely regret my action. The contents were horribly disturbing but, please, you have my assurance, there was nothing supernatural to them. The box was simply a decorated funerary casket, like those of the ancient pharaohs."

Harker was growing more terrified and more furious by the second. "Where is Gull? Effective action will likely require his influence. Take me to him! Now!"

"I thought I'd catch up with him here, but he must have already returned home, he has a meeting with business associates there before dinner. Wretched nuisance, I only left his house a few hours ago."

"Ladies and gentlemen! In her extended season with us, the formidable, the fabulous, the phenomenal, Ruby Wester!"

There was a sharp cry as the man with the unlit cigar accidentally slipped free of his boots and dropped to the floor with a bone-snapping crack. The pianist at the side of the stage played as loudly and rousingly as he could to cover the noise. At the same moment, Harker was hastening Flemming down the staircase and out of the building.

IX

The air had felt clotted all day and Lily Murray felt grimy and tired. She looked down at the smart attire she'd paid 3d to rent first thing that morning, and was relieved to see no damage beyond the ordinary mud and dirt of the street.

From 8am to 10am: she'd ridden buses up and down the Strand, any bus on which Clipper's mate Tom The Thumb was the conductor. She sat next to respectable ladies, with a smile and a polite word, and while Tom staged distractions, she used her skills as a dip to relieve the respectable ladies of the contents of their voluminous skirt pockets. Result, minus expenses, minus Tom's cut: 8s 9d, plus a snuff box and a fancy fountain pen sold to a fence in Lugg Street.

From 10am to 1pm: she swam the undulating ocean of people and vehicles from Nelson's monument to Fleet Street, dipping wherever she could, cadging as a lady in distress from worshippers leaving the Exeter Hall, lifting from the smarter shops. Result, minus heavy losses sustained in a short altercation with an officer of the Metropolitan Police: 4s 2d.

From 1pm: she joined Clipper at the Northumberland

House end of the Strand to run the Melon Drop on any unsuspecting newcomer to London who was leaving Charing Cross. She walked at speed towards her chosen mark, careful to collide with him only when his attention was diverted by the glittering splendour of the nation's capital. Her securely wrapped parcel of broken old junk tumbled to the ground with a loud internal crash.

Miss Lily Murray: Oh! Great heavens! My dear mother's vase!

Unsuspecting Newcomer: I'm most dreadfully sorry!

Miss Lily Murray: Smashed to pieces!

Clipper (arriving heroically upon the scene): Are you all right, Miss? Sir, such clumsiness!

Unsuspecting Newcomer: I was looking at— I do apologise!

Miss Lily Murray (fetching a handkerchief to stem her copious tears): I was to pawn it, to provide the little ones with a meagre supper of bread and milk! But now. . .! O, we are ruined!

Clipper: As a lawyer, Miss, I advise you to bring a legal action against this bungling and infelicitous gentleman!

Unsuspecting Newcomer: No! Sir, it was but an unfortunate accident!

Miss Lily Murray: No harm was intended, I'm sure. I shall explain as much to the little ones, and to my dear, dying mother. . .

Clipper: You are kindness itself, Miss. However, sir, I am less forgiving when it comes to negligence and injustice! Your name?

Unsuspecting Newcomer (producing whatever cash he

has about his person): Here! Please! For the children! It's all I have! I apologise unreservedly! Good day to you! Good day!

Clipper followed each mark for a few hundred yards, to make sure they were fleeing in shame. By the time he returned, Lily had picked up her parcel and was scanning the crowd for the next dupe.

Result, minus sundries: £6 18s 7d.

Throughout the afternoon's successes, Lily's mind kept flicking back to her child. She didn't like having Jack at her side when she was working, but certainly didn't want him mudlarking or in the factories, no matter what some people said. Some people could keep their fat, runny noses out of her business. He was perfectly fine with Mrs Potter. Their room mate was a respectable old lady, and grateful for the two shillings a week, and if *she* couldn't be trusted then who the devil could?

Lily felt the late sun on her face. What was left from her share of today's takings, she reckoned, might even buy a few weeks' school for Jack at the nearby National, if she was careful.

Above her, a patchwork of ragged, yellow-brown clouds slowly swirled in a hot blue sky. Three roads met close to where she crossed King William Street. Around the junction, to keep the dust at bay, kids pushed brooms and men sprinkled water from carts, their hands extending for a tip from every passer-by. They fought a losing battle with the dirt kicked up by the workmen digging a branch line into the railway station.

A group of sharp young men, adorned in fashion and money, were making slow progress along the pavement, partly because they were more intent on chanting than walking, and partly because they were trying to force brandy down the throats of the two prostitutes who laughed and brayed too. Lily and Clipper kept eyes on them, while watching the roar of the human river and eating fried fish and pea soup from a stall on the Strand.

Clipper's gaze narrowed and his head swung. "Look," he muttered with a nod, "here comes a pack of Jolly Dogs. Out early. Must be celebrating. A chance to invest."

Lily knew both girls by sight, but didn't recognise them for a minute or two with their faces as unpainted as posher customers preferred. "There's no need," she groaned, "we've got today's take, and there's what Bert Maurice owes us. I can pay off my rent, Mrs Potter said Gull hisself has turned demander."

"We'll double our money. More."

"Why risk it?"

"Look at these swells, you can see they hold a candle to the Devil. Why should those two rollers have it all? We can just clip the loosest of 'em."

"I want to go home to Jack."

"He's fine and dandy. Come on, I can't do one on me own, even if he likes a she-shirt. Come oooon, let's do a bit of bug hunting."

Clipper marched, Lily reluctantly trailing in his wake. She was distracted for a moment by the sudden bellow of a cow being pushed into the basement slaughter house across the road. As she turned, she was surprised to see the brusque-and-sad gentleman who'd helped her out the other night at Holmwood's.

He was hurrying as if his life depended on it, a paper

clutched tightly in his hand, and scampering at his side was a slender, rattled-looking bloke with a beaky nose. She was close enough to hear the brusque-and-sad gentleman cursing the traffic and the slender bloke demanding explanations.

"Lily!" hissed Clipper. "Come on!"

Harker hadn't seen Lily at all, his attention fixed on finding some form of transport that might move at quicker than walking pace. Flemming, patting dust off his sleeves, pulled a face as they passed through the aroma of the fried fish stall. They turned into a side street and sped north.

Within a minute, they were unknowingly observed for a second time. Mrs Potter had seen Arthur Flemming once or twice before, in that bastard Gull's company. She paused in the shadows until he and that angry-looking sort were out of sight.

Mrs Potter was heading for the Haymarket. She'd left home almost an hour ago and, to avoid any chance of being spotted either by Lily's cronies or by Lily herself, had taken a route well out of her way. Eight-year-old Jack's hand was firmly grasped in hers. They inched through the press of Covent Garden market, where they could be invisible among the porters shouting a path to the produce carts and the costermongers with tall stacks of fruit and veg baskets balanced on their heads. They walked through the quieter streets that ran parallel to Long Acre, avoiding the stares that clustered in doorways like wild toadstool blooms, the derelicts in a waking sleep on watch for toe-nibbling rats.

It was only once they reached the area around Leicester

Square that little Jack began to weep. Mrs Potter's lack of conversation was unusual enough in itself to tell him that something was wrong. Unease started to flutter in his stomach and he cried, overcome by a jittery, unfocussed dread.

Some sections of the Haymarket were lined with beggars, others with women who'd soon be seeking toffs to accompany into the glitter and velvet of the Argyll Rooms. Mrs Potter gravitated towards the hidden corners where ragged, starving parents with eyes like death discreetly sold their youngest ones into the service of the Haymarket Hectors.

"Stop snivelling," she hissed. "Stand up straight."

Jack's tears rose into a bawl of fright. He hadn't the faintest clue where he was, or why, but instinct howled at him that this was no place to be. Strangers looked him up and down. Some were seedy men in bowler hats who smelled of tobacco and teeth.

"Shut yer noise," spat Mrs Potter under her breath. "It's for everyone's good. This way yer get to live with a higher class of people, *and* yer mother is relieved of a burden, *and* I pays the bastard Gull. I pays me nethers, I do."

Jack, his hand still held tightly in Mrs Potter's, stood motionless with his other hand limp at his side. He wailed and sobbed.

Mrs Potter jabbed his shoulder. "Listen, I got bills to pay. I got outgoings. I'm doing you a favour, y'ungrateful little sod. Yer mother allus says she wants a better life for yer, don't she? Most would've put yer in a baby farm, soon as yer was born. When you go I lose two shilling a week off me money, think on that!"

She'd counted on getting ten or twelve pounds for Jack from the ponces. She planned on telling Lily that Jack had run away. The silly girl'd believe it once he didn't come back.

The sun pushed a final beam through the hot broil overhead, throwing a last gasp of glory against the grandeur of Her Majesty's Theatre and the Theatre Royal, before sinking from sight behind the rise and fall of roofs. With lengthening shadows, extra players from the lowest caste of characters gradually made their entrances.

Jack's unceasing tears were all that saved him. The drizzle of pimps who inspected him for lice, or checked his bones for deformities, sneered at his snotty face and demanded money from Mrs Potter to take him off her hands.

Before it was fully dark, she gave up and dragged him away, muttering in despair through gritted teeth. Several times on the walk home, she stopped and slapped him hard across the face.

"You say one word to yer mam, and I'll get a knife and I'll slit yer miserable throat! And hers! Right? *Right?*" She shook him until he nodded. "What do I do now, eh? Yer a selfish little shit!"

X

"Mr Flemming arrived a few minutes ago, sir, in company with another gentleman," whispered the polished butler. "Her ladyship advised me to show them into the study."

Gull nodded. "Very well."

The butler melted into the background while Gull continued his farewells to the line of colleagues filing out of the fraught meeting which had just concluded in the sitting room. One of the last out, a rotund and heavily whiskered man, leaned in close to Gull as he passed.

"Better make some progress, old chap," he said softly. "Board of Works'll be making a final decision. Chop chop, eh?"

Gull's ice-cold eyes followed him for a moment. The slight rouge of Gull's cheeks could have been either rage or embarrassment, it was impossible to tell.

Once his guests had departed, Gull stalked along a wide, carpeted corridor which led past a number of elegantly appointed rooms. As he marched into his study, Flemming rose quickly to his feet. Harker remained seated, pondering a painting that was one of a dozen or more propped up together against a bookcase. It was the eerie Fragonard that Flemming had admired in Transylvania. Gull caught the direction of Harker's gaze.

"Flemming, what's all this doing here?"

"These are the remaining items from the vault that Lady Gull did not wish to keep," said Flemming. "They'll be collected and prepared for sale in the morning."

"Mm. Captain Harker, are we to hear more tales from Mr Andersen and the Brothers Grimm?"

Harker's earlier anger had hardened into a brooding, saturnine calm. He sat with his hands clawed on both armrests, quietly burning.

"I think, sir," stumbled Flemming, "in view of recent events, um, evidence which has come to light, we should hear what my friend has to say. He has done a great deal of scholastic research, following his experiences in the Far East—"

"Unless he has experience that will solve my immediate problem and give my consortium control over the Board of Works, I'm not particularly inclined to hear anything your friend has to say."

Harker suddenly slammed his fists down on the arms of the chair. He spoke with tightly controlled menace. "Damn you, sir, I have no wish to associate myself with odious predators like you, but you have the ear of the authorities and as a public servant you have public duties. Unless urgent steps are taken, every citizen of London may be in danger. I am in deadly earnest. Do you not understand me, man?"

Flemming leapt to defuse the explosive silence. "Sir, I felt a terrible presence in that vault. For less than a heart's beat but, if you'll please forgive my candour, Sir Edwin,

I'd venture to suppose you felt it too. I can personally attest to Captain Harker's courageous service for queen and country and, while I have never pried into his private griefs, I do believe his knowledge of supernatural matters could be of immediate value."

Gull slumped wearily into a chair. If his meeting hadn't left him feeling bruised, he'd have thrown the pair of them out of the house. As it was, he reached for the embroidered bell-pull to summon a servant, and had a decanter of whiskey and three crystal glasses brought to the study.

Harker drank several while he told them about the jiāngshī attack he'd witnessed in China. Gull slouched in silence, his brow gradually knitting. Flemming sat with his knees together and his glass cupped in both hands, growing paler as he listened to the details of Harker's narrow escape.

"As soon as I returned to England," said Harker, his mood tempered with alcohol, "I resolved to understand the nature of the evil that had so thoroughly destroyed my nerve and my professionalism as a soldier. To that end and. . . particularly after I lost my family. . . I have amassed testimonies, histories and other documents from far afield, some of great antiquity.

"The phenomenon of the vampyr is both real and worldwide. Their phantom-like form, once described to me as 'living smoke,' feeds on fresh blood via its host organism. I retain the customary categorisation of them as supernatural entities for the simple reason that they display characteristics far beyond our present understanding. For example, they can, should they need to, exert a mesmeric influence on the human mind, which helps them to escape danger and evade detection, rather like the ink of an octopus. How such a faculty operates is a mystery, although texts I have studied in vitalism, and works by Faria, Deleuze and others, provide a few clues. This faculty, combined with an ability to lie dormant for long periods, is what I believe accounts for their absorption into folklore rather than into science. As folklore, details of their nature vary from region to region, but they are a matter of historical record and have plagued mankind for centuries."

He poured himself another glass of whiskey. "In ancient Greece and Rome, the *lamia* was known as a creature that habitually drank the blood of children in the night. The Vikings called them *draugr*. South America has several overlapping vampyr traditions, in particular that of the *tunda* in Colombia and the *peuchen* in Chile, which is said to favour large snakes as hosts, since this enables them to stalk and subdue their human victims efficiently. West African peoples speak of the *adze*, which hunts the young and the weak, in India the *vetalas*. Across the Philippines and Malaysia, the *mannangal* or 'self-segmenter' is reported as being able to occupy separated body parts. On the islands of Japan these are known as *nukekubi*. Europe has at least three distinct, localised vampyr legends, including the *strigoi* which is native to the area around Croatia. Significant outbreaks have occurred on the Continent roughly once in every century, the last being in East Prussia in 1721. A few notorious names from Eastern European history, including Vlad the Impaler, Eleonore von Schwarzenberg and the

Countess Báthory, have been rumoured as hosts, but nothing is certain.

"Our own culture has had little to say on the subject. England's relative freedom from the vampyr scourge, to date, has seen the creature treated only as florid, inaccurate fiction. Dr Polidori's *The Vampyre* of 1819 made a complete nonsense of the truth, and there was a penny dreadful twenty years ago entitled *Varney The Vampire* which was even worse. These fictions are filled with idiotic romanticism in which aristocrats grow fangs, fear the holy cross, turn to dust in sunlight and other such foolery. A real vampyr has no such weaknesses. A biologist would consider them parasites, like tapeworms or ticks." He emptied his glass and refilled it again.

"How long do these creatures live?" said Flemming weakly.

Harker stared into his drink. "Hundreds of years, it's said, perhaps even thousands, but nobody really knows. They are unaffected by fire or explosion, that much is known."

Gull shifted in his chair with a grunt. "There must be some defence against them, surely?"

"Vampyrs can be driven out of a host, but only at the cost of the host's life. The host must be decapitated, or buried, preferably head down, or pierced with spikes that pin him to the ground. This is because, if a host dies while occupied, the vampyr can power the corpse for a short while like a marionette on strings, until it finds a new home. Vampyrs don't lightly leave a host so, for one to be driven out, the host body must be made useless to it. Loss of limbs, that sort of thing. How and why a vampyr chooses a particular host in the first place is a matter of pure speculation."

"Are you saying," squeaked Flemming, "there is no way to prevent yourself being occupied by one of these fiends, should it find you?"

"Some traditions advocate specific garlands, claiming that vampyrs avoid certain plants. Others say they won't enter running water, and advocate isolation in river or sea, but these are superstitions at best. However, despite their nebulous existence, they must in *some* sense be corporeal . . ." Harker paused and directed meaningful looks at the other two men, ". . . because a vampyr *can* be trapped."

A sickly chill ran through both Gull and Flemming. Gull overcame his first.

"Trapped how?" he said.

"By being sealed into something from which no air or liquid can escape. It takes a good few seconds for this parasite to wriggle free from a host, and therein lies an opportunity to catch it. There is a Spanish account, for example, of a host being dropped into molten iron; another from Mexico of a host being rolled into layers of thickly tarred linen; another of entrapment in a vessel used for brewing, of all things. That was in the Baltic, if I remember correctly. While I was still in China, I discovered that some rural villages keep a readily sealable box or container, a *xīxuèguǐ hézi*, for exactly this purpose. You'll notice that, again, a host's fate is unavoidable."

"Does trapping the vampyr not kill it?" breathed Flemming.

"Eventually, yes," said Harker. "Entrapment weakens

and disorients them, but they can survive in a dormant state for very a long time. For decades, certainly, possibly far longer. Until then, they wait."

"For what?" mumbled Gull.

"For someone to let them out. I don't believe that the box you found, Flemming, was intended to be used as a *xīxuèguǐ hézi*. They're normally much larger and rather different in shape, hence my uncertainty when I saw it. In this instance, I'd say that box was simply a decorative item picked up by someone on their travels which was fortuitously to hand when the crisis came. In other words, an item Chinese in origin but filled and sealed in Transylvania."

From his pocket, Harker took the letter he'd received at Holmwood's and smoothed it out on his knee. "What human host this particular vampyr was previously driven from, I cannot say, but the nature of the host in which it was then trapped. . . is less uncertain. I pray to God, gentlemen, that ignoring my instructions revealed only the body of some small animal which the vampyr intended as a temporary hiding place."

Flemming's throat felt as if it was coated in sand, but his glass remained absolutely still. Gull's gaze wavered.

Harker, knowing he'd made his point, continued, "I sent my transcription of those words scratched into the seal to a diplomatic contact I made some time ago as part of my work for the War Office. I told him nothing of where the words had come from." He tapped at the paper on his knee. "He says they're in a Hungarian dialect used widely in the rural parts of the Carpathians, and take the form of three concise warnings: *óvakodj a vérivótól*, beware the drinker of blood; *halál csap le, ha feltöröd ezt a pecsétet*, death will follow the breaking of this seal; *ez a doboz tartalmaz Dracul*; this box contains – the last word here means 'the dragon' or 'the devil' but is written as a name, Dracul."

"And we let this Dracul out," moaned Flemming.

"It was likely in a weakened and confused state after its confinement. Think yourself lucky it didn't choose either of you two as a host."

Gull sat upright. "How do we know it didn't?"

"If one of us was host to a vampyr," said Harker, "then the others would already be dead upon this rug. From what you were telling me on our way here, Flemming, I doubt if – well, we'll refer to it as Dracul for the sake of clarity, shall we? – I doubt if Dracul was trapped for more than a few months. Had it been years, my guess is that it would have attacked you instantly."

Flemming's quivering fingers dabbed at his chin. "The consequences of our actions may be incalculable, Sir Edwin."

Gull's mouth mashed at his thoughts and he stretched forward making his chair creak. "I am prepared to admit that I am somewhat less sceptical of Captain Harker's claims than I was half an hour ago. However, if these claims are true, this demonic monster has been at large for well over twenty-four hours, yet there is no panic in the streets, no blood-letting, no gleefully illustrated reports in the *Examiner*."

"Dracul's new host will not be walking the streets acting like some raving madman," said Harker, running a hand through his hair. "A vampyr's instinct is to operate by stealth. It is a wolf stalking sheep. If it were not, it would scarcely have stayed a creature of myth. It becomes frenzied, like those jiāngshī I encountered, only when its lust to feed is fully aroused. It will already have killed at least once, and it will do so again and again."

"One killer, no matter how vicious or elusive, does not constitute an emergency."

"It will draw others," said Harker impatiently. "The continued success of one vampyr seems to somehow light up its occult power such that more are attracted to it. Documented cases from the past confirm this, they even use the language of disease: outbreak, epidemic, pestilence. This is why those vampyrs in China, those jiāngshī, had come together in the first place. Leave this thing unchecked and London will *crawl* with these horrors! I'm not asking for any kind of alarm to be raised, such a thing would only cause panic and send Dracul into hiding, what we need is discreet, co-ordinated action."

Gull snorted gruffly to himself and set his chair creaking again. His mind fought itself, one side commanding him not to take this macabre yarn-spinning seriously, the other remembering the terrible feeling of dread that had washed over him when the box was opened. At last, he took a deep breath. "As you have said, quite correctly, I have the ear of the authorities. However, we are fortunate to live in an age of rational science and so I will rapidly lose that ear if I start to tell it ghost stories. In order to take action, I require proof, and as yet there is none. None, that is, to support your specific assertions."

"That will change," growled Harker.

"True or not," said Gull, "you are making an assumption, namely that the authorities will take a view identical to yours. That is unlikely since this devil, this Dracul, has been released in an area of grossly congested population. I can name a dozen of my fellow Members of Parliament – and many others! – who would remind you that overcrowding lies at the root of poverty and all similar moral failings, and thus a periodic cleansing of the gutters by disease, accident, or war is both natural and an unfortunate necessity. They would see this matter as akin to an outbreak of cholera, a regrettable but unavoidable culling of society's economically inactive. They would see no cause for concern unless it got out of hand by threatening commerce or civil unrest."

"Unless it threatened themselves, you mean!" spat Harker, leaping to his feet. "How large a cull might be tolerated, pray tell? A hundred? A thousand?"

"I assure you, Captain Harker, the prevailing view of the authorities would be one of wait-and-see until a palpable situation of civil disturbance arises. The public purse is limited."

"For pity's sake!" cried Harker, his hands almost reaching to tear his hair. "I have never heard such contemptible, purblind stupidity! I can see I am wasting my time!" With that, he swept out of the room.

Above him, on the landing that overlooked the hallway, Lady Gull peeped over the bannisters to take a look at this peculiarly rough, fuming visitor leaving the house. She'd been standing there for a few minutes, on the exact spot where discussions in the study could best be overheard, short of putting an ear to the door, but she had gathered very little. Sir Edwin's earlier meeting, on the other hand, she'd heard more than enough of. The grille in the chimney stack in the third bedroom conveyed sounds from the sitting room downstairs with admirable clarity.

Frances Gull was a few years older than her husband, an austere *grande dame* of polite London society whose distinguished lineage had its deepest roots in the robber barons of the early Middle Ages. She was a matronly, humourless person whose stare could spear a chambermaid from ten paces and who had taken some years to admit to herself that her husband married her for her money and her influence.

While Sir Edwin's meeting had still been in its early, less accusatory stage, Lady Gull had taken the opportunity to spend a few minutes perusing her husband's private papers in the study, as she often did when she knew she wouldn't be disturbed. She had unlocked his desk drawers with her duplicate set of keys. Among the items she looked through were Gull's increasingly sour correspondences with the Metropolitan Board of Works, and his pocketbook.

She'd turned the pocketbook's pages slowly, all but certain of what would be revealed when she got to the loose items that could be felt tucked into the back of it. Sure enough, there were three photographs mounted on thin card, taken on Herbert Maurice's new chaise. She'd believed the whispered rumours from a trusted informant, that Gull had a mistress, some tawdry tart on the make who sang in the West End music halls. And here was confirmation. A striking, dark-haired young woman.

Three indelicate poses, one of them signed on the back "Love, your Ruby."

Lady Gull had put everything back exactly where she found it, locked up the desk and silently returned to eavesdropping Sir Edwin's meeting. Her expression was fixed and grim.

The continued piling of *her* money into *his* business affairs was bad enough. A problem that rankled beyond endurance, but one she was confident of solving, given time. However, one cheap slut might easily precipitate matters, and *that* she would not tolerate. She would not have her name dragged through mud!

Now, as that oily stick insect Flemming followed the other man out, and the house closed up for the night, she retired to her room. She took comfort from the secure, concealed hatch in the base of her bed frame. Inside was her insurance against Sir Edwin's folly, collected over a decade, to use if she ever needed to plead ignorance of his actions, or ditch him to avoid scandal: bank promissory notes proving his involvement in fraud, a few legal letters and other incriminating documents, and a small blue phial of arsenic.

XI

The last thing young Hugo remembered was— What was the last thing he remembered? He began to raise his head but the sloshing throb inside his skull stopped him. He groaned in pain and slowly ungummed his eyes.

What were these funny shapes? His mind finally ticked over enough for him to realise he was looking up at the night sky, from between two tall buildings. Lying down, looking up at the night sky. He felt cold, and there was, *urgh*, what was that terrible smell?

Emitting a half-moan, half-whine, he turned onto his side and his nose dipped into the puddle that was the source of the smell. He sat bolt upright with a yelp, which sent the world spinning around him.

He'd been out with his friends. Yes, all Jolly Dogs together! That was it. He remembered. . . er. . . some girls. Nice girls.

It was only when he looked down at himself that he understood why he was feeling cold. He'd been stripped down to his underwear. He reached out to steady himself and his hands mushed into the slimy dirt which coated the cobbles beneath him. Then he was sick.

Wait, wait, wait. Underwear?

His clothes! His money! Ye gods, all his money!

They had. . . passed Charing Cross. Yes, he remembered that. Him and his friends, out for a good time, not a care in the world. There were those nice girls. Two of them. C'mon, ladies, catch us up, we've been downing the stuff since midday! We're celebrating, for our chum here has bought a naval commission and leaves for— Wait a minute, was that *me* leaving? Oh, no, thank heavens, it was good old Jamie-boy. I'm. . . Hugo. That's it, I'm Hugo.

And another girl joined the fun! Pretty girl. Fair hair. She had a friend with her. He seemed like a thoroughly decent chap. They suggested. . . something. Then just the three of us, went off to. . . a night house? There was dancing! Polkas and quadrilles! Another drink, don't mind if I do, to your good health, sir.

Upstairs, some other place. Quieter, some card games. Oooh, not to worry, I've got loads, look, let's bet on another hand. Drink up, bottle's still half full, you're right.

Did the pretty fair girl argue with the decent chap? There was a vague recollection of disagreement. No, can't have, they were both there in the quiet room, nice and peaceful, sleepy time, look after me, my angel, for I think I may have overindulged, any chance of a. . .

Young Hugo slapped his hands to his forehead, forgetting they were caked in muck. He looked around at the dark, dripping alleyway into which he'd been dumped, cursing his stupidity over and over again. What were their names? Couple of common mutchers! *Cl*-something. Claude? Whoever they were, by God he'd roast them alive! He'd bring the full weight of the law down on their thieving, miserable heads!

After he'd done something about his own miserable head. *Owww...*

He wiped his hands on his vest and tried to stand up, but he was too weary and wet and fed up. He could hear the sounds of people, of revels, not too far away. He considered shouting for help, but was sick again.

He suddenly heard a soft scraping sound, coming from somewhere behind him. He twisted painfully to see a stout middle-aged man appear from the shadows.

"What on earth has happened here?" said Maurice-Dracul. "Have you been robbed, sir?"

Hugo gasped with relief. "Indeed I have, and left for dead by a pair of armed ruffians. Can you help me?"

"Of course, sir, of course."

"I put up one hell of a fight, but they knocked me unconscious."

Maurice-Dracul tutted. "Such brazen villainy is the curse of our times." He scuttled closer to the young man.

Hugo felt a little better now his stomach was empty. He didn't look up until Maurice-Dracul's face was only a hand's width from his own, and then it was too late to cry out.

Maurice-Dracul descended on young Hugo like a dead weight, slashing his throat with a kitchen knife. The vampyr burned hot with hunger, eyes wide and mouth gaping, burned with the need to soak in the blood of his prey, to have it fill his throat, his belly, his whole body.

He clamped his mouth over the wound, pulling blood into himself in long, gluttonous gulps. With his free hand, he sliced at his prey's chest to make a second feeding hole. Hugo was quickly reduced to a sunken, grey shell of skin and bone.

Gathering up the corpse's withered legs, Maurice-Dracul began to drag the remains away. A few hours earlier, he'd jammed the husk of Mrs Maurice into the oven back at home, and now this second body would have to be hidden too, if he was to keep feeding in peace.

He was interrupted by the noise of approaching drunks, too many to fend off without attracting more attention. Cursing his bad luck, he left the corpse and scurried away into the darkness.

Over the course of the evening, Hugo's friends had lost him, then found him coming out of one of the seedier pubs with those two hangers-on in tow, then lost him again. Now they were following a suggestion made by those – just a moment, where *had* those charming girls gone all of a sudden? Those charming girls had slipped away quietly, before any Jolly Dog noticed that their cash, four rings and a hip flask had slipped away as well.

"Is that him over there? Down the alley? Look at the fellow! Ready for action!"

"Huuuugo! The theatres are turning out, we might catch the last hour at the Argyll!"

"Or there's Mott's."

"Yes, or Mott's. Or Evans's."

"The night is not quite as young as it was, old chap, but it's still got a decent pair of tits on it!"

Laughing raucously at their own rapier wit, they swayed along the alley, slipping here and there on the cobbles and singing the odd line or two from a couple of songs they could almost recall. It was only as they got closer to what was left of their friend that they subsided into silence, wondering why he was so still and why he lay in that strange position.

They blinked woozily down at him for a moment, through the swirling gloom, until they could focus properly. The noise of their reaction could clearly be heard on the Strand.

XII

from the *London Daily Examiner*, dated Friday 29th May 1868

HORRIBLE MURDER IN THE WEST END

Dreadful injuries inflicted – Peculiar condition of the victim – Suspects sought

by Wm Browning,
staff reporter

Persons in the area of the Strand close to Southampton Street and Lemmly Court were much alarmed at a few minutes to 11 o'clock last night by a series of loud cries emanating from a small alleyway branching off Maiden Lane. These cries were the result of a gruesome and disturbing discovery, namely the victim of a shocking and bizarre murder.

The body of the deceased, Mr Hugo Pell, nephew of the industrialist Jabez Pell, had been violently torn on the neck, chest and upper thigh. These wounds were of such severity that the victim had little blood remaining, and was in a hideously emaciated state that was terrible to behold.

BLOOD LOSS

To compound the mystery, the amount of blood evident at the scene of death could account for only a proportion of that which had been lost from the body. With no sign of the deceased having been dragged from another location, and no wheel tracks nearby to indicate any similar movement, the dreadful, yet logical, conclusion must therefore be that three or four pints had been extracted and removed.

To compound the mystery still further, it was later ascertained by police examination that the grievous wounds, while having been initially inflicted with a knife, had been added to by deep and penetrating bite marks. The flesh around the wounds was ragged and somewhat puckered, but none appears to have been cut away.

Your reporter can personally verify the details of this grisly crime as I was among those who first responded to the cries of alarm. I had left Holmwood's Music Hall, a short walk away, only a few minutes earlier.

SUSPECTS

The body was discovered by friends of the unfortunate Mr Pell. All had spent the evening enjoying local hospitality, during which time they became separated. However, these friends later saw the victim in the company of two suspicious persons, described by them as being an unshaven man in refined dress and a fair-haired woman of respectable appearance.

The suspects are being urgently sought by the police, who strongly advise that members of the public should not attempt to approach or apprehend them. However, the police also stress that violent criminals of this kind quickly run from the threat of capture and are highly likely to have left the city by train.

It is clear that this brutal event presents facets of unique obscurity and conjecture, principal among which is the apparent theft of human blood. Why any assailant, no matter how deranged, should burden themselves by carrying off a large container of liquid is beyond sense.

• • •

Maurice-Dracul was on his hands and knees behind the counter of his bookshop, plucking at the plump beetles coming up between the floorboards and crunching them in his jaw, when the shop bell rang. His head popped up to see who'd arrived.

"Oh, good morning, Mr Maurice. I am William Browning, perhaps you may remember me? We exchanged cards the other evening at Holmwood's?" He took off his hat and brushed absently at his moustaches and the sandy waves of his hair.

Maurice-Dracul got to his feet, beaming. "Of course, sir, of course I remember, the toiler in the Street of Ink."

Browning gave a diffident half-bow and smiled. Maurice-Dracul swept a hand around the shelves. "In what may I interest you?"

"Unfortunately, Mr Maurice, I'm here on what might

be called official business. Have you by any chance read my piece in today's *Examiner*? Relating to last night's tragedy?"

"I'm afraid I've been rather busy of late, Mr Browning. Tragedy?"

"A most—" Browning suddenly paused and asked in a whisper if there were any sensitive ears present. Maurice-Dracul assured him that Mrs Maurice would not overhear anything. "A murder took place, in an alley not thirty yards from this very spot."

"One is not safe anywhere these days," gasped Maurice-Dracul. "Has the culprit been caught?"

"Not as yet. At the moment, I fear that the police have too little information on which to base an arrest. I am making further enquiries myself, with a view to publishing a second article. My editor is hopeful of a series, should progress be made in the investigation."

"Then I wish you success, Mr Browning," smiled Maurice-Dracul, "for both your sake and the sake of justice. One man's misfortune is another's gold. T'was ever thus."

"To that end, Mr Maurice, I'm calling at local addresses to discover if anyone saw or heard suspicious activity. My particular interest is to ascertain whether someone was seen carrying a large jug or basin, or any similar vessel, at around an hour before midnight."

"Last night I went out for a substantial dinner, then came home and slept it off till dawn."

Strategies crackled through Maurice-Dracul's head. He'd have to stop this idiot's snooping! Kill him now? No, he has colleagues. Lay blame elsewhere? Uncertain outcomes. Substantial dinner was a mistake! Police? Disposal of Mrs Maurice's corpse becomes urgent. Serious risk! So keep this idiot close. Then drink him at leisure.

"Mr Browning, I recall from our first meeting you were in need of local accommodation? Are you by any chance still looking for new lodgings?"

"That I am," said Browning, turning the brim of his hat in his hands. "All the rooms I've applied for have been outrageously expensive or of deplorable quality, often both! You know of something suitable?"

"Why not take the two rooms on my own second floor? They are clean, and available at a nominal rent since the shop provides enough money for my needs. I would be a quiet neighbour and my only stipulation would be respecting the privacy of my personal sanctum behind that curtain you can glimpse back there."

Browning beamed, raising his hat high. "I accept, sight unseen! That is most uncommonly generous of you, sir. With Fleet Street so near, I shall save a small fortune in omnibus journeys and I'll be close to Holm—er, to the Strand too."

"You see, misfortune into gold, Mr Browning. A bizarrely bloody death has brought you to my door, yet it has profited us both! I'm sure our mutual love of the written word will make you a highly agreeable tenant. I know Mrs Maurice will feel the same. When she returns from her sister's. Next week. On that subject, I assume the accommodation will be for you alone? You are not married?"

Browning blushed so deeply that his cheeks felt hot. "No, sadly romance has not come my way. My heart is pledged where it has no business to be. I wonder, Mr Maurice, if I may install my few belongings here later today? If it's convenient."

"By all means." They parted with a hearty handshake and William Browning went about his business with a spring in his step.

His mood sobered when he returned to the bustling, noisy offices of the *Examiner*. He was told that two men were waiting for him, had been waiting for some time, would speak to no-one else, were a sombre-looking pair. Nervously, he introduced himself to Arthur Flemming and Valentine Harker, who asked to talk to him in private and in confidence.

They told him a story he was, at first, strongly inclined to dismiss as a practical joke played on him by his fellow reporters. But as its details gradually answered all the questions in his published article, his normally ruddy complexion grew pale.

XIII

The barrow's squeaking wheel threatened to draw attention. Maurice-Dracul had dragged the shrivelled remains of Mrs Maurice from the cold kitchen oven, and tied them securely in a weighted sack, but he had no oil at hand to silence her short journey down to the river.

He'd thought about burning her up in the oven, but he couldn't get the thing re-lit. He'd thought about finding a public burial pit in which to dump the corpse, but the sack was sure to be opened by scavengers. He'd thought about paying for disposal by a couple of underworld ruffians, but he knew they'd never resist searching the body either. The bottom of the Thames it would have to be.

Even in the mist and shadows of four o'clock in the morning, there were too many people and vehicles about to make the trip in complete secrecy. There were knots of ladybirds, in finery borrowed on commission, heading home to Limehouse or Brick Lane; stubborn merrymakers fighting and emptying their bladders; cabs clopping through the soot-laden miasma that draped itself around the gas lights; mug-hunters and lurkers owning the early hours; wanderers owning nothing; tradesmen setting out for early markets.

The bookseller's natural nervousness stirred up thoughts from deep inside his head as he steered the barrow towards the Thames. Memories struggled to assert themselves and tried to wriggle free of. . .

the. . . thing that controlled?. . .

His mind spun with random thoughts about his shop. . . his life. . . his past. . . He recalled. . . his previous sideline in photography, before his current, more profitable one. . . Photographs for grieving families, with siblings and cousins and fathers posed beside their dear departed, a precious keepsake available from Mr Herbert Maurice esq, Purveyor of New & Divers Books, for one guinea.

Mrs Maurice had always handled those particular customers, she had a gift for tact and sympathy, and now she. . .

. . .was dead, cold in this sack, drained and staring, to feed his vile thirst, *his* thirst, *his!*

He had done this to his wife! To his dear *wife*!

Oh dear God, help me! Get it out of my head! Get this nightmare out of my head!

He paused near the corner of Arundel Street. For several seconds his face squinched and turned, like a baby unwilling to be fed, until the vampyr re-tightened its grip inside his mind and Maurice-Dracul resumed his task.

He wheeled his load onto the broad, steadfast Embankment, which for the six years of its construction had been systematically sweeping away all the old wharves and steps that used to back onto the river. The eyes of beggars and rough sleepers followed him from wherever the gaslight couldn't reach. If they saw him slink out onto Waterloo Bridge, past the toll stop, they took no notice. If they saw a hazy shape raised up, and heard the dull splash when it dropped into the pitch-black river water below, it was none of their business.

Maurice-Dracul abandoned the barrow on the bridge, knowing it would be snatched within a minute or two. Better to return home less conspicuously, and by a more circuitous route. He turned left off the bridge and soon found himself approaching a place he'd seen vilified in the press but which he'd never dared venture to discover for himself.

For decades, the Adelphi Arches had been the city's most squalid and notorious cesspit of criminals, the dispossessed, the forgotten, the reviled. A series of immense open brick arcs faced the Thames, behind which were passages, tunnels, steep steps and sudden turnings reaching hundreds of feet back into what had once been the slope of the river bank. This vaulted labyrinth was built to support the tall, grand houses of the Adelphi directly above, so that the houses could command a better position, level with the Strand. It was used as warehouses, serving trade ships and other commercial enterprises, but floods had regularly filled the tunnels with stinking silt and now the continued construction of the Embankment was rapidly cutting the Arches off from the river entirely.

The huge semi-circles were barely visible in the smothered moonlight. Maurice-Dracul looked up at them with awe and crept over to the nearest, to investigate further. Cold, damp air breathed slowly and continuously from the cavernous darkness, merging with the faecal smell of the river.

The sound of a sudden movement echoed off the curved walls. A bulky figure stepped into the half-light, with a heavy cudgel raised above his head. "Welcome, stranger," he hissed quietly.

Maurice-Dracul snatched him by the throat. This tea leaf fancied his chances, did he? Perhaps he'd like a better look at who he was threatening? A look into the psyche of the vampyr, into the lust of a thousand feedings through the catalogue of years?

Look into the dreaming of the dead! Look into your own despair! Look into the eye of Death and feel the pain of all things! Let every mug-hunter and cracksman in this place do his worst, every footpad and prig!

The thief crumpled to the mud, his face fixed in terror and his mind diseased by nightmare. He curled up on the ground and began to weep.

Maurice-Dracul stepped deeper into the dripping chamber. Forlorn cries and harsh shouts reverberated now and again from distant niches, cutting across the continuous patter and scuttle of rats. Haggard figures huddled around meagre fires, some of them barely clothed, their filth-smeared faces battered and etched by their own histories. An enclosed cart, a decaying old prison transport, had been deprived of its wheels and wedged into an alcove to form a shelter packed with elderly men, hollow-eyed young women, children staring into the dark, a mewling baby.

The deeper Maurice-Dracul went, the fouler became the air and the more numerous the inhabitants. Nobody dared go near him, as if the evil he carried inside was seeping visibly through the pores of his skin. Bony wretches clawed at each other over edible scraps, or over rags and stolen trinkets that could be resold. Others slept while the rats sniffed at their fingers. Some inflicted their urges and aggressions on those too weak to defend themselves.

The vampyr was exultant. What a discovery! Here was the reeking underbelly of London, the collective gutter where the vilest muck snipes squirmed! There had to be hundreds of humans in these tunnels, all of them the scum of society, not one of them likely to be missed.

Not one of them! A *perfect* feeding ground, a secret larder of blood. This city of grandeur and toil was indeed the greatest in the world!

The vampyr closed his eyes and held his trembling hands to his breast. If he listened to the delicate vibrations of the ether, he could sense the distant, yearning calls of his kind, rising faintly from the netherworld far away. He whispered into the ear of loneliness, told the faintly echoing breeze about a modern, stately metropolis that teemed with prey, a shining place of true abundance, the mighty heart of an empire which fed itself through pulsing veins of human life.

Those of his kind who heard him slipped like phantoms into the space between realities – seeking, flowing, thirsting. They too would come to this paradise, soon. . . soon. . .

XIV

Since the day he'd been sent by the *Examiner* to report on new artistes for the Spring season, the day he met Ruby Wester, William Browning had missed only three evenings at Holmwood's. Checking the time by the clonking grandfather clock in Mr Maurice's bookshop, he was vexed to see he'd be late for curtain-up tonight, but strengthened his resolve with stern self-rebuke, a reminder that he had important work to do.

He reminded himself how utterly unnerved he'd been the previous day by his meeting with Harker and Flemming at the *Examiner*'s offices in Fleet Street. Although he agreed with them that public warnings might do more harm than good, until the identity of the vampyr's host could be discovered, he also privately resolved to continue his own investigations, while Harker and Flemming made further efforts to wake the authorities. After all, his editor had heaped praise on his account of the murder, and further exclusives might enhance his professional reputation no end. Might even, well, you never know, impress a certain lady.

Browning was pleased with his new rooms, which were every bit as airy and comfortable as promised, and Mr

Maurice's welcome to them was warmly effusive. However, with horrifying thoughts of the supernatural freshly shrieking in his mind, he passed a sleepless first night above the bookshop. Wide awake in the stillness of the early hours, he very faintly heard Maurice – it must have been him, there was nobody else in the building – leave by the back gate. Pushing some sort of small cart or wheelbarrow, to judge by the soft squeak.

At first, the reporter told himself that Maurice's eccentric nocturnal activities were none of his concern, but as the bookseller returned some time later, unaccompanied by the squeak, Browning suddenly recalled something his new landlord had said to him that morning: "a bizarrely bloody death has brought you to my door," he said. Using the word 'bizarre' hadn't struck Browning as odd at the time, because that's exactly what the murder had been, but it now occurred to him that he hadn't actually described the killing to Maurice, and Maurice had claimed no knowledge of the crime.

How, then, did he know it had been 'bizarre'? Any murder might be 'dreadful' or 'shocking' or 'horrible' but surely not 'bizarre.' Not 'bizarrely bloody.' Did Maurice know something he didn't want to admit? What on earth *would* he be carting around in the dead of night? Browning's thoughts began to gallop as fast as his heartbeat.

In the morning, hiding his tentative suspicions from the bookseller, and mindful of his decision to investigate for himself, Browning left the shop before breakfast. Once at his work, he arranged a wild goose chase: an anonymous note, to be handed to Mr Maurice that afternoon, worded in vague terms about spilt blood, and night-time comings and goings, requesting words on the matter, at a specified time, at a fictitious address on the outskirts of the city. A note designed to disturb any man with something to hide.

Now the grandfather clock struck the hour. The sonorous *clong* made Browning jump, but a quick recalculation of distances reassured him that Mr Maurice wouldn't be back for quite a while yet.

Where to begin? He quickly toured the shop but nothing appeared to be amiss or unusual. Behind the counter were pen, ink, paper, some printed receipts, some invoices received, nothing unexpected. Looking closer, he noticed a tiny lock set into the wall panelling beneath what he thought was no more than a join in the wood, but which his fingers soon identified as an edge to some sort of disguised cupboard or hatch. With no key, no handle and a few pushes producing no result, he moved on.

He went upstairs and painstakingly worked his way through Mr Maurice's rooms. Washstand, chairs beside the fireplace, wardrobes – where was it Mrs Maurice had gone? Her sister's, that was it – chamber pot under the bed, nothing strange or suspicious. He went back downstairs, quietly pulled back the curtain and stepped into the photographic studio. He didn't dare make more than a cursory inspection, since he wasn't familiar with technological machinery and was sure he'd leave signs of disturbance, but even here nothing seemed peculiar or untoward.

He told himself he'd let his night-time imagination run

away with him. He was feeling perturbed, being over-zealous, grasping at straws.

It was only when he looked around the little kitchen under the stairs that his heart began to thud. The empty oven was stone cold, and its door was lolling open. He approached it with caution because it was giving off an unpleasant odour, as if it hadn't been lit for months. On one of its stout metal legs was a dried-up splash, reddish-brown and elongated. Gravy. No, not blood, surely. Gravy. Bending right down to peer into the dark recesses of the oven, he noticed something small and crumpled wedged into a top corner at the back. Fetching a long fork, he poked at it until it fell with a clatter and he could fish it out.

It was a small ladies' shoe, squashed almost out of recognition. It wasn't burnt, or even singed. Merely hidden out of sight. It too was stained. The wearer must have been very careless indeed with her gravy. He stared at it for a moment, his thoughts tumbling over each other.

With increasingly jittering nerves, he quickly set it to one side and strode back into the shop. There had to be more here, he was sure of it.

He checked the time again. There should be at least another fifteen minutes, possibly twenty, before Maurice's return. He hurried over to the little keyhole he'd found earlier. It was a small mechanism and shouldn't need much force to jimmy. He pushed and thumped at the wall panel but nothing would move. Looking around for something to use as a pick, he retrieved the fork from the kitchen and bent back all but one of its tines.

His hand shook as he pressed the fork into the lock.

If there was a dead body in here, like the one in the alley, or a container full of blood, he would run to fetch the police immediately. No, he would run to fetch Harker and Flemming, and then the police.

He jabbed the fork with greater urgency, and with a twist it clicked. The lower section of the wall panel slid out, revealing the wheeled rack that held the shop's mostly-illegal stock of pornography.

For a few seconds, Browning didn't quite understand what he was looking at. He picked up some of the bound volumes and illustrated booklets. It was only as he leafed through them that his eyes began to widen and his jaw grew slack.

Available for the Discerning Gentleman were editions of *Charley Wag* and *Memoirs of a Woman of Pleasure*; pictorial lists, set out like menus, of West End toffers and where to find them; old issues of *Paul Pry*, *Swell's London* and *Peter Spy*, filled with True Adventures. Above them was a row of securely wrapped packets, lightly marked in pencil with customers' initials.

Browning dropped them all back in place, confusion and disgust folding his features. Then he flicked through the thick stack of photos.

Who were all these girls? Oh good God, Maurice must have photographed them *himself*, in that studio over there! Had he no shame, no decency? Hadn't *they*?

Wait. This one was the pretty blonde girl he'd seen talk to Maurice at Holmwood's the other night! Lily Murray smiled knowingly up at him, from her Roman Venus pose, then her Cupid pose, then her Greek athlete pose. He flipped past Lily and was suddenly frozen in shock.

In that terrible, crystalline moment he felt his heart break – actually break, like a physical splitting apart from the blow of an axe. His stomach turned inside out as his trembling hands pulled pictures of Ruby Wester from the stack.

No. No, no, no.

His Ruby, his darling, treated like a common street walker! Led astray by the louche promises of rich, exploitive beaux and the sick leeches who did their bidding!

He fought hard to control his grief and his outrage, and lost both battles. He snatched every photo of Ruby from the rack, tearfully ripping them to shreds and crushing them into his pockets, vowing revenge on Herbert Maurice, on Ruby's mystery lover – whoever that foul wastrel was! – on anyone who dared sully his angel.

Any thought or theory concerning murders or vampyrs was temporarily blotted from his mind. That malignance Maurice was a nasty little bludger, no more, no less! A verminous fungus who deserved the rope for what he'd done!

Practicalities eventually pulled Browning to his senses and a calmer frame of mind. He carefully pushed the rack back into place and, with a heave of relief, heard the lock click shut. To prevent alerting Maurice to his snooping, he bent the fork back into shape and tossed the bloodstained shoe back into the oven.

There was more than enough evidence behind that panel to put the worm in prison for the rest of his days. Shocking evidence of a scandalous double life. Crimes which must be exposed. Crimes which could be exclusively revealed to readers of the *Examiner* even as the Bow Street peelers were hauling him away.

Browning soon had the swine's downfall planned out in his head, but there was a more important task that he needed to do first. He left the shop by the front entrance, locking it with his tenant's key while the ringing of the bell faded into silence. He was around the nearest corner a fraction of a blink before Maurice came stalking into Frye Court from the opposite direction. The bookseller unlocked the shop, barged angrily inside, and the bell faded into silence once more.

XV

It took only a few shillings for William Browning to bribe his way into the backstage area of Holmwood's Music Hall. An assortment of performers smoked, or drank, or tugged at their costumes, surrounded by muffled sounds from the auditorium, which swirled with laughter at The Tottering Toff and his new song about the h-unfortunate h-ablutionary habits of the h-artistocracy.

Jacob Renfield the magician grouched at the laughs and cheers. "I worked with Arthur Lloyd at the Marylebone. I worked with George Leybourne, I did, Champagne Charlie himself. Proper *Lions Comique*, not this rubbish."

"Excuse me," said Browning, trying to flatten his uncooperative hair. "I recognise you from the stage, you are The Sensational Swami?"

Renfield sat upright and a glint shone in his eye. "I am."

"I need to speak to Miss Wester, I assume she's here somewhere?"

"Oh." The glint faded. He jabbed a thumb over his shoulder. "In the store room, last I saw."

"Thank you. Your current turn is most entertaining, by the way."

The glint reignited. "You think so?"

"Ingenious."

"You may be interested to know I'm developing a billet reading act, since demonstrations of second sight are always well received and, now that some of the spiritualist presentations have attracted certain criticisms—" He stopped in mid-flow, suddenly conscious that he was talking to himself.

Browning knocked on the open door of the store room and Ruby answered without looking up from the trunk of old coats through which she was rooting. "Hmm?"

He cleared his throat. "Miss Wester."

Something in his tone made her pause and she stood up. "Yes?"

"Miss Wester." He swallowed and wrung his hat. "Miss Wester . . ."

"Are you nervous or simply have a shockingly limited vocabulary?"

He laughed nervously. "My name is William Browning."

"You're from the. . . *Illustrated News*?"

"*Examiner*. It's very kind of you to remember, we met when I wrote about the Spring season artistes."

"I'm unlikely to forget," she smiled warmly, "when you've spent all your evenings here since. I do hope the repertoire hasn't bored you."

"Not at all, quite the contrary," said Browning earnestly, his cheeks beginning their short journey from ruddy to scarlet. "I come before you with a request. A request which is both serious and sincere."

"And concise?" said Ruby, hearing applause. "I'll be on in a few minutes, after the tightrope walker."

Browning twitched in an agony of conflicting instincts. "Since we met, er, briefly, Miss Wester, I have taken the keenest interest in your career, as you have, er, so kindly noticed. To that end, I have been alert to, er, all circumstances with which your name has been associated. Until this moment, I have quite properly kept my feelings to myself. To do otherwise would have been the grossest impertinence since I cannot possibly offer you the same advantages you currently enjoy. However, it is my belief that such advantages may have been gained at too great a cost. You may have been led into a world which is unworthy of your presence, and in which I fear you may find much unhappiness. Therefore, Miss Wester, with all the humility I am able to muster, I ask for your hand in marriage. My income is modest, but it may well increase in light of recent developments. I know I cannot give you a life of luxury, but I *can* give you my undying devotion."

Ruby swayed slightly, her rouged lips contorting. She shut the lid of the trunk through which she'd been rummaging and sat on it with a rustle of skirts, indicating for Browning to sit on one of the trunks opposite her. She spoke gently, through a gossamer screen of emotion.

"Mr Browning. William. I've no wish to reject such a tender appeal, really, I haven't. Only a heart of stone could fail to be moved. But I don't know you. And you don't know me. What could possibly have prompted such sudden affections?"

Browning nodded rapidly. "I understand how very absurd and irresponsible I must sound. My heart has always been an open one, I fear. If a plea of marriage is foolish, might it be amended to one of fellowship? Trust me, I would cross a thousand oceans, brave a thousand dangers, to keep you from harm, Miss, er, Ruby. I would consider my life well spent if I could be your guardian and friend."

"But why?" she whispered.

"I wish to... to save you." His eyes squeezed shut for a moment. He couldn't speak the necessary words. "I fear for your future, that is all I can say."

Ruby leaned forward and held his hand. The sensation of her touch was a memory he would treasure and revisit until his dying day.

"William, I would be nothing short of cruel if I didn't give such a heartfelt proposal the consideration it deserves. Let me think about what you've said."

"That is all I have any right to ask," he beamed, his hands cutting a joyful underline in the air.

Renfield's voice warbled from his rickety chair. "Ruby! Five minutes!" he cried over the applause for Albert Hayes and his Dancing Dogs.

"Alright!" called Ruby. She smiled at her earnest, fidgeting suitor. "You're a very kind man, William. A knight errant. But some princesses might be quite at home with their dragons."

Once Browning had left to take his seat in the auditorium, in a whirlpool of hope, Ruby found herself profoundly troubled by what he'd said. Not so much by his clumsy ardour as by his implied awareness of her relationship with Sir Edwin Gull. Whatever connections this journalist had made, whether by accident or investigation, a trail had clearly been followed, and if Browning had followed it then so could others.

She should never have picked a miserly old goat like Gull in the first place! Clothes, trinkets, money, he'd coughed up nowhere near enough. He'd had the best of the bargain!

Well, no more. She'd decided. If he wouldn't pay her fairly, it was high time he was made to pay in other ways. She had the means. And Lily would be glad of the work.

She smiled to herself. Half an hour later, during her song, she looked for William Browning in the audience, to give him a wink, but he wasn't in his usual seat. He'd suddenly remembered, with a lurch in his stomach, that he still had vitally important detective work demanding his attention.

XVI

It took Maurice-Dracul only a few minutes to discover that someone had been peeking around his shop, and only a few minutes more to discover who it was. He'd suspected a ruse to keep him away as soon as he realised he'd been sent on a wild goose chase across the city. Now, in a fury, he fussed over every inch of the place, sniffing, feeling, dipping his eyes to examine things close-to.

In his photographic studio, he noticed the faintest trace of a familiar, oddly medicinal scent, one which wasn't part of the room's usual chemical fog. He caught another, more elusive hint of the same scent lingering in his private apartments.

It was soap, Gossage's, the blue mottled variety. He'd used it himself, in the past.

And it was used rigorously, so he'd noticed that morning, by his new lodger. The idiot Browning was onto him!

The fire in his head made him seethe and spit, told him to hunt the idiot down, to kill him, to drink him dry, but cooler thoughts eventually took command. He uncurled himself, his tongue lapping at the back of his teeth.

He shouldn't act rashly. He should prepare to flee, if necessary, but it would be madness to abandon this plump, bounteous city without a fight. There were no policemen on the doorstep, so it was possible that the idiot had reached entirely the wrong conclusions. On the other hand, it was equally possible that the idiot was in collusion with others, who might have different plans.

He was hungry. The need for hot, fresh blood was beginning to growl in his belly again.

Locking up the shop, and taking deep breaths to regain his composure and straighten his back, Maurice-Dracul hurried away into the night, in search of food. He considered making the short walk down to the Dark Arches again, but changed his mind. Until his uncertainties about the idiot were answered, he'd be wise to keep away from busy streets.

He'd leave the Arches to his guests, a feast for them to enjoy upon their arrival. He closed his eyes for a few seconds and stilled his thoughts. He could sense them approaching London, a dozen vampyrs or more, answering his call, and once they were established here, then more would come, and more.

The sun had set but the hot, insect-laden fuzziness of the day had yet to dissipate. Maurice-Dracul dabbed at his forehead with a sleeve and weaved through the alleys and passageways between Frye Court and Seward Walk. He walked purposefully, to give a business-like impression of familiarity to the locals he passed sloping silently on corners or gossiping in small groups at rusty water pumps.

Once he was sure there were no eyes on him, he ducked into a run-down lodging house. Inside, the only light in the tiny hallway came through the transom above the front door. Beside the staircase, a little wooden doll had been wrapped in a rag and settled down to sleep by its absent owner. A froth of brown woodlice skirted around it.

Slowly, he climbed the steps, which cracked and sighed beneath his feet. Scattered here and there across the stairwell walls, in letters that were mostly still legible, were the testaments of yesterday's tenants.

". . . Dutch Harry, bound for Liverpool, by Gods good grace . . ."

". . . Jim – no longr I ware the brord arrow – this, my crib with my moll . . ."

". . . A fair ken sais Mil and his razor . . ."

In the first room he came to, a sticky drone of flies announced a resident who'd lain dead for a month or more, waiting until his fellow lodgers could raise enough cash to have him moved. From the next room came voices arguing about a pub in Whitechapel. Further up the house, a warm mist of onions and fatty meat was stirred with the nasty flatulence of an inexpertly tapped gas pipe.

On the top floor, Lily's son Jack listened to the vampyr's slow, approaching footsteps with increasing alarm. The sound was neither familiar nor friendly.

He quietly closed the battered *Fun* he was dutifully pretending to read and clutched it tightly. On the other side of the grey bedsheet that hung from a string mid-room, Mrs Potter sat snoring on her thin mattress, her face resting flat on the cool surface of the wall under a narrow, smeary window.

At each footstep, Jack's pulse beat a little harder.

Slow implied a stranger. A stranger implied bad intentions.

The creaks stopped outside the open doorway. Jack could tell by the shifting of shadow over shadow that there was someone standing there, just out of sight. He stayed absolutely still, feeling his scalp prickle and his insides turn. Mrs Potter snorted and snuffled in a fitful doze.

Gradually revealing itself, inch by inch, a face appeared slowly around the edge of the door frame. Its eyes were round and unblinking, its mouth stretched into a broad grin. The face was chubby, with tiny spectacles.

Jack gulped back tiny gasps of fright, not daring to make a sound. He felt paper crackle in his fists.

The man from the bookshop. The well-spoken one, his mother's friend. He couldn't be sure, because the man's face had an expression he'd never seen before, on any adult, gleefully evil like the snakes in Regent's Park when he'd gone to see Jumbo the elephant.

The man slid quietly into the room, shutting the door behind him. Jack pressed himself into a corner, his eyes flicking from the man's face to the man's writhing, clawing hands and back again.

What did he want? Why was he here?

"Why, it's young Jack, is it not?" said the man softly. "Lily's boy." Mrs Potter stirred in her sleep with a grunt.

"Yessir," muttered Jack.

Whatdidhewant? Whatdidhewant?

The man pushed back the makeshift screen that divided the room, then stood over Mrs Potter with his fingers knitting in anticipation. "Let's see now. This one first . . ."

He looked over at Jack, ". . . and then a sweet taste of pudding."

Jack's chest fluttered like a sparrow.

Was he here because Mum had stolen magazines from his shop? Had Jack been bad, done something wrong? He hadn't told on Mrs Potter! He hadn't! He hadn't!

Maurice-Dracul hauled Mrs Potter off her mattress. As she wriggled and squawked into consciousness, he swung her around and knocked her out of it again with a hefty punch to the jaw. She dropped heavily in front of the door, cutting off any chance for Jack to escape down the stairs.

Jack's feet scrambled backwards against the floorboards. Maurice-Dracul descended on Mrs Potter with a shuddering cry. Ripping aside layers of clothing, he bit into her skin, tearing raggedly into the flesh of her neck, and then her thigh, until he'd opened the main blood vessels.

He drank, filling the room with a hideously rhythmic sucking. Mrs Potter's rapidly dying body heaved at each gulp, her skin becoming discoloured and creased. Maurice-Dracul's mouth enveloped every gush and spurt of blood. Any that pooled on the floor was slurped dry.

At last he rocked back on his knees, breathing heavily, red stains covering his face and chest. He wiped his lips with the back of his hand and spun around to grab at Jack.

The boy had opened the window above Mrs Potter's mattress and was most of the way out. Only fear was stopping him from sliding down onto the thick, angled pipe a few inches beneath his dangling legs.

With a sharp growl, Maurice-Dracul lunged at him. Jack let go of the sill and dropped.

The hard impact of the pipe on the crumbling soles of his shoes sent a shock up his spine, and he almost toppled backwards. He ducked down, finally yelling for help, and gripped the encrusted pipe with both arms as the vampyr stretched to snatch him. Jack was small enough to stay out of reach but relief vanished when he glanced down. The distance to the pavement was at least a thousand miles.

His yells, and the clanking of his movement of the pipe, was noticed in the street below. Raised faces quickly drew other raised faces. Some laughed, some shouted about helping the lad, some placed bets. Maurice-Dracul quickly withdrew behind the window and slunk into shadow. The blood on him would be easily visible, even in the smoggy twilight.

Jack clung to the pipe, telling himself over and over again that he'd been brave, hadn't cried, hadn't been a baby this time. A ladder was found by one of the onlookers and he inched his way to safety.

XVII

William Browning's stomach had lurched exactly three times since he'd finished pouring out his heart to Ruby backstage. The first lurch came as he took his seat in the auditorium, when he suddenly realised he still had vitally important detective work demanding his attention. The second came as he sent an urgent summons to Captain Harker, when he suddenly realised Herbert Maurice might, at that very moment, be planning to hide evidence of criminal activity and would have to be watched immediately. The third came as he marched back to the bookshop, when he suddenly realised that until Harker's arrival he would have to contain his true feelings and play the innocent with the foul blackguard as if nothing was amiss.

Once in the shop, his calls of greeting went unanswered and he felt deeply relieved. Although Mr Maurice was evidently not at home, Browning's return to the lair of the contemptible villain was rapidly eroding his nerves. He was finding it difficult to stop his hands shaking.

He decided to make use of the ink and paper behind the shop counter and compose a piece for submission to his editor while he was waiting. He would expose the bookseller not only as a suspect in the recent murder case but also, in shocking revelations exclusive to the *Examiner*, as a supplier of illicit *curiosa* on a scale not seen in this country since the scandalous London publishing careers of Dugdale, Vickers &c.

Browning bolted the shop door. Several times, while he was bent over the counter with furiously scratching pen, customers knocked and peered through the glass, saw an unfamiliar face heavy with petulance, and went away again. Each time it happened, the journalist wondered with repugnance if that had been the face of an innocent browser seeking innocent entertainment, or—

His thoughts were interrupted as a loud crash came from somewhere behind him. Startled, he spun around and listened intently.

For long, empty seconds all he could hear was the rush of his own pulse. Then a sudden crunching, like shards of glass being trodden, set his mouth dry and the hairs of his neck bristling. The sound had come from the photographic studio, behind the curtain.

He jumped as the curtain was flung aside. Maurice-Dracul didn't notice him at first, busy picking splinters from his clothes. When he looked up and saw Browning, he recoiled in surprise but then gave his new lodger a broad smile.

"Mr Browning," he said, indicating his blood-soaked and glass-snicked clothing, "you find me at something of a disadvantage. In my haste, I foolishly put my full weight on a single pane in the studio ceiling."

Browning pointed, assuming that the blood stains were all the bookseller's injuries, and his thoughts showed on his face. Maurice-Dracul glanced back at the litter of debris visible on the floor beyond the curtain and chuckled. "Don't worry, the damage to both myself and the ceiling is minor. A couple of streets from here, I was forced to make my exit via an attic and over several roofs. Quite exhilarating."

"Over roofs?"

"To keep off the streets. Due to my soiled appearance. I shimmied down a drainpipe or two and over a wall, and I thought to approach the back gate with equal stealth, but . . ." He held out his arms in mock helplessness.

Browning's surprise flipped over into outrage, any need to play the innocent forgotten. "You, sir, are under arrest! I have called for assistance, and it will be here momentarily! I have discovered all your filthy secrets, and shall have no hesitation in seeing you clapped in irons!"

"Indeed?" said Maurice-Dracul softly. He took a step towards Browning, and Browning took a step back. "I anticipated an action of this kind. I generally do. I've returned here only to furnish myself with a temporary source of income from my stock, to use as I re-establish myself elsewhere. How brave of you to face me alone."

"Alone? Assistance will be here momentarily, of that you can be assured."

Another step forward, and back, in their dance to the death. "I don't doubt it. But your presence hinders the swift exit I desire, so my best course of action is to kill you without delay and be about my business."

Browning stumbled around the counter and backed awkwardly across the shop. Maurice-Dracul began a slow, steady pace in pursuit. "I have had," he said, gently patting his stomach with both hands, "a decent main course, but I missed my pudding. I'm still hungry for a torn-out throat or an opened belly or two."

Browning finally grasped the razor-edged reality of the vampyr's existence. He grabbed the handle of the shop's front door, rattling it in panic, forgetting he'd bolted it himself, the bell tinkling on its wire. As Maurice-Dracul advanced on him smilingly, he dashed to one side and sped into the photographic studio.

His heavy breath ended in a heave of terror when it dawned on him that he'd run into a room with no exit but the broken roof. Maurice-Dracul, his patience at an end, marched at his prey with outstretched arms. Browning grabbed the camera and tripod from the middle of the floor and swung them wildly, knocking the bookseller clean off his feet.

He jumped over Maurice-Dracul's thrashing limbs, but in one lightning movement the bookseller grabbed one of the shards of glass that had fallen from the smashed pane and slashed the back of Browning's leg. Browning dropped with a yell, bumping against the heavily laden table of photographic equipment which stood beside the curtain.

Maurice-Dracul scrambled across the floor like a huge spider, aroused by the smell of blood, his eyes dancing. He clawed at the hems of Browning's trousers and dragged himself up the journalist's body, giggling and gasping.

Browning, his face distorted with horror, reached up onto the table and grabbed whatever his shuddering fingers could grasp. With all his strength, he smashed a glass bottle on Maurice-Dracul's head. The noxious liquid inside splashed down the bookseller's face and he bounded aside with a screech like a scalded cat.

Quickly, trembling with nerves, Browning got to his feet and limped as fast as he could down the passage which led past the kitchen and out to the back gate. Maurice-Dracul burst through the curtain, his face alight with rage and streaked with chemical burns.

Browning glanced over his shoulder, expecting to find Maurice-Dracul's glaring eyes right behind him, but instead he saw a brief flurry of movement disappearing up the stairs. He stopped dead, listening to footsteps race for the upper floors.

The murderous fiend was probably making for the roof, hoping to evade the forces of justice! If he'd successfully escaped by that method before, then he could do so again. There was only William Browning of the *Examiner* here to stop him!

For the briefest of moments, he was torn between the desire to escape with his life and the desire to mete out retribution on Ruby's behalf. Wincing, he slipped off one shoe, hurriedly used his sock as a bandage for his leg, and chased after the bookseller. Gripping the bannisters for support as he went, he took two or three steps at a time.

Up on the landing outside his rooms, Maurice-Dracul had dragged a large wardrobe across the top of the stairs to prevent pursuit. As soon as Browning appeared from below, he flung down a chair which crashed against the wall inches from the journalist's head. Browning raced forward, threw all his weight against the wardrobe and shifted it far enough for him to squeeze past onto a landing which overlooked the stairwell.

Maurice-Dracul suddenly emerged from the bedroom carrying an antique night stand. With a ferocious growl, he raised it up in front of him like a battering ram and charged. With a yelp, Browning threw his arms around his face and dropped to the floor. Maurice-Dracul, too bull-like to swerve quickly, tripped over Browning's curled-up body and crashed headlong into the handrail at the landing's edge.

The balustrade burst apart. The vampyr pitched over with a howling scream and fell head first to the bottom of the stairwell, hitting the lowest step in a deafening shatter of timber. Browning, kicked over by the impact of Maurice-Dracul's feet, almost toppled after him. He scratched desperately at the dusty rug laid across the landing. He finally managed to pull his balance in the right direction only because half the rug was held down by the weight of the wardrobe.

For a moment or two, Browning lay still, trying to steady his thundering heart. The only sound was the rasping gasp of his own breath.

He sat up, feeling the cut in his leg throb painfully. The blood had stopped dripping, but some of it had trickled past his ankle and his sock-less shoe felt tacky and uncomfortable.

Rocking forward onto all fours, he crept up to the now-open edge of the landing and slowly peeped over. Twenty or more feet below, Maurice-Dracul was face up, motionless in the middle of a smashed spray of wood. His arms and legs dangled in an X-shape, and his eyes were open, but it was the angle of his head, skewed sharply to one side, which caught Browning's attention. The impact had clearly broken his neck.

Browning smiled cautiously to himself. Fleeing Killer Caught – Brave Action By *Examiner* Staff Writer – He Is My Hero, Says Writer's Betrothed, Singer Ruby Wester.

But, as he looked down, his stomach suddenly lurched for a fourth time that evening. Maurice-Dracul blinked. He blinked again, then began struggling to free himself from the broken tangle into which he was wedged. Browning gaped at him, cold jets of fear freezing his senses.

The dead body of Herbert Maurice, forced into animation by the vampyr that lived in his brain, kicked debris aside and grunted with the effort of turning over onto his knees. With sections of broken bannisters cracking under him, he heaved himself up onto his feet and tried to straighten the awkward tilt of his head. It lolled and twisted with a creaking grind of ligaments.

Browning watched him step carefully over the strewn fragments surrounding him and stalk off down the passage leading to the back gate. Seconds later, still unable to believe his eyes, he heard a stream of urgent knocking coming from the shop door and the raised voices of Captain Harker and Arthur Flemming.

XVIII

Harker elbowed a pane in the door and reached through to unbolt it. He and Flemming were halfway to the detritus at the bottom of the stairwell when William Browning came staggering down to meet them.

"He's still alive!" cried Browning. "He fell and broke his neck, and he's still alive."

"Proof he's host to the vampyr," said Harker. "Where is he?"

Browning had a hand to his forehead. "At first I doubted you, but I have seen it with my own eyes, it's astounding—"

"Browning!" demanded Captain Harker. "Where is he?"

"He went down there, just a moment ago. You can get out to the back gate. He can't have gone far, he seemed unsteady on his feet."

Harker marched along the passageway with Flemming trotting nervously at his heels. He barely slowed when he noticed Browning's hobble. "You're hurt? Do you need attention?"

"I'll live," said Browning. "Keep going, we must be quick!" The three men sped out of the building and along the narrow gap which took them into a long side street.

Flemming spoke as he hurried to keep up. "What if the vampyr should merely leave its present host? Might it not elude us with ease?"

Harker called over his shoulder. "Mr Browning, did the creature attempt to drink your blood?"

"He claimed to be hungry, but I was able—"

"Good. It should remain in its host until it can feed again," said Harker. "It will wish to restore its strength before the uncertainty and risk of detaching itself. My guess is that it will attempt to lose itself amongst the West End throng, and seek out a fresh victim."

Flemming untied his cravat as he hurried along, and used it to dab the cold sweat from his face and neck. "Perhaps, Harker, I'd be better employed preparing the trap? The strongroom? Make sure it's opened up and ready to seal?"

Harker's brief glance at him was enough to assess Flemming's ragged state of mind. "Yes, an excellent idea." Flemming nodded rapidly and stopped to rest for a moment before setting off in the direction of Seward Walk.

"A trap?" said Browning, quickly limping to Harker's side. "Do you mean the box you and Mr Flemming told me about?"

"No," said Harker, "the small vault in which it was stored. I examined it more fully earlier today and its seams are tight as a drum. It should make an ideal *xīxuèguǐ hézi*."

"Would the monster not remember being released there?"

"Probably not. It would have been weak after months in the box, little concerned about where it was until it had found a host."

Browning felt a professional urge to take notes, but he couldn't hobble and write at the same time. "So how do you propose to get it into this vault?"

"At present," sighed Harker, "I haven't even the vaguest notion."

"And once the monster is trapped, what is to be done with the vault itself?"

Harker looked at him. "I haven't the vaguest notion about that either. Are you sure your injury. . .?"

"Our work is far more important than my personal comfort. By the way, I've been meaning to ask, would Mr Flemming be related to the owners of Flemming & Pratt Ltd, the bankers?"

Harker barked a laugh. "Good heavens, no, Arthur's family are all Dutch academics. His father is a professor with enough letters after his name to furnish an entire alphabet, but for some reason the man disowned him. An aunt living in Chiswick took him in as a child."

"Dutch, you say?" said Browning.

"He was born in Amsterdam. His original name was Abraham Van Helsing."

XIX

Lily kept a tight grip on her son's hand, and Jack in turn kept a tight grip on her skirts. The boy's breathless account of Mrs Potter's horrible death and his escape from Maurice-Dracul's clutches had reduced his mother to a wide-eyed panic. They loitered in the open doorway of the bookshop while Clipper paced inside.

"For the last ruddy time," said Clipper, "Bert is not at home. We saw those two blokes break in here, playing the jack, so the murdering bastard must have legged it. The coppers will be all over this place soon, this is our last chance to get what we're owed. What a mess! Look over here!"

He rifled through the drawers behind the counter, kicking the locked ones until they split. "The stingy old duffer must have piles of finnies around here, the amount he makes."

"There's more value in the stash," said Lily, pointing to the hidden panel in the wall.

"Yeh, but we'll have to fence it," moaned Clipper. "We'll be lucky to get a thrummer an item." He pulled back the curtain to the photographic studio and spat out a stream of vitriol when he saw the valuable camera and much of the equipment smashed to pieces.

Lily went over to the wall panel. She took a folded burlap bag from her skirt pocket, handed it to Jack and started to lever the lock apart with the small crowbar she'd brought with her. Clipper, muttering moodily to himself, decided to search the kitchen for hidden cash, then make a quick trawl through the rooms upstairs. He hurried into the shadows of the passageway and had no inkling that Maurice-Dracul had stepped out behind him until a blood-stained hand was over his mouth and he was being dragged into the darkness.

He wasn't able to struggle for long. Lily assumed the bumps and thuds coming from the kitchen were the sound of Clipper grumpily ferreting through tins and jars.

The bag was quickly filled, Jack holding it open while Lily heaped handfuls of pictures and pamphlets into it. "When we've finished here, sweetheart," she said, with the forced brightness only a parent can muster, "we'll go to see Ruby, yeah? Get out the way till this blows over. We're not going back to our room, not ever."

Jack nodded severely, to show her how serious and grown-up and sensible he was. His downturned mouth vibrated like warnings of a coming earthquake. The bag scratched against his bare, twig-like legs.

Lily pushed the half-empty rack back into the wall. "Anything?" she called down the passage.

She was answered only by the clatter of a pot falling off the stove. "Come on, we'd better go. . . Oi, are you listening to me?" With a heavy sigh, she told Jack to tie up the bag while she went to check on Clipper.

She paused when she saw a heaped shape moving on the tiled kitchen floor. What was Clipper doing down there, squirming about like that?

Part of the squirming shape appeared to elongate itself. She backed away, her insides turning to water, as Maurice-Dracul raised his lop-sided head. His mouth was smeared with Clipper's blood and his fingers held open a deep wound above the man's heart.

Lily's shattering scream made Jack flinch and stare. She ran to the boy, scooped him up in her arms and fled, out into the street, into the night, Jack peering back over her shoulder in case the monster was chasing after them.

Angrily, Maurice-Dracul flung Clipper's body aside. He'd had barely a taste! His concealment in the pantry, his ruse to evade the idiot Browning and those other men, had worked so well, but now that wretched howling female would bring a crowd!

Keeping a wary eye on the front of the shop, he quickly fetched a scarf from the hooks outside the studio and tied it firmly around his neck so that his head would sit straight on his broken neck. An overcoat to hide the bloodstains on his clothes, a bowler pulled low over his eyes to hide his face. With curiosity-seekers already beginning to gather at the open front door, he slipped out of the back gate.

XX

Captain Harker and William Browning walked within sight of each other, one on each side of the wide, crowded Strand. Packed omnibuses clip-clopped back and forth with their male passengers hanging onto the open seats up top; cacophonous flocks of young toffs flung ha'pennies at dirty faces; countless women fished for wandering eyes to catch or unguarded hands to clasp; shopkeepers put up "Beds" signs for some by-the-hour evening income.

Harker and Browning scanned the crowds, looking for any trace of their quarry. Lily's screams in Frye Court were a few hundred yards away, lost in voices and traffic, so their inaccurate impression of Maurice-Dracul's whereabouts was starting to make them think they'd missed him completely.

It was Harker who spotted the top of a bowler hat moving rapidly across the road, close to Ivy Bridge Lane. He wouldn't have given it a second look, but a gap between two passing carts gave him a momentary view of the person wearing it. He caught up with Browning.

"That man there! You see?"

"That's not him, is it?"

"It's a very warm night, and he's not only got that hat

pulled down, he's wearing an overcoat and a scarf. He's trying to conceal his identity. Come on, we'll keep pace, he's moving away from us. Stay back a short distance."

"Perhaps it's merely someone with a summer chill?"

"And rattling along at that speed?" grumbled Harker. "No, he's looking for something. I say that's our vampyr hunting his supper."

At that moment, the bowler hat disappeared behind a vendor calling today's Billingsgate leftovers of eels and fish. Harker raced ahead and saw the hat and the back of the overcoat duck into a slender opening at the side of a pub and climb narrow, enclosed steps to the pub's upper floor.

"Stay here, in case he comes back this way," said Harker.

Browning nodded. When Harker had gone, he propped himself up and, with a fearful expression, raised his leg to examine it. The sock he'd used as a bandage was soaked, but the pain had eased into a nagging ache and the cut itself, now he looked at it more carefully, was quite small. Sighing, he took off his other sock to make a fresh dressing.

At the top of the steps, Harker was confronted with the low roar of an expectant gathering and the hot pungent air of pressed bodies and tobacco. A grimly towering man, who looked like he was built from offcuts of meat, held out a hand at him.

"Shilling," he belched.

Harker paid the admission and entered a very large room with a low ceiling, filled with a rowdy gathering of a hundred people or more. He immediately had an uneasy feeling that the vampyr may have sensed he was being followed and had come in here to throw off his pursuers. He moved through the room cautiously.

Drinks were raised, drunk, re-poured, raised again. The lumpen patrons of this establishment were predominantly male, but crossed every divide of age and income. Lurkers and dippers jostled drunks, who begged from costers and clerks, who guarded their coins from pawnbrokers, who ignored factory hands, who sneered at swells in clean clothes.

The floor was tacky with spilt beer. On one wall was a chalkboard where a sinewy arm, rising up above the flow, was writing names and betting odds. The other walls were bare except for a few stalactite strips of the Scheele's green wallpaper which had once covered them.

In the middle of the room, underneath a cluster of gas lamps which between them threw down a sharply dazzling light, was a ring about six feet in diameter. Its solid sides rose to roughly elbow height, and the whitewash that covered its inside surfaces was criss-crossed with scratches and dark, dippled stains.

The resident umpire, a scruffy man with a twist of skin in place of one eye, rapped for silence with his walking stick. The patrons drank up and shut up, their mood swiftly focussed on the important business of the evening.

"Sportsmen! In contention for the pot, an elimination competition for dogs of four pounds in weight or less! The rounds to be furnished with one dozen opponents apiece, rising to fifteen, thence to twenty!"

Beside the umpire were gathered half a dozen men holding muzzled terriers to their chests. The umpire tapped the one closest to him and the dog's owner clambered into the ring. He removed the muzzle with a ceremonial flourish but kept the dog's leash wrapped around his fist. The terrier began to pull against it and lick its chops, its toenails scrabbling at the floor.

"First, the champion of no less than two previous contests, Billy!"

A cheer rose up which quickly transformed itself into the frantic placing of bets, shouting of odds, exchanges of money, arguments about form and athletic ability. Billy looked up at it all with bright-eyed interest.

Captain Harker slowly circled the room, anxiously surveying every face and figure. Once the contest began, there'd be enough noise and distraction for Maurice-Dracul to grab one of these onlookers and drag them away, or even kill them there and then. Harker stuffed his hands into his pockets to stop himself skittishly flexing his fingers.

The umpire raised a silver stopwatch above his head and the din subsided. "Each round to be timed, each kill to be verified, and mine is the final word on all matters of adjudication! Time to commence from the removal of the tether!"

The crowd parted to allow through a man carrying a heavy cage, from which poured a powerful stink of drains. He heaved it over the side of the pit, the light from above making the squirming contents of the cage glisten wetly. A dozen rats rolled and clambered over each other until a string was pulled and they tumbled out.

Billy began to bark and snarl, pulling hard on his rope leash. The rats scattered and bunched in panic. Billy's owner reached down, paused to savour his moment, then in one swift movement unhooked Billy's leash and jumped over the side of the pit to safety.

A triumphant, continuous roar burst through the room. Billy flashed around the pit, his jaws snapping at fur and tails. The roar rose in pitch for a moment every time the dog's teeth made contact and a rat was shaken then flung aside in a spray of blood. Hands waved betting slips, hats slapped at the pit's edge.

The deafening tumult made Harker unconsciously speed up his patrol. In his eagerness to pick out the hat and coat he'd followed, he overlooked the possibility that the hat and coat had been replaced.

"Time!" yelled the umpire. "Billy... ten kills!" The terrier, his nose red and torn by nips from the rats, was scooped up by his owner as the onlookers cheered their winnings or bemoaned their losses.

Harker saw a figure in a John Bull and a pale linen duster, splitting off from the melee around the pit and heading back towards the stairs. It was only the unseasonable scarf Maurice-Dracul had to retain, to keep his head straight, which gave him away. By the time Harker reached the top step, Maurice-Dracul had almost descended to street level.

Harker, hands framing his mouth, yelled a warning to Browning. Clattering down, he heard sharp voices and the sounds of a struggle.

Out on the Strand, Browning aimed a punch a split second too late. Maurice-Dracul grabbed hold of him by his outstretched arm and swung him around with enough force to pull him off his feet. He barrelled into Captain

Harker and they hit the damp pavement in a tangle of limbs.

With an angry cry of frustration, Harker pushed Browning aside. He sat up in time to see Maurice-Dracul, already across the road, scuttling into a side street. He was also in time to see Arthur Flemming on the opposite pavement, returned from checking the vault in Seward Walk and in search of his companions.

"Arthur! *There*! For God's sake, stop him!"

Flemming looked nonplussed for a second, switching back and forth between Harker and the rapidly retreating vampyr. His legs felt as weak as his will power. His first few steps down the side street were hesitant but, finally seeing that the portly bookseller was no match for him in speed, he broke into a gangling run.

They raced past the entrance to Holmwood's Music Hall, Flemming gaining all the time. Cabs and carriages clattered, dropping off and picking up. Maurice-Dracul dashed through the patchy glow of one street lamp after another, watched blankly by passers-by.

As Flemming caught up, he momentarily baulked at the need to grab hold of the vampyr. The thought of tackling anyone to the ground was utterly alien to him and he reached forward hesitantly, as if trying to grab hold of a feral cat. On the third attempt, he took a tight grip of the bookseller's collar.

Not expecting to be caught so easily, Maurice-Dracul twitched to a halt in surprise and squirmed around, forcing Flemming to let go. Running had inched his scarf down past his nose and mouth, exposing the drawn, sallow skin left behind by the pooling of blood in his dead body.

He suddenly lunged at Flemming, hissing at the back of his throat, his bloodstained teeth clacking hungrily, his eyes lit only by the creature within. Flemming, with a yelp and a rush of fright, gave him a hard shove against his chest. He fell backwards, heels missing the edge of the pavement, and dropped onto his back in the road, falling behind the hooves of a passing hansom.

The cab was going too fast to avoid him. There was a bump as the wheel hit the side of his head, and a terrible cracking sound mixed with the driver's undulating yell as he tugged hard at the reins to stop. Within seconds, people were gathering, shouting, screaming, jostling each other for a better look.

Harker and Browning appeared at Flemming's side. Only the three of them knew the true cause of the weird, uneasy ambiance which had suddenly begun to seep through the street. It had nothing to do with the sight of Maurice's dead body. The vampyr Dracul had abandoned its spent host and was free again.

Flemming beat his fists at his temples. "How could I be so stupid? So damn cowardly? It's my fault! Great heavens, Sir Edwin was right, it's all my fault!"

Captain Harker, his saturnine expression turning to dread, looked up at the night sky. Thin beams of waxy moonlight lanced through cracks in the layers of sulphurous fog and cloud.

Everything he thought he'd conquered, all the rage and helplessness which had haunted him for years, was burning into his mind again. He felt powerless, overwhelmed by an evil he had no way to control and for which, as yet, he had no remedy.

– THE SECOND HOST –

XXI

Ruby Wester put a warm cup of milk and a piece of cake into Jack's lap. He smiled at her and she placed a hand around his unkempt hair. Lily sat in a sagging chair beside them, brooding in the flickery candle-glow, lost in thoughts that kept spilling onto her face.

Ruby, like Renfield and one or two of the other performers, was renting space in the airless maze above the music hall's backstage area. The last acts of the night had taken their bows, and now Ruby's room thrummed with the hollow clashing which reverberated up through the building from the washroom-kitchen way down in the basement.

Lily rubbed at her cheeks. "Clipper was a pain in the arse," she muttered, "a ramper, for all his flash, and I barely even. . . but he didn't deserve that." She dipped her head for a minute while she fought back tears. "I left the damn bag," she sighed at last. "And there's no chance of getting the money Bert owed me. God almighty, his face, the look on his face. Like a raving maniac. Why did I leave the damn bag?"

"With a raving maniac on your tail?" said Ruby. "I'd have left the damn bag."

"It's not funny," said Lily. She seemed to shrink into herself. "You didn't see him. You think you know someone, and they're. . . I'll see that face till my dying day, I know I will. Jack saw it too, didn't you, sweetheart?"

Jack nodded. "I was too scared to fight him," he said softly, in a tone filled with shame.

"You did the right thing, darling, you were very brave," said Lily, sniffing and batting swiftly at her eyes. She turned to Ruby. "All the demons of Hell were behind those eyes. Like he was possessed by the Devil hisself."

"Let's leave the ghost stories with Mr Dickens at the Royal," said Ruby. "Have you got no money, then?"

"A few shillings," said Lily. "Real, I mean, not snide. I'm going to have to do a scoot on the rent, there's no way I can pay it in time. There's no way we're going back to that house in any case."

"Then tonight, dear Lil, I am your faerie familiar," said Ruby, the candlelight twinkling in her eyes. "I've got a job for you. If you want it."

"What sort of job?"

"Sir Edwin Gull," said Ruby, leaning forward. "I've got more than enough to get him on the black. Mace him thoroughly."

Lily looked doubtful. "I'd need backup, wouldn't I? I'm not sure who I could trust."

"Gull doesn't need to keep muscle, he has a Home Secretary in his pocket. Anyway, he's too miserly. Take Jack."

The boy sat up eagerly, but his mother waved him down. "No. You know I don't like involving him. I want it to be better for my boy."

"Mamaaaa," pleaded Jack. "I want to help. Please let me help." He knew the way to his mother's heart went right through his own. "You said if we get some money we could ride on the train, to the sea."

Lily knew that her son knew that the way to her heart went right through his own. She shut her eyes for a moment and sighed. "What's the convincer?"

Ruby fetched a cloth bag from under her cot bed. Inside was an old cigar tin. Ruby handed her friend a handkerchief and a pair of knee-length flannel underpants, both of which bore the embroidered monogram 'E.G.'

"He's far too sharp to write me letters, or sign anything," said Ruby. "These I took from right under his nose. And from right under his backside."

Lily cackled. Jack didn't get the joke.

An hour later, when all three were tucked into the one bed and asleep, their shared blankets kept them from feeling the chill that accompanied Dracul's arrival in the room. The vampyr had fluxed and waned, dizzied by its sudden, enforced freedom. Along the street, into Holmwood's, through the emptied auditorium and the corridors backstage. Once it steadied its senses, it started searching for a new host.

It drifted, like cold breath on a winter's night, beneath the door of Ruby's room. A mist that was not a mist, a phantasm of no shape and unreal substance.

There were humans here, their minds turned inward. Dreaming. Three.

This one: young male. Small. Healthy but not very strong. Encountered before, recently. When hungry and feeding. It ran. Would be good host. Subtle. Not believed.

Next one: also encountered before. See it through last host's desires. Looking, looking. Female. Rejected before. Smell of recent disease in the organs.

Last one: free of blemish and canker. Smell of strength. Smell of cunning. The possibility of *co-operation*. Understanding. *Acceptance* of a new life.

Rare and wonderful. An *ideal* host.

Dracul wormed softly into Ruby's ear, caressing her dreams, soothing her doubts. They communed in the unconscious, sharing visions from the distant past and distant lives, existence from beyond death.

Power. Escape. Love.

Yes.

All these gifts I offer you.

Give them.

Ruby felt a sharp stab behind her eye. A tightening inside her head, a pressure forcing itself outward.

She was drowning in empty space, gasping for thought. Twisting, in a pain which dissolved as soon as it began, and suddenly awake.

Lily turned her head. "Are you having a nightmare?" she said in a fug of semi-consciousness.

"No," smiled Ruby-Dracul. "You go back to sleep."

XXII

from the *London Daily Examiner*, dated Thursday 4th June 1868

WEST END MURDERER EXPOSED

Culprit's secret life of moral degradation –
Meets accidental death during pursuit

by Wm Browning,
staff reporter

The grisly and mysterious case of murder, recently reported as having been committed in an alley close to Southampton Street and Lemmly Court, has now come to a shocking and dramatic conclusion. The culprit, tracked down by a party of concerned citizens, was Mr Herbert Maurice, local bookseller, a man of previous respectability and good name.

SECRETS
This fiend, it has been disclosed, was responsible for at least three deaths in all, the last two killings having been carried out in the course of yesterday alone: that

of Mrs E Potter, widow, and that of an un-named man thought to be of the criminal classes. Both suffered the same horrible and bewildering fate as the first victim.

Moreover, Maurice's exposure as the perpetrator of these crimes has led directly to the discovery that he was also, and had been for some years, a secret purveyor of materials now seized by police under Parliament's Obscene Publications Act, in force for almost eleven years. A considerable cache of these materials has been recovered and destroyed.

CHASE

This contemptible villain was cornered near the Strand last evening. A chase on foot followed, the climax of which was witnessed by persons outside the premises of Holmwood's Music Hall at approximately 10 o'clock. A member of the public, Mr Arthur Flemming, bravely tackled the fleeing Maurice, who then met his end beneath the wheels of a cab while attempting to escape justice.

INVESTIGATION

The peculiarity of the blood loss suffered by the murderer's victims is still under official investigation, as are his motives for engaging in such frenzied attacks. The police are inclined to the opinion that the balance of his mind was overturned due to the illegal and furtive nature of his publishing activities, but enquiries are ongoing and more complete details will follow in future numbers of this paper.

• • •

The early morning editions of the newspapers were being pored over at coffee kiosks and shops all along Fleet Street and the Strand but, standing at a canopied stall near Holmwood's, Jacob Renfield only skipped through the stall's copy of the *Examiner* before setting it aside and concentrating on his cup and his slice of bread and butter.

"The state of the world today." He took a sip of his coffee and pulled a face. "Can't even get decent coffee. All ruddy carrot and chicory, this." He glanced up to find the stallholder glaring flatly at him, so he turned to his assistant. "You not having any breakfast, girl?"

"I'm not hungry any more," said Ruby-Dracul. "I ate earlier." She unconsciously checked her hands and dress for blood or other evidence of the two drained bodies she'd dumped into the new sewerage system shortly before dawn.

Renfield thought about leaving the coffee, but he'd paid his hard-earned penny now and he was going to get his money's worth if it was the last thing he ever did. He bit into his bread. "Is there something different about you? Changed your hair or something?"

"Different? There certainly is," said Ruby-Dracul with a smile. She tilted her head back and let the soot-filtered morning sunshine lick her face. "It's going to be a beautiful day," she said. The street's crush of people and transport seemed to exhilarate her. She took it all in as if seeing it for the first time. "Each life is fresh, each host unique."

"Eh?" said Renfield. Butter from his bread was spreading to his gnarly fingers.

Ruby-Dracul flicked flakes of dandruff from his shoulder.

"I've been thinking. I've got some new ideas for our act."

"I say what goes in the act."

"Of course you do, but these are very good ideas. I'll show you."

She led him back to Holmwood's. Despite the staff and hangers-on in the building, the place felt deserted at that hour of the day, resting and waiting for the public to fill its cavernous innards. They clumped up the long flight of open steps behind the stage.

"Holmwood wants to put one of those big diorama things in the foyer," said Renfield, "charge a ha'penny a go. A view of Venice from a gondola, he wants. I told him, those things are old hat now, they're not the novelty they were."

"And what did he say?"

". . . Can't remember. Don't you need props?"

"No."

Renfield's room was sparse and dusty, with none of the comforts of Ruby-Dracul's. Everything the magician owned was gathered onto and inside a dressing table, a shambolic assortment of make-ups, costume parts and personal memorabilia. He lit an oil lamp and hung it up, then creaked to perch on the end of his bed.

"I've learned I need . . ." She searched for the word. "A confederate. A lieutenant. An aide-de-camp. In order to thrive in a city this crowded. A lackey, that's it. A faithful retainer."

Renfield scratched at his neck. "I don't get you."

She sat cross-legged on the floor, under the lamp, and patted her knees. "Come on, sit beside me."

"You trying to put my hip out?" he grumbled.

"Sit. . . There you go. Now. . . Look at me, Renfield. Look at my eyes. Look at these deep and beautiful eyes of mine."

He screwed up his face, unimpressed, but did as he was told. To tell the truth, her eyes were indeed beautiful. Why hadn't he noticed that before? Her dark hair seemed. . . to curl around them. Her face. . . lustrous. How could he not have properly appreciated her charms until now?

She extended her arms. "Here's a trick," she whispered. "Watch this."

The light from the lamp dimmed for a moment, then slowly increased until it was brighter than Renfield had ever seen it before, and then brighter than any lamp, and then brighter than the sun itself, radiating light and warmth down upon him.

But he had no need to shield his eyes. All he needed to do was bask in the comfort and serenity which flowed over him, around him, through him.

Ruby was at the heart of the light. She was its source and its power. From her came hope, joy, safety, a future that was assured and not to be feared. She was the mother he'd never had and the friend he'd never kept. She was wisdom, she was the beginning of all things and their end. She was warmth in the bitter cold, relief from the raging storm. How had he not realised all this?

He was hers, truly and forever. He was hers, body and soul, flesh and bone.

"Mistress," he mouthed, his eyes streaming gratitude, the lamp back to its normal luminance once more. "Bless you. O, bless you, Mistress." His bony hands clutched reverently at the folds of her skirts.

Ruby-Dracul smiled her benevolence upon him. With one hand, she held him to her tenderly. With the other, she scooped a spider off the floor and popped it between her teeth, enjoying the squish and the snuffing of a life.

"Come with me, Renfield," she said soothingly.

"Yes. Oh yes," nodded Renfield gently. He cupped her hand and kissed it several times. She turned down the lamp and they left.

As soon as they'd descended to the backstage area, Lily and Jack appeared from the storage room and hurried over. "There you are, Ruby! We wondered where you'd gone."

"I got up very early," said Ruby-Dracul. "I was hungry. Well, you two look splendid."

"Holmwood won't mind us borrowing these?" Lily twirled in her smart dress and Jack bowed in his jacket and cloth hat.

"If he does, he can take it up with me, can't he?" said Ruby-Dracul.

"It'll save us a gen or two. The posher we can look today, the better." She put a hand on Ruby-Dracul's arm and lowered her voice. "Thanks, again. For giving us a lurk for the night, I mean. I'll sort us a new place later. I've friends already sharing at Lambeth."

"I'm hardly going to leave my best friend and her little boy out on the streets, am I?" smiled Ruby-Dracul. "I'm not a monster."

"You look different today."

"So I've heard."

"Yes," said Lily approvingly. "You've got a rosy glow in your cheeks. Hasn't she, Jack?"

"You look very pretty, Miss Ruby," said Jack with a shy grin.

She bent down to his level and gently tweaked his nose. "You're the proper gentleman. I could eat you up, I could, if I'd not already had my breakfast!"

"Come on, Jack," laughed Lily. "Let's get to work. Couple of swells today, ain't we, eh? Look at us, washed faces, washed hands, all out of twig."

Renfield waved at them from behind Ruby-Dracul's shoulder as they departed. "Nice people."

He was equally pleased half an hour later when, attending his Mistress in the stage wings, he saw William Browning approaching them through the unlit, echoing auditorium with a folded newspaper tucked under his arm.

"Good morning to you, Mr Renfield," said Browning. "Would Miss Wester be, er. . .?"

Renfield beckoned and Ruby-Dracul emerged onto the stage wrapped in a voluminous damask dressing gown. "William! How lovely."

At the sight of her, Browning blushed as only he could. Theatrical people, so daringly bohemian! And how fresh she looked. How newly vibrant. "I do apologise if I've caught you at an inconvenient time . . ."

"Of course not, my dear William. Renfield is helping me prepare an entirely new act which will premiere tonight."

Renfield nodded vigorously. "It promises to be unlike anything seen before on the London stage." His expression became wistful, as if he could hear distant traces of music echoing from the past. "I saw the Great Wizard of the North, Mr John Henry Anderson, perform his bullet catch trick. I had the privilege of being witness to Monsieur Robert-Houdin's 'Marvellous Orange Tree' illusion at the Palais Royale in Paris. These will melt into history after this evening, when the name of Miss Ruby Wester will shine as the brightest star in the theatrical firmament."

"Well, then I shall secure the best seat in the house," said Browning brightly. "Miss Wes—Ruby, might I speak to you in confidence? Forgive me, there is another matter of some urgency—"

"Another? You do lead a frantic life, William."

She waved a hand to dismiss Renfield and sat down on the edge of the stage, her bare feet dangling at the level of Browning's chest. He fought back the urge to admire their daintiness.

Instead, he cleared his throat and plucked today's *Examiner* from under his arm. He handed it to her, folded back to show the short piece he'd written. "Despite my editor's approval of these reports, they do not make a full disclosure of the facts, and much information must stay outside the public domain. I have to warn you that the perpetrator of these crimes eluded capture and is still at liberty, although I am actively engaged in seeking his demise."

"How disturbing. Who is it?"

"I— By now, his identity will have changed. No, that's not— how should I put it?"

She enjoyed watching reluctance and necessity wrestle

on his face. "This murderer," he said, "is of so distressing and peculiar a type you may think me insane for voicing my concerns."

"Never, William," said Ruby-Dracul, with a brush of consoling fingers along his cheek. "If you have a warning to impart, I'd be foolish not to listen."

A smile half-flickered across Browning's agonised expression. "Each night, on this very stage with Mr Renfield, you conjure up the dead. The true nature of this murderer is somewhat— No, perhaps, rather, what I mean is, just as the performers in this music hall adopt costumes and characters for effect, so this murderer is, shall we say, a master of disguise. He may appear before you as a stranger, or may have the appearance of someone you know and trust. Please. I beg you. Be especially vigilant if you notice any alteration in a person you know well, any change of behaviour for which you cannot account. Be wary of *everyone* until I and my colleagues can make sure this devil is despatched. A terrible evil stalks London, and it can lurk inside any one of us."

She took his hands in hers. "I will be careful, dear William, for your sake. I promise." As he looked at her, he felt a strange portent, deep in his soul, as if the Fates of ancient myth were blowing wisps of foreboding from the darkness of a bottomless pit. "Isn't there something else you want from me?" she said, her crystal voice breaking up his thoughts like a hand through his reflection in water. "An answer to that other question you asked?"

"Oh, yes," he stumbled, "but I would never presume to—"

"The answer is yes," she said softly. "I have considered carefully, as I said I would, and the answer is yes. I will be yours."

Browning felt his heart mend.

"My valiant prince," she whispered, lifting his chin with one finger and planting a delicate kiss on his trembling lips. "Come and see me, upstairs, after tonight's performance. I will show you the true measure of my love."

He was in a daze as they parted. He was unaware of anything except his own happiness until he was outside in the sunlight again, standing motionless while a ragged man worked around him, shovelling horse dung off the road and into the basket on his back.

How well Ruby had taken his alarming news. How wonderful that she'd made up her mind. How alive she seemed, how radiant, how glowing.

XXIII

". . . at a Coming Out ball, no less, at Bath House. Never on time, that man, and one has to practically shout at his wife in order to be heard."

The trustees were politely amused. They'd been politely amused by the President of the Society's remarks on gardening, on the London traffic, and on the Irish question, and now they were being politely amused by his remarks on the poor state of the monarchy. "One despairs for international relations once he's on the throne."

There were twelve around the dining table at Sir Edwin Gull's house, seven ladies and five gentlemen. Twice a year, Lady Gull hosted a luncheon for the organising committee of the Society for the Suppression of Vice, of which she was a senior member. Sir Edwin attended in his unofficial role as the Society's voice in Parliament.

Beneath the glittering crystal Montgolfière and the periwinkle draperies, spoons clinked on rapidly emptying plates of spotted dick and vanilla custard. Dappled sunshine filtered through the lites of the French doors, from a rose garden freshly cleaned of smog residue. A selection of Lady Gull's ancestors peered down at the diners from their portraits on the panelled walls.

"More wine, your grace?"

The President of the Society pointed to his glass and it was filled immediately. "Mr Secretary, as time is pressing a little, would you be so kind as to enumerate the Society's recent successes?"

The Secretary, a dapper muttonchop-whiskered man, cleared his throat and addressed himself to the whole table, checking numbers on a slip of card as he went. "We have seven separate prosecutions currently before the courts, three of which are due a hearing within the month. More specifically, these relate to the appropriation of vicious periodicals numbering two thousand two hundred and eleven, licentious publications in volume form numbering nine hundred and sixty, song sheets numbering eight hundred and four, handbills numbering two thousand seven hundred and sixty, lithographic engravings numbering one thousand five hundred and twenty-two, packs of cards numbering eight hundred and nineteen, and another three hundred and thirty-seven sundry articles of a vile nature. A total for photographic materials is yet to be calculated."

The trustees exchanged congratulatory looks and nods. One of them, a broad lady with skin like a parsnip, leaned forward to level her gaze at Sir Edwin. "I propose we thank Mr Gull for his efforts recommending harder punishments for offences of this type."

"Mm, I merely do my duty," said Gull, bowing his head in answer to murmurs of agreement but certain, beyond all doubt, that he'd never recommended any such thing to anyone. "In my work, I see enough of the city's gutters to know that only the strongest penalties deter the stubborn fecklessness in which vice thrives. When filth is stirred up it merely circulates and settles back in its original position. It must be cleared away entirely."

"Like that open patch at the top of the Strand," said the President. "Every time I pass it, it's refilled with vagabonds, no sign of a start to building these new Royal Courts of Justice—"

"The contract is very soon to be awarded," said Gull, gripping his napkin under the table. "My consortium is in contention." He chewed at his pudding.

The President was suddenly reminded of a question he'd meant to ask earlier. "Speaking of that district, Sir Edwin, what's this about your factotum Flemming in the papers today?"

"Mr Flemming? In the papers?" said Lady Gull, looking back and forth between the President and her husband.

"As I understand it," said the President, "good old Flemming contributed to the successes of which we've just been hearing, by single-handedly tackling a peddler of obscene literature to the ground."

A ripple of admiration and approval circled the table. Far off, at the front of the house, the doorbell clanged.

"Although, of course," he added with a sly smile, "we should perhaps hesitate to follow his example since our recourse is to the law rather than to fisticuffs."

The trustees were politely amused again. "Perhaps we should make him an honorary associate of the Society?" said the Secretary, expecting more amusement but causing none.

Raised voices sounded in the distance.

"You should have invited him to join us, Edwin," said

Lady Gull. "He could have told us all about his adventure."

Sir Edwin swallowed the last of his pudding. "As you know, my dear, Flemming's duties keep him fully occupied."

The raised voices drew closer. In a stage whisper, a servant announced to Lady Gull that tea and coffee were being served informally in the sitting room. The trustees, chatting amongst themselves, were halfway to the door when it was shoved open.

Lily wrenched herself free of the butler who was grabbing at her arms, but pulled herself up short for a second when she saw that Sir Edwin and Lady Gull had so many guests. Only for a second, because years of persuading coins to leave other people's pockets had made her nothing if not adaptable.

"So!" she declared in the posh voice she used for this sort of occasion, straightening the front of her dress with a sharp tug and directing an indignant glare at Sir Edwin. "I've found you at last, Ezra! Or, as I now discover, Edwin! That is your real name, is it?"

Gull was too bemused to do anything but gape at her. Lady Gull stepped between Lily and the President of the Society. "I am Lady Frances Gull," she said with icy calm, "and may I ask *your* name, Miss? This is private property and you are rudely interrupting a private luncheon."

Lily toned down the anger a little and stressed the emotional turmoil instead. "I have no wish to offend innocent parties, Lady, but I have no other choice but to rudely interrupt when I am roughly manhandled by your servants." She flashed a scowl at the butler, who raised an eyebrow. "I have come seeking justice. Justice! Eight long years I have searched! Eight hard and painful years." She flung a finger at Sir Edwin. "This man! Abandoned me to a pauper's fate!"

Gull finally found his voice, and it made the trustees jump. "What? Who in blazes *are* you, Madam? I've never seen this woman in my life!"

Lady Gull, her face visibly draining, made attempts to move the guests along to the sitting room, but they dithered and fussed at a snail's pace. The woman with skin like a parsnip rested a corded pince-nez on her nose.

"My name," said Lily, striking a pose of contained and dignified rage, "is Constance Mary Heartwell, resident of Leamington Spa, far to the north, in the Midlands of England. This man! Claimed to be a Mr Ezra Golightly, in town to take the waters. He plied me with gifts, seduced me, then deserted me."

"Get out, you lying slattern!" brayed Sir Edwin. He turned to the slow-shuffling guests. Two of them had left the room by now but were hanging around in the hallway. "This is a feeble attempt to cause me embarrassment, made by some unscrupulous business rival or political enemy. Take no notice."

"Unpleasant enemies," muttered the President of the Society. "Makes you wonder."

"Why did he desert you, Miss Heartwell?" said the woman with skin like a parsnip.

Lily pulled Jack out from behind the butler. There was a low gasp from the trustees. "He learned I was with child, and fled, all promises of marriage forgotten.

Tracking him down has been the work of eight years, eight hard, distressing years."

"Mama," said Jack, angelic and innocent, "is this kind gentleman my papa?"

"Yes, Gabriel, he is."

Lady Gull, with calm but firm insistence, herded the rest of the guests towards the door. They continued to dither because, well, this *woman* and *child*, surely, by their appearance, decent people, their cleanliness and speech, surely, and a *child*, hardly looked like rough slum dwellers chancing their luck, surely, would be unimaginable impertinence...

"Miss Heartwell," said Lady Gull sharply, "perhaps you would care to provide us with evidence of your claims?"

"Precisely. She can't," said Sir Edwin.

Lily reached into her dress pocket and flourished the monogrammed handkerchief she'd been given by Ruby. "If you and I have never met, how could I be in possession of this?"

"The initials *E* and *G* are common enough," snorted Sir Edwin.

"But I'll wager you any sum that the lettering matches many another item in this house," said Lily.

"And so what if it does? I could have dropped that by mistake in any one of a hundred places!"

"Oh yes? And these?"

The moment Lily produced the monogrammed underwear, she knew she'd hooked her fish. The trustees were no longer amused, politely or otherwise. "Would I care to provide you with evidence? Well, Lady, here's evidence your husband's been on the randy with me."

There was a tense silence, broken when Lady Gull spoke quietly to the butler. "Take the child down to Cook, please Chilvers, I'm sure she can spare something from the pantry," she said, adding a whispered instruction to fetch the household accounting box from her bureau in the morning room.

Smiling only with her lips, she ushered the trustees along the tastefully decorated hallway that led to the front door. "My dear friends, I have so enjoyed our little gathering. I will have sharp words with our housekeeper on the subject of thefts from the laundry. As my husband suggests, a political opponent is playing an outlandish practical joke, I'm sure we all appreciate that important men of state can be the target of such antics from time to time. A simple misunderstanding, easily dealt with. Do mind the step, Lady Bitterlea. Thank you."

In the dining room, Gull loomed over Lily, bellowing into her face without making a sound or moving a muscle. Lily met his stare, but her legs made a slow retreat, like a nervous cat's. She suddenly felt the lack of backup brawn that she'd feared.

"Who sent you?" he said in a low growl.

"Someone you won't be dabbing it up with no more," she whispered cheerfully.

The butler reappeared carrying a plain metal box. He put it on the table, and withdrew as Lady Gull returned. She spoke to Lily while she unlocked the box with a key from around her neck. "Would you like some tea? The pot has been warmed."

"No, thank you, Lady."

"How much do you require, Miss Heartwell? To go

home to Leamington Spa, or wherever it is you come from, and permanently lose all knowledge of my husband."

"What?" roared Sir Edwin. "Pay her off? Are you mad? We'll have every gutter whore in London at our door!"

Lady Gull counted half a dozen banknotes out of the box. "I'm sure Miss Heartwell understands the terms of the arrangement."

"A bargain struck is a bargain honoured, far as I'm concerned, Mrs Gull," said Lily sweetly.

Lady Gull handed her the money. "Is this enough?" It was more than five times the amount Lily had hoped for, but she covered her delight with a sneery wrinkle of her nose before giving a curt nod and throwing the handkerchief and underwear onto the dining table.

"Thank you," said Lady Gull. "Now I'd like you to leave via the kitchen, if you'd be so kind." She summoned the butler and Lily was shown out.

As soon as they were alone, Sir Edwin transferred his looming to his wife. "You're acting as if you believe that piece of trash," he snarled.

"Don't be absurd," said Lady Gull calmly. "Nobody genuinely in such a position would accept a token payment like that."

"Then why in God's name make one? Let her shout from the hilltops! Who would take the word of a worthless harlot over mine? The truth would soon be apparent."

"Truth is only a point of view efficiently repeated, my dear, as you very well know and as that dreadful girl has just demonstrated. The point of the matter is that it might have been your friend Ruby who turned up instead, and told a more plausible story. Be grateful her opinion of you is so low that she passed her chance at blackmail to an associate."

At the mention of Ruby, Sir Edwin blanched. His lips pressed tightly together and he took a step back without meaning to.

"Now that the luncheon is over," said Lady Gull, "I'm sure you have plenty to keep you busy. There's a vote in the House later today, isn't there?" She rang the bell, walked sedately across the hall to arrange for a light supper to be served on Sir Edwin's return from Westminster, and went to her bedroom.

She sat in silence for long minutes, with her back straight and her hands folded in her lap. As Daddy had so resolutely required. Thin tears began to fall from her shuddering face, no matter how hard she tried to stop them, and her fingers rose to delicately cover her eyes.

Immediately and forthwith, if she didn't act swiftly and if luck was not on her side, she would find herself at the centre of a public scandal. Even the least venomous of the trustees were capable of idle gossip, no matter how outlandish. A situation she'd dreaded for years had been suddenly thrust at her like a mewling infant.

A mess she'd have to manage with care, a mess caused by her husband. One more grievance to add to Sir Edwin's continued draining of her family's money into his consortium. Already, her finances needed a rapid reversal of fortune to avert ruin. Now, after today's luncheon, they'd need a miracle.

She allowed herself a few moments' nauseous emotion, then with a shake of her head she dried her eyes and tweaked at her hair in the mirror. From its hiding place in the bed, she took out her secret insurance cache. She picked through the contents – the papers, the accounts, the small blue phial of arsenic.

It had gone too far and now there was no other choice. He'd have to go.

XXIV

She'd have to go. Sir Edwin glared out of the brougham that rattled him away from Westminster, consumed with thoughts about how he could rid himself of Ruby Wester. When the hell had she stolen those monogrammed items? The effrontery – the damned impudence! – to set up that scene at his home. After all he'd done for her! Ungrateful bitch!

A thickening evening mist blurred his view of Trafalgar Square, making ghostly shapes out of the drifters, and those who preyed on them, already gathering there for the night. Gull checked that his top button was done up. How much money would it take to make that greedy jumped-up bawd stop bothering him?

Once the brougham had arrived at Holmwood's, he heaved himself out onto the pavement and told the driver to wait. The show had started and he found a lounge seat on the balcony, where he could brood until he'd worked out an acceptable bargaining position. The scowl on his face kept the nightly circulation of smiles at a distance.

The audience, William Browning among them, applauded as the players bowed following their re-enactment of The

Notorious Bermondsey Horror And The Burial Of O'Connor Beneath The Scullery. Browning's eager face glowed with anticipation, highlighted in beams that spilt from the limes at the front of the stage.

> *"Ladies! Gentlemen! One and all! For the very first time, on any stage, in any country of the world, Holmwood's Music Hall presents to you a performance unparalleled in history! Our regular patrons will be familiar with the marvellous mystic Renfield and his journeys into the unknown, but now he stands eclipsed as Master of Magic and Mesmerism! Eclipsed by our very own Songstress of Sorcery! The fabulous! The fantastical! Ruby Wester!"*

The band struck up an air of mystery, the red curtains parted just enough to let her through, and to an enthusiastic but slightly puzzled welcome, Ruby-Dracul stepped into view. She wore a long gown in a vaguely medieval style, with a huge feathered collar and a headpiece like a frozen fountain of shining particles. Claps and whistles died away into silence. She spread her arms and a single violin began to play a song of mourning.

Her head tilted back slightly, her mouth opened . . .

My gift to you, whispered the vampyr

. . . and the long, high notes rising from her throat took a gentle hold of every heart that heard them. Her song wrapped every soul in an aching glow of love and loss, a yearning for things gone by and things yet to be. She sung in a conjuration of language unheard, words of sorrow and hope, of longing and passion, to a fluid melody so strange it thrilled the senses and bedazzled the mind.

Every human smiled and melted. William Browning's vision swam with joy. Up on the balcony, Gull's anger at his ex-lover kept him detached enough to understand what was happening. He remembered what Harker had said about vampyrs, and with a flush of terror squeezed his eyes shut, turned his head away, pressed his hands tightly to his ears.

As Ruby-Dracul sang, she rose up onto the balls of her feet. From her back unfurled enormous, diaphanous wings, curling outwards in shimmering colours. They began to beat slowly, in time with the music, and her toes lifted off the stage.

She drifted in mid-air, like a gorgeous and iridescent butterfly, singing with unbearable beauty, with the train of her gown flowing and rippling behind her. Slowly, higher and higher, rising way above the stage and out over the people, pouring breathless sounds of heartbreak and wonderment over all, like a balm for the soul, a kiss of absolution. The people were filled with inexpressible joy, some of them on their feet, some on their knees in the aisles, some of them clasping their hands together in rapture.

. . .*your lifelong desire*, whispered the vampyr.

William Browning felt a pride so glorious, an admiration so intense, that he barely dared to breathe in case the enchantment of the moment might be lost. Gull, whose feelings were equally strong, but of fear and awe, risked a brief glimpse down at the stage. Ruby-Dracul's feet were firmly planted there, and her singing voice was no different to how it had always been, while the audience looked up at empty space and heard ethereal sounds with amazement and delight. Renfield stood beside the violins, eyes aloft and swaying slowly, his bony fingers circling and fluttering.

The song was reaching its conclusion, trembling notes in a cascade sad and magnificent. Ruby-Dracul's body weaved and rolled, like a reed lost in a river's current. She descended in a graceful swirl, her own Ophelia, her dying swan.

I love you so, her mind whispered to her inner self, her truth, her vampyr.

Her toes alighted, her arms reached wide, she sighed a last, extended note, and with a flourish the music ended. For a thin splinter of time there was a silence as delicate as spun glass.

Applause rose like a tidal wave.

A thunderous, unstoppable swell of elation burst forth, a cheering, calling, hat-throwing, deafening radiance of approval that seemed to shake the walls. It cascaded through the auditorium, a living celebration of one person. Ruby-Dracul bathed in their appreciation, bowing and bowing again, her face beaming.

I love you so.

With a wave, she disappeared behind the curtain. Unable to wait any longer, William Browning left his seat to head for the promised rendezvous with his fiancée. On second thoughts, he'd head for the bar and a little Dutch courage first, and *then* the promised rendezvous with his fiancée. He picked his way through the thronging crowd, surrounded by chatter.

". . . most marvellous, look at me, I can't stop crying . . ."

". . . the angels themselves couldn't hold a candle . . ."

". . . much better than the French magician at St James's. Done with wires, possibly . . ."

". . . never seen anything so beautiful in all my life . . ."

Gull inched forward in his seat and glowered over the balustrade at the excited audience, the band playing a jaunty tune to calm them down and get them re-seated. His nerves stung with icy needles of horror. It was almost incredible but, according to Harker's blathering, Ruby Wester was clearly host to this. . . this supernatural creature!

He gripped the balustrade, conscious that he was shivering despite the summer heat. Cold fear pleaded with him to contact Flemming at once, to raise the alarm as Harker had demanded, but far too many years had passed since he'd last considered needs beyond his own. His instincts, as a politician and as a businessman, readily suggested to him the acceptable bargaining position he'd been looking for. He hastily strode out of Holmwood's and into his waiting brougham, just as Browning was hastily taking the steps, gazelle-like, up to Ruby-Dracul's room.

He knocked with a single knuckle. Renfield, grinning and diffident, showed him in.

"William!" trilled Ruby-Dracul. "Come in, come in!" She had peeled herself out of her costume, which was pegged up on a coat hook, and was wrapped in the same robe she'd been wearing that morning. A freshly filled candelabra danced shadows around the walls.

She bounced to a kneeling position on her bed and stretched forward, head tilted to one side, her face alight with triumph. "Well? What did you think?"

"It was sublime," said Browning, his mouth dry. "Truly. I'd venture to say that it was a performance every bit as innovative as it was moving and beautiful. I cannot even begin to guess how such effects are achieved. Extremely clever."

He looked askance at Renfield, who smiled and dipped his wrinkled head. "Oh, her talent far surpasses mine, Mr Browning, I would not presume to offer advice and none was requested of me."

"Then I congratulate you with all my heart, Miss Wes— Ruby, on a remarkable achievement. The first of many, I am sure."

"You're a lamb, William." She swung her legs around so that she was lying on her front and looking up at him. "After such exertions, I'm absolutely ravenous."

"Perhaps I might escort you to one of the better restaurants?" said Browning. "Or perhaps you'd prefer The Café Royal? The Holborn Casino?"

"I was thinking of dining right here, in the candlelight."

"Oh," said Browning, fresh blushes blooming, "of course, you must be very tired. Should I leave you to rest?"

"No, William, no," said Ruby-Dracul softly, raising herself up towards him so that the folds of her robe began to part. "After all, I promised that I would show you the true measure of my love. And a promise is a promise."

Browning glanced uncomfortably back and forth between Ruby-Dracul's gown and Renfield, now standing in front of the door, a portrait in unctuous pleasantry.

Until that precise moment, it hadn't even occurred to Browning that his devotion had glossed over any awkward questions he might have asked about Miss Wes— Ruby, but now there was a twist to her smile, an odd catch in her voice, that made him swallow skittishly.

She had a strange and unsettling charisma, here in the candlelight. There was an uncanny otherness about her, a peculiar quality which made his skin bristle.

He looked down at the long curve of warm flesh visible between the open edges of her gown. She drew closer to him. "You may kiss me, William. Renfield won't mind." She took hold of his lapels and pulled her face up level with his.

Fear inched up his spine but he tried to deny it. "I burned every fragment of the photographs," he muttered feebly, "I swear. To defend your honour. Please believe that I love you, Ruby."

Her lips brushed his ear. "My name is Death, I am the dragon, I am the devil."

Her teeth snapped together a hair's width from his nose and he tried to pull away. At last he saw the truth. There was nothing he could do, and terror overwhelmed him when her lips pressed tenderly against his.

She bit hard into his face, her mouth working to get a better grip and to crush open more blood vessels. She drank and bit, deeply and greedily, and when all of William Browning's blood was in her belly, or smeared around her mouth and chest, she dropped his body to the floor and sat at her dressing table, panting.

She adjusted the angle of the candelabra and looked at herself in her mirror while she began to wipe herself clean. "When I went out in the early hours of this morning, Renfield, and breakfasted on two whores, I found a convenient place for disposal I hadn't considered before. The sewerage system."

"Ingenious, Mistress," smiled Renfield. "Up goes the lid, down goes the rubbish."

"At a quieter moment, Mr Browning can go the same way."

"I will attend to it, Mistress. Do you require any more sustenance?"

"Not for the time being, thank you, Renfield."

XXV

from the journal of Arthur Flemming

5th day of June 1868

I thank Providence for the <u>solace</u> afforded me by my journal. These past days have been no less than torment and, what's more, torment for which I bear a heavy responsibility. The decision to bring the box to London was mine alone. Moreover, my nerves have fallen into such a dreadful state that I allowed the fiend Dracul to escape its host the bookseller! I cannot rid myself of <u>constant</u> self-recrimination and regret.

I find relief in the pouring out of my heart upon these pages (since <u>recording</u> and <u>organising</u> my troubles has always helped to alleviate them) but now the effect is temporary at best. Naturally, it is impossible for me to confide in my aunt in Chiswick. Her health is far too flighty and prone to disturbance. Only this week she has suffered extended paroxysms of agitation over the uneven drape of her tablecloth and the pallor of the meat delivered by the butcher's boy. One dare not even guess at her reaction to accounts of the murderous undead!

Sir Edwin's reaction is all too clear. His casual (yes! indeed! <u>casual</u>!) attitude to the ongoing crisis has, it shocks me to say, done considerable damage to the high regard in which I've always held my employer. Until now, I have thought of him as a serious man; a thoughtful man; a principled, steadfast man; perhaps, it's true, a hard-headed man. Above all, a man of success to whom I have been proud to offer my services.

However, in his dismissal of the dangers currently faced, and in particular his dismissal of the potential damage to the broader *populus*, I am beginning to question many of the opinions that he and I have hitherto shared. I will re-evaluate both my attitudes and my current employment if – no, <u>when</u> – the nightmare passes. I pray it will pass, fervently, every hour of every day, to whatever god may deign to hear my prayer.

I am prompted to set down these latest words because of the horrifying developments which have today taken place in our quest to vanquish the vampyr foe. Valentine Harker and I have, over the past days, made relentless efforts to persuade persons capable of mobilising an official force that there exists a threat. Harker's contacts through the War Office (possibly because they know his history and are predisposed to disbelieve him?) have been of <u>no</u> <u>help</u> <u>whatsoever</u>; our independent attempts to enlighten some of Sir Edwin's colleagues have met with <u>bafflement</u>; the police have proved themselves little more than a collection of mutton-headed <u>fools</u>. One entirely understands that, in our modern age of advanced science, talk of mythical horrors might be greeted with scepticism, yet one might reasonably think that our modern age of advanced science should have bred minds capable of open enquiry!

In all our efforts, we have been careful not to generate any personal notoriety for ourselves (which may <u>alert</u> our quarry) and not to cause a wider public alarm (which may alert our quarry <u>and</u> make the fiend's capture all the more difficult). The journalist, Browning, and a single Bow Street officer, one Sgt Barré, have been the <u>only</u> people to offer us useful aid! Of course, all such efforts might not have been necessary, had Sir Edwin exerted his influence as requested, but I shall set my feelings on that matter aside.

Appalling Discoveries

The mention of Browning and Barré forces me into an account of this morning's terrible events, since it was the latter who told us of a find by the river and it was the former to whom the trail led. Shortly after dawn, Harker called at my house in a cab and we made haste to the Charing Cross bridge.

The area of river bank to the north of the bridge is fully viewable from the bridge itself and so, fortunately, there was no need for us to descend the short iron ladders to the river's edge. I held my hand to my face to reduce the unutterable stench that rose from the pitch-black waters. Below us was one of the many outlets into the

Thames from the recently finished sewer tunnels. A covering mesh, to catch any large objects that might stray into or out of the outlet, churned the river into a hissing froth. Bobbing grotesquely in this turbulence, held back behind the mesh, were three dead.

Two were women, young from the general look of them, and one a man. All exhibited the exact same characteristics as the vampyr's known victims to date: the shrivelled appearance, the ghostly skin, the open wounds. The man, floating on his back, had received grievous injuries to the lower half of his face, and his clothes and hair were sodden with effluvia, but still he was recognisably William Browning.

I shut my eyes, overcome with nausea and sorrow. There was a solitary policeman standing guard close by, waiting for someone to come with a boathook and pull the corpses free. A steady push of curiosity seekers, on both bridge and bank, were craning their necks, pulling faces and pointing out gruesome details for the benefit of their neighbours – <u>ghoulish</u> <u>swine</u>, the lot of them, every bit as reprehensible as that slavering mob at the hanging!

Harker, ever the one for practical action, tugged at my sleeve and took me aside. "It seems the vampyr has not only acquired a new host, but regular habits."

"In what way?" I asked, my head still spinning with disgust.

Harker nodded in the direction of the deceased. "Even at this distance," he said, "you can see from the state of these corpses that they've been in the water for different lengths of time, the women for at least a day longer than

Browning. Since all three have ended up here, and on that side of the railing, it's reasonable to suppose that they were all disposed of in the same fashion, possibly from the same location. Such regularity may be to our advantage."

I felt a glutinous knot in my stomach. "You're surely not proposing that we investigate the sewerage system?"

"No, only that we mount observations of local accesses."

"Surely, these unfortunates might have been placed in the sewers at any point? From what I've read in the newspapers, don't they intersect for several miles?"

Harker fixed me with that reproachful, sullen gaze of his. "It would be the most extraordinary coincidence for them to end up exactly here, close to the area we've already been searching, if they had been deposited any appreciable distance away. No, I think fortune may be on our side for once. I think Dracul's new host is still close by, like our bookseller friend."

He broke off abruptly, frowning at something over my shoulder. I spun on my heels, expecting some lurid monster to be staring, wild eyed, directly behind me! Once my heart stopped racing, I perceived that his brooding was directed some hundred yards or more downriver at the Adelphi Arches, the old storage vaults behind the new Embankment, originally erected for the benefit of seagoing trade.

"What is it?" I ventured.

"I'm sure you've heard of the Dark Arches' reputation for squalor and criminality. If Dracul is still close by, perhaps there's a reason, a useful source of fresh blood.

We should direct our attention to those tunnels. I have a sudden suspicion."

We made our way down precarious steps and walkways, Harker taking the lead while I supplied a series of well-founded and level-headed arguments for pursuing an entirely different course, for none of which he had an answer. Until, that is, I eventually said: "And what is more, we are completely undefended! The brigands lurking in those tunnels may be armed to the teeth!"

At this, he produced a revolver from concealment inside his coat and held it up in front of me! "Since when have you carried a gun?" I gasped.

"Since Herbert Maurice escaped me on the Strand. If only I'd been carrying it, I might have brought him down with a shot to the leg. This is my old service pistol, I dug it out of my military effects yesterday." He eyed the firearm in his hand for a moment. "I'd vowed never to carry it again."

The vast brick arches rose high above us. Even in full daylight, only a few yards of their interiors were visible. Beyond was nothing but a Stygian blackness. Even Harker hesitated, but then proceeded into the cold shadows at a slow and steady pace.

Destitutes are a daily and unavoidable sight in our city – indeed, in any modern city of these isles – but in those dank vaults was the most dreadful and pitiful human wreckage I have ever seen. (Even as I record this experience, strong feelings akin to the self-opprobrium already detailed stand as herald to a change in attitudes).

Hostility came at us on all sides, in the form of scowls and threats. Metallic clangs and horrible cries echoed from deep chambers up ahead. However, nobody approached Harker, probably due as much to his stern, no-nonsense bearing as to the gun in his hand! We continued further into the tunnels – into this strange, <u>macabre</u> rabbit-warren of tomb-like proportions! – and once our eyes had fully adjusted to the dark, and the huge semi-circle of our entry point was back past half a dozen turns and junctions, we found the evidence that Harker had feared.

Another body, stuffed into a corner to rot. Another human being fallen prey to hideous vampyr appetites.

"Your suspicion was right," I hissed, *sotto voce*, "Dracul does indeed live down here."

"*That* wasn't my suspicion," said Harker.

I was suddenly startled by a voice like cracked leather. "You have come to take him? You are alienists?"

With an expert crack of flint beside us, a meagre stub of candle was lit. Holding it was an old man, his white beard thin and streaked, who sat wrapped in layers of rags on a protruding stone platform nearby. He had a small, greasy bag tied around his neck with string, which I presume contained his few possessions. "You are the delegation from the Bethlem?" His words echoed around the dismal chamber in which we found ourselves.

"I'm afraid not, sir," said Harker. "You're expecting one?"

"My brother is quite mad," said the old man in a conspiratorial manner, indicating the corpse. "He thinks he is dead! He puckers his lips and lies still. No words of mine will persuade him to the contrary."

The poor fellow's wits had completely deserted him. I

would have moved on, but Harker spoke to the wretch in an understanding tone: "Why might he believe this, sir?"

The old man wagged his ancient head sadly. "I've seen death in my time. Fat Peg only bit him. Three, four bites. A few bites won't kill you. He's pretending. Always was a sulky bugger. Don't know what he'd done to upset her. Not like her at all."

"This Fat Peg," said Harker. "Her actions were out of character?"

His face began to twitch, or it may have been the trembling of the candle in his hand. "Peg's been right sour. Not like her at all. And young Sammy too. And the boy with the squinny. Funny moods. And the woman with the hair. Funny noises. Not normal. My brother, he's copying that lot. Always copied off me too."

"That lot?"

"Don't know any of them. Take them to the Bedlam too. They all think they're dead. I know they're fooling. You don't die that way."

His shaky fingers held the candle out at arm's length. We turned to follow the glow and my blood ran like ice in my veins: a few yards away, hitherto hidden in the dark, was a stack of at least a dozen cadavers, exactly similar to the mutilated corpse at our feet, arranged in a haphazard pile as one sees at the paupers' burial sites.

I could not prevent an exclamation of pure horror from escaping my lips. It was evident that even Harker was severely rattled.

"I seen worse," shrugged the old man. "Saw worse, I was at Waterloo. Boney's Imperial Guard come at us, at the charge. I was a slip of a lad, newly press ganged, thought I'd be sent to sea. Pissed me uniform when the bayonets started cutting."

I counselled an immediate retreat into the light of day, but Harker delayed our departure by pressing a few coins into the mad old man's hand and urging him to find food and safer shelter. At last, with my friend's pistol providing us safe passage, we emerged onto the Embankment and I picked up a hurried pace to take us well away. By now, the dead (including the ill-fated Mr Browning) had been fished from the Thames and the ghoulish onlookers had dispersed.

"What other conclusion is to be drawn," I declared, "than that Dracul is now established in that hell-hole of a place?"

Harker seemed every bit as disturbed as I, with none of the introspection that was his usual aspect and countenance. "If Dracul's host was resident in the Dark Arches, then there would be no need for disposing of bodies into the sewer system. No, Dracul is very much amongst us. What we have down there are the additional vampyrs which Dracul has already attracted to London."

"Attracted? How? Attracted why?" (My mind was in such a turbulent state of emotion that it issued words by instinct alone, before common sense had any chance to edit them!)

"As I explained to you, and to Sir Edwin Gull," said Harker, regaining a hint of his restlessness, "vampyrs communicate with their own kind just like most other creatures. How they entice each other to new hunting grounds is anyone's guess, but entice each other they do. It seems there are at least another three or four of them back there, and I have no doubt there'll be more soon."

"Why lurk in those caverns?" I ventured.

Harker's eyebrows rose and he shook his head. "The easy availability of prey, no doubt. Or they may be waiting, either to gather in larger numbers before spreading across the city, or obeying some organising influence of Dracul's." He whistled and a cab swerved over to the side of the road to pick us up.

"It feels as if this perilous hydra grows more heads by the hour!" I shuddered, climbing up into the two-seater. I watched the city drift past for a minute or two. "I fear that my nerves will get the better of me, Valentine. My moral fibre is not the strongest, even at the best of times. Should I let you down, I apologise in advance."

"There is no need," said Harker. "I thought I knew fear, but I look at these familiar streets today, and I think what they may become if they fall under Dracul's control, and I'm more afraid than I have words to describe. Finding Dracul's current host and putting an end to this creature's potential for terror consumes my every thought, believe me."

"What about these other vampyrs? Even if we trap their – leader, should we say? – then won't the rest of them realise that we're after them? Attack us? Become impossible to catch?"

"Dracul's influence over them works in our favour, remember. Their first instinct is to operate by stealth and if the majority of historical records are accurate, we may be able to act like a cat among the pigeons. Snatch one, and the rest take flight. If Dracul were to be trapped, the others are likely to run like hyenas from a lion."

To quell the continued tremors in my mind, I told myself in the sternest terms that there is <u>every hope</u> of a satisfactory conclusion to this horrifying affair. Every hope, despite the considerable, so far solution-less, and apparently intractable problem of how to accomplish the monster's <u>entombment</u> (within the prepared vault, in the derelict shop)! Every hope.

"Since he had the misfortune to cross paths with Dracul's host," I said, pushing back my unease, "perhaps we should trace Browning's last known activities?"

"I agree," said Harker. "We should speak to his colleagues at the *Examiner*. And who else? It's a pity we didn't know the poor chap better. I think I recall seeing him at Holmwood's?"

"Very possibly, but I doubt his tastes in entertainment would yield much information."

XXVI

Sir Edwin Gull stepped out of his brougham onto the Strand and was instantly on his guard. The sudden burst of voices and movement around him made him shrink back, fearful that reporters or other gossip-mongers were about to cause trouble until, a few seconds later, it was evident that the ruckus had nothing to do with his presence. Two women, one with her hair flopping in disarray, were being hauled along the street by a bulldog in human form.

"He's yer cash carrier and yer owe him—"

"But the white-choker wouldn't pay! You'd think, him a man of the cloth, but noooo—"

"No gilt, no tail! You know the rule—"

"Aar, shut yer bellows!—"

Gull watched them jostle and push their way out of sight. "Parasites," he muttered.

He strode into Simpson's Grand Divan Tavern and was met in the lobby by immaculately liveried staff, who escorted him to a booth table in the Ladies' Dining Room to await his guest, and handed him the Bill of Fare. Around him, more than a hundred diners talked, laughed, appreciated the silverware, eyed the room for traces of the famous or infamous, made sure they were seen by the right people, exchanged identical opinions and even, here and there, ate and drank. Boiled potatoes soaked up gravy and the plush red carpet soaked up the subdued gaggle of refined conversation.

Gull had already ordered for himself by the time Ruby-Dracul arrived. She looked in perfect harmony with her surroundings, her face and hair fastidiously tended, the rest of her dressed in expensive, fashionably cut silk, paid for from her acolyte Renfield's savings.

Immediately, right across the wide, sunlit room, she was the object of both male and female attention. Very little of that attention was concerned with the novelty of a lady entering the establishment unescorted. She radiated a presence that was almost spiritual in its purity and grace.

"Am I late, Sir Edwin, or were you early?" she said, sitting opposite him.

He ignored the question. A waiter hovered. "For the lady. . .?"

"Oh, nothing for me at the moment, thank you. I might have a little something in a while."

Once the waiter had glided from view, and the diners had returned to their own business, Ruby-Dracul smiled wryly. "You've never taken me anywhere like this before, Winnie."

Gull glared hot coals at her. "It rarely welcomes women of your class. I haven't the time or the inclination for social niceties, Miss Wester, I'm perfectly well aware that it was you who sent that cheap trollop to my home. You may be interested to know that she caused only minor embarrassment to the household and had nowhere near the effect you obviously intended."

"I don't know what you're talking about," said Ruby-Dracul innocently, one hand to her throat.

"If you wished to sever relations, I am a reasonable man, there was no need for spite."

"You look a little nervous. . . Mr Gull. Or is it stuffy in here? I've never seen inside this building before, it's certainly a cut above all the other cigar divans around here. Is it true it's full of chess players?"

"Mm. It was. Not quite so much now."

A silver trolley was wheeled smoothly to their table. Its dome was opened to reveal a hefty, glistening side of beef from which wafer thin slices were cut. Waiters danced their ballet of wine and vegetables while Gull watched the plate in front of him fill, waiting awkwardly.

"Yes . . ." he rumbled, vaguely in Ruby-Dracul's direction, purely to break his own silence and mirror the animation of neighbouring diners, "this place is very reputable . . . Of all people, Gladstone recommended it to me. Mind you, he also recommended the grilled turbot, so at least his record of being wrong is still largely safe . . ."

Ruby-Dracul, despite enjoying her invigorated self-confidence and her capacity to turn heads, felt unsure of Gull's motive for inviting her here. In hindsight, she was equally uncertain about the wisdom of letting Lily loose on Gull, and any unintended consequences that might yet come from it. She decided to step out on the front foot.

"Have you heard, Mr Gull? I'm an overnight sensation. I have an entirely new act playing at Holmwood's and it's the talk of the West End. There were notices in more than half the dailies this morning."

The waiters concluded their pirouettes and pliés, and withdrew. Gull attacked his beef as if it was still alive and needing to be defeated.

"I saw it," he said flatly. "That's why we're here."

She was genuinely surprised. "You were there? Were you hiding, I didn't see you? I hope you liked it."

"I was there because your friend the slattern had opened my eyes to what a devious, petty-minded, grasping little vixen you really are. I was there to send you packing. Run you out of London, out of the country if necessary."

She pursed her richly red lips. "Oh? Yet, you did not. Could it be that the spectacle of my new act won you over?"

He paused and looked at her for as long as he dared, a flap of meat dangling from his fork. "No," he said. "I changed my mind for other reasons . . ." He chose his words carefully. "My opinion altered because of certain recent events, and certain information which has been made known to me. When I witnessed your theatrical trickery, I at once knew precisely how it was achieved. Precisely. How."

Ruby-Dracul was genuinely surprised all over again, and slightly flustered. She eyed him levelly across the white tablecloth, her slender fingers drumming against it very slowly. "I'm afraid you're going to have to be a little more forthcoming than that, Mr Gull," she said brightly, hoping that she'd read too much into his words, or that he'd misinterpreted whatever he might have been told.

Gull roundly chewed some cabbage and potato before he answered. "I am aware, Miss Wester, that your mind and body have become host to a preternatural form of life, known as a 'vampyr.' I am also aware that it is the mesmeric powers of this vampyr which accomplish this... new act of yours."

She delicately closed her eyes for a moment. "Of course. Now I understand why we're here. And why you're so nervous. You're frightened of me. You wanted to meet me in a public place, in case I try to pull out your innards."

"A sensible precaution, surely?" said Gull, feeling a sudden chill in his stomach and putting down his knife and fork. "I thought it best not to allow you an opportunity for violence."

"What makes you think the mesmeric powers of a vampyr can't influence you here and now? Make you forget you ever met me?"

"I am aware of the danger you pose. Therefore, I am on my guard. You don't fool me. Your prowess has limits, otherwise your kind wouldn't need to operate as they do."

"But if I pose such a danger, why put yourself in its path? Why not run away?"

The watery shadows of clouds smeared their way across all the tables in the dining room. Gull's heart was in a drum roll as he tried not to look away from the vampyr's host. He couldn't shake a sudden resurgence of the sensation he'd had when Flemming's Transylvanian box had opened – the feeling he was in the presence of a serpentine evil, something horribly cold and predatory with no affinity for the broad spectrum of human emotions.

"Because—" He cleared his throat.

"Because you think you know me?" she said.

"But I don't know you, not any more." He looked at his mostly emptied plate, at the gliding waiters, at the glamorous and well-heeled diners. "Is there anything left of you in there, Ruby?"

She perched forward a little. "We are legion," she smiled softly. "But, tell me, who's been sniffing and snitching into vampyrs then, eh? William Browning mentioned allies, but I'd have thought you unsuited to a role like that."

"I don't know any Browning, William or otherwise," said Gull. He fingered the top button of his coat and set himself to the business at hand. "That isn't the point. I haven't 'run away,' as you put it, for the simple reason that I have a proposition to put to you. A business transaction."

Ruby-Dracul sat back, intrigued. "Business?"

"Another thing I learned from a recent discussion is that your kind are capable of being—"

"Tamed? Domesticated?"

"Reasoned with. I was told of a conflict, on the other side of the world, in which vampyrs were successfully employed as an engine of war. I'm not interested in anything of that sort, but circumstances have arisen in which I think you'd be prepared to—"

"Obey orders?"

"Co-operate. For our mutual benefit, but if your only interest is in flippancy then we can go our separate ways."

Their waiter reappeared. Gull's plate whirled away,

thank you, sir. In its place, the Bakewell pudding, at the requested temperature, thank you very much, sir.

"Oh, no, please, dearest Winnie, you have my fullest attention. Truly."

He suppressed the notion that he'd have been better off making a pact with the anacondas of the South American jungle. Larger issues were at stake. "You're an ambitious woman," he said, hacking with his spoon, "but until now your talents have been, shall we say, too modest to advance your career on the London stage very far. However, that situation has changed. You have the potential to become a major attraction, not only in England but on the Continent as well, and possibly even the Americas, for all I know. Potential which may well go to waste without money to back it. I am not particularly well-informed on the subject of theatrical finance, but it hardly takes an expert to see that performers require promotion and endorsement commensurate with their intended status. I can provide the necessary resources. Every penny."

A fly landed on the tablecloth, close to Ruby-Dracul's hand. She watched it, motionless. "You're right," she said, "I've always wanted to be a success. It's ironic that the means to achieve it should come at a time when I'm forced to avoid too much scrutiny of what I get up to. Are you going to pay my way out of trouble when my messy table manners are noticed?"

The fly busied itself with its front legs. Ruby-Dracul's hand began to move towards it with infinite care.

"In a manner of speaking, yes," said Gull. "You can live privately, even secretly, in a set of rooms I own in

Wenham Gardens, and I propose that your. . . nutrition be organised on a more structured basis. I will arrange for two or three men with tightened lips to be employed as procurers, finding you. . . sources of food, keeping them until required, and clearing up afterwards."

"I'd be denied the thrill of the chase, I suppose, but it would be ungracious to turn down professional help when it's offered."

"Of course, an arrangement of this kind could only be expected to provide food from among those of insufficient worth to arouse comment. I trust this is an acceptable condition?"

"Selective breeding only troubles those who've been selectively bred. It means nothing to me."

Her hand was slowly descending on the fly as she spoke. Except for the occasional shudder of a leg or two, the insect remained still.

"Then such is your half of my business proposal," said Gull, spooning the last of his pudding. "A career of great potential, and continuous personal protection, underwritten by me."

"And in return. . .?"

The nails of her thumb and middle finger suddenly closed like tweezers on the fly's wing. It flicked and shook, but couldn't free itself.

"In return, Miss Wester," said Gull, noticing the fly for the first time and frowning, "you are to bring your considerable gifts to bear on any person or persons of my choosing. You are to bring them under your influence, by whatever peculiar methods you used on that audience at Holmwood's, and get them to do as they're told. To agree with my point of view, to vote in my favour, to act in my best interests. I take it that's possible?"

"Perfectly."

"The first thing I'll require of you is to ensure that the Metropolitan Board of Works accepts my consortium's bid to build the new Courts of Justice. This is a matter of great urgency."

Ruby-Dracul raised up the fly to examine its frantic flicking and buzzing. She spoke in a low, calm tone. "Oh, Winnie, you never offered me wealth and fame when you were snapping the hoops of my skirts. When I was grasping my knees. When you sent me to spend the afternoon with Mr Herbert Maurice." She considered for a moment. "What an interesting collection of memories I now have of that day."

"Do you agree to the arrangement?" said Gull from beneath a hooded brow. A deeper tension was peeking through his bravado, one born out of hard necessity. He kept glancing at the fly.

"You have no other terms?" said Ruby-Dracul. "Then I agree, although I seem to be getting the better end of the bargain."

Her lips parted. With a deft flick she shot the fly into her mouth and imprisoned it behind her teeth. It buzzed and darted for a few moments, until it stuck to saliva and slid, shivering, down her throat.

Gull felt the beef and pudding turn sluggishly in his stomach. "Make no mistake," he muttered, "I'll get my money's worth. You forget, my parliamentary duties place me alongside those who make the law and enforce the law. I, and a number of like-minded MPs, will make full use of your services. In the meantime, the Board of Works. You're to meet me at exactly five minutes to two, at the Spring Gardens building, that is in just over one hour. You will not be late."

"Your approach to business is most original, I'll give you that," said Ruby-Dracul, pushing back her chair and rising to her feet. "Your mama and papa must be so proud."

"My parents are long in their graves."

Her red lips curled in a smile as ancient as the human race. "Sooner or later, we are all children of the dead. We live on top of their remains." She was followed out by the same eyes that had followed her in.

As soon as she'd gone, Gull felt half the muscles in his back and legs sigh with relief. He snapped into a better mood, all the vexing anxieties which had weighed him down suddenly brushed away like hairs off his collar.

His partners in the consortium, he grinned, would soon be offering him congratulations instead of snide comments and veiled demands for money. Those among his business partners who were also among his colleagues in the Commons would soon be praising him to Disraeli's spineless ministers on the front bench.

In a speech or two, in a month or two, he would lament the steady decline of this country ever since the European insurrections of '48; he would lambaste the House for its craven – yes! craven and cowardly! – appeasement of Reform League violence and disorder; he would satirise the Reform Act and the absurdity of extending the vote to the illiterate and the ill-informed, to so-called 'working men' who surely mustn't run a government when they evidently cannot run a bath (a pause here, while hilarity ensues); he would, in conclusion, stand firm against Fenians, against trade unions, against all foreigners and Liberal Party radicals who seek to overturn proper governance by the educated and the experienced, the governance which forged the might and prosperity of Great Britain – we must regain control, before it is too late!

"Is everything to your satisfaction, sir?"

"Mm. It is. You may tell Mr Davey that his kitchen has excelled itself today."

"Thank you, sir."

• • •

The Spring Gardens offices, home to a number of municipal organisations, had a grandeur that was purely visual. In every room, the stained floorboards groaned incessantly, like the shrieking of the damned, and a strong smell of wet dust haunted the corridors.

Seven of the forty-five men of the Metropolitan Board of Works were gathered to end two years of speculation and lobbying. They sat sipping tea around one end of a long table, placed between a wall of bookshelves and a pleasant view of the street, expecting their deliberations to take no more than a few minutes. The architect George Edmund Street's design for the new Royal Courts was eminently the best of the dozen, and had been since the day it was submitted.

When Sir Edwin Gull, and a lady, were unexpectedly shown in, there was a certain amount of leaning to one side and looking over the top of spectacles.

"A pleasure as always, Sir Edwin, but I'm afraid our decision has now been reached—"

". . . 'fraid you're too late . . ."

". . . any amendments to submissions were halted some months ago . . ."

Gull took a seat at the far end of the table. Ruby-Dracul stood at his shoulder. "Excuse my interruption, Sir John, gentlemen, but I'd like you to meet Miss Ruby Wester." She gave a brief curtsy. "She has important information about the bidding process, to which you should listen very carefully."

There was a certain amount of glance exchanging and paper shuffling.

". . . rather irregular . . ."

". . . not sure we can accept anything at this late stage . . ."

". . . I suppose it never hurts to hear what a handsome young woman has to say?"

Ruby-Dracul paused slightly to ensure she had their attention. Her smile made them smile in return. As she spoke, she walked slowly around the table, seven heads following. Gull quietly got up and left the room with his chest thumping uneasily.

"Gentlemen," said Ruby-Dracul, her voice the distant pealing of church bells on a warm Sunday morning, "I won't take up any more of your time than strictly necessary. I've been asked to tell you that the bid put forward by Sir Edwin Gull is the one you will accept."

"I'm sorry, Miss Whatever-your-name-is, we cannot be influenced—"

". . . would be contrary to the Courts of Justice

Building Act of 1865, and the Courts of Justice Site Act . . ."

". . . decision has already been made . . ."

She spoke softly as her steps creaked a gentle pace around them. In her words was the shining glow of eternal truth. In her movement was the soft embrace of loving arms. In the dark, liquid flow of her hair was the passing of history.

She circled the table with the steadiness of common sense, a sensible argument, making sense of what was sensible. A reasonable request, just listen, listen. A reasonable and reasoned reasoning, certainly. It was as clear as day, Sir John, you see, as clear as the clearest water in a clear, fresh mountain stream, now that the clarity had been clarified, now that the full explanation had been explained. Thank heaven for a timely intervention, intervening just in time. Her preference was preferable, it prefaced the preferred preferment, did it not? It was thanks to this lady – this lady – that we could be thankful in our thanks. A revision of the decision was in order, to revise previous revisions and decide on a decision that was to be decided.

Ruby-Dracul grinned at the seven men of the Metropolitan Board of Works and the seven men of the Metropolitan Board of Works grinned back at her. "I believe there are legal documents involved?" she said.

There was a certain amount of flustering and nodding. Papers were produced and sorted. Gull returned cautiously, surveying the room and the corridor outside. Warily, he eyed his enemies with contempt, these pen-pushing sheep, these mulish and vacuous functionaries whom he'd fought with all the weapons at his command.

"Ah, Sir Edwin, do come in—"

". . . contracts already prepared, if you'd be so kind . . ."

". . . some redactions and insertions now being made, evidently clerical error . . ."

He felt a sudden child-like delight which was quickly stifled by the creeping sensations of fear and awe that chilled his spine. The supernatural creature stood beside the seven men while they muttered amongst themselves. One of them, acting as secretary, scratched new details in copperplate onto the vellum contracts.

"It's astounding," whispered Gull, delight regaining the upper hand for a moment.

"It's temporary," said Ruby-Dracul, at his shoulder. "They're only dreaming."

"Don't worry, I'll have the site at the top of the Strand swarmed with workers by nightfall. By the time they start to question themselves, there will be a *fait accompli*. They won't remember this?"

"I told you, they're dreaming. The memory will be like dust in the wind."

Gull shuddered to himself, remembering how that Harker chap had described a vampyr's defences. Like the ink of an octopus, he'd said. The revised papers were signed on behalf of the Board, and the acting secretary slid them across the table at Gull.

"Approved by Sir John, requires only your assent . . ."

". . . congratulations on a successful bid . . ."

". . . progress report due at the end of the year . . ."

Gull added his signature to the papers with his heart trotting like a pony. He quickly pocketed one of the copies, and flinched as Ruby-Dracul's lips suddenly appeared at his ear.

"You owe me blood, Sir Edwin Gull. I'm hungry. I had only a light lunch."

XXVII

In the sweeping foyer of Holmwood's Music Hall, Captain Harker had spent the past hour questioning every employee or visitor to the place he could find, seeking information on the last hours of the unfortunate William Browning. None were of any help.

Near the grand staircase, under the curve which rose gracefully to the balcony, Mr Holmwood himself was supervising the installation of a large, circular diorama. Patrons would be able to step inside and view, ladies and gentlemen, an accurately rendered, entertaining and educative panorama of Vienna.

"No, no!" cried Holmwood, flaring at the young lad delivering a boldly lettered painted sign, "*Venice*! It's *Venice*! Take that damn thing away and put it right! And tell your dad if he charges me twice, I'll kick his arse!"

Harker sat on the bottom step, dwarfed by the flamboyantly decorated space around him, rubbing his face in his hands. Every avenue of investigation seemed to be a dead end, every clue seemed to trickle through his fingers, every chance to stop the fiend seemed to dissolve into defeat.

His mind ached with the throbbing pain of memories

which the last few days had stirred up inside him, of his military failures, of his wife and daughter's final days. His head drooped on his shoulders and he stared blankly at his scuffed and muddy boots, the leather frayed at the tops below his knees. He wanted a drink.

"You alright?"

He looked up to see a fair-haired, plainly dressed young woman standing a few feet away from him, her head cocked at an enquiring angle. She seemed vaguely familiar. "I beg your pardon?"

"You look a bit upset," said Lily.

"Oh. No, thank you, I'm quite alright. A trying day," he said, attempting a smile. She didn't move on, and after a moment he looked askance at her.

"I was on my way out, and I saw you," she said. "I never thanked you properly. For getting that drunken letch's paws off me the other night."

The penny dropped. He remembered her smile, and the pies in her pocket. "There's no need for thanks." His face regained its usual brooding and saturnine composure.

"I've seen you around, with that fella who works for Gull."

"Arthur Flemming," said Harker, heaving his back straight and glancing at the grand entrance into the auditorium. "He's around here, somewhere, asking questions backstage. As you're here, Miss. . .?"

"Lily Murray," she beamed. "Mr. . .?"

"My name is Harker. As you're here, Miss Murray, may I ask you a few questions of my own?"

"You may."

"Do you know a journalist on the *Examiner* called

William Browning? I believe he visited this music hall regularly?"

Lily scrunched her face. "If that's so, I'd likely know him by sight, I don't know the name."

"But you do work here?"

"No," she smiled, "my friend does, I came to tell her that the tip she gave me paid off handsomely, but she's not here. I'll come back later, I've heard she's got some great new act."

"Might she know Browning?"

"Does this fella owe you money?"

"I'm afraid he's dead, killed by a murderer who's struck in this area several times over the last few days." Harker saw the instant change in Lily's demeanour. "You know of this?"

She nodded. "He terrified my little boy. I saw him too, like he was possessed by the devil."

Harker quickly got to his feet, just as Flemming appeared from the auditorium. "Several recognised his description as a regular customer, Harker, but none were acquainted with him personally or could testify as to his recent movements. It's quite bedevilling."

"Miss Murray," said Harker, "it seems you have details about the creature we're trying to track down, beyond what's already known to us. Please, if you'd be so kind . . ." The three of them quietly exchanged information for several minutes, each gradually growing more sombre, while Mr Holmwood berated the workmen who'd installed one of the diorama's painted panels upside down.

Lily suddenly halted mid-sentence, flashed an apology and hurried out of sight under the staircase. Harker and

Flemming stared after her for a moment before turning to see Sir Edwin Gull stalk into the foyer from the street entrance. As he came closer, he glared at his employee.

"Flemming?" he snorted. "Once again, I find you loitering in this plebeian establishment. Am I to assume you'll soon also be spitting in the street and boiling sheep's trotters? Why aren't you at the Chief Cashier's office?"

Flemming's mouth and brow struggled in vain to devise a barbed reply involving streets and sheep. "Er, I was, er, had a small matter with Mr Holmwood," stumbled Flemming, with a vague gesture in the direction of the diorama.

"As do I," said Gull, watching Holmwood pass comment with imploring arms. "Flemming, I want you overseeing labour costs on the Royal Courts site up the road. Work must move apace, I'm on my way there myself." He nodded at Harker. "Captain Harker, so nice to see you again, I trust I find you in a more balanced mood than at our last encounter?"

"Yours seems to have improved no end," said Harker.

"Sir Edwin," said Flemming, confused, "am I to understand that the contract—?"

"Is safe and sound, Mr Flemming, but time is pressing and a fortune stands ready to be made. By the way, gentlemen, since you are both here, I'm pleased to inform you that the business we discussed the other day has now been successfully concluded. Neither of you need cry wolf and doomsday any more."

"What?" gasped Harker.

"Dracul's current host is captured?" said Flemming. "But this is marvellous!"

Harker raised a hand. "Flemming and I have evidence that more vampyrs are gathering close to the river, and that would not be happening if their ringleader were trapped."

"The situation is under full control," said Gull. "The creature has been brought to heel, the matter is closed. You have my personal guarantee. Now, I want a word with Holmwood."

Harker blocked his way. "Who is it? Who became the creature's host?"

"Nobody of consequence. Now I—"

"You must know his name, surely? You'd consign him to a living death without a name?"

"The name escapes my memory for the moment," growled Gull.

"And the method used to catch the vampyr? Did you devise it yourself? How did you seal the container? Is it at a safe location? Or have these details also escaped your memory?"

"Captain Harker," said Gull, as if calming a disobedient child, "we have all been witness to some shocking events. Those events are at an end. There will be no more murders, that much is certain. You'll need only look around and wait a while to discover this fact for yourself. The problem is solved. There will be no panic in the streets. What more could you want?"

"I want an explanation," said Harker. He stepped uncomfortably close to Gull. "You haven't caught it at all, have you? You've made some sort of pact with it."

Gull turned his head defensively. "Your own testimony, of the war in China, demonstrates that a bargain can be struck. Even a domestic pet can be trained to obey its master."

"You cannot master a vampyr!"

"Oh, but I can, and I have. I have agreed to the creature's terms, and it has agreed to mine."

"Terms?" spat Harker. "Is it to be your personal assassin?"

"Don't be ridiculous, this isn't the Middle Ages!"

"Then of what possible use can it be to you?"

"I repeat, the animal is under control, which is a perfectly acceptable and practical state of affairs. You, Harker, have succeeded only in chasing shadows and throwing booksellers under cartwheels. I have applied simple business acumen to your problem and have solved it."

"For your own gain! Good God, have you *no* conscience, sir? Do you expect us to believe that you've gone to this trouble for the benefit of society?"

"Society, I think you'll find, would far prefer the matter was entrusted to a responsible public representative than left in the hands of an emotional hysteric. Be grateful that I've had the courtesy to keep you informed at all, I might just as well have left you to run around the farmyard like headless chickens."

Harker fought to keep his temper. "If, as you claim, everything is so firmly under control, you can have no reason to deny me the name of the host. Do your 'terms' allow it to run free, or is it locked up? Under what 'terms' is it supplied with blood?" Without thinking, he grabbed the lapels of Gull's coat. "I demand you answer!"

Gull's expression twisted into a sneer. "And I shall demand your arrest if you don't unhand me."

Harker shook him. "Then call the police! Call them! Under how large a rock do you think you can hide your deadly pet?"

Mr Holmwood, seeing the scuffle and his landlord in the middle of it, broke off from his reprimands and began to stride across the foyer. Flemming hopped at Harker's side, his hands trying to mark a dividing line.

"Please, Valentine, this is not the way," he said nervously. "We both know that Sir Edwin's word holds far greater sway than our own. I beg of you."

With a final push, Harker let go. Gull straightened his coat and checked his top button. As Mr Holmwood marched towards them, Gull dipped to Harker's shoulder and spoke in a low, even tone.

"You have lost this particular battle, Captain Harker. Accept it with good grace."

"Mr Gull?" boomed Holmwood. "Is everything in order?"

"Quite in order," said Gull. "My employee Mr Flemming is escorting his friend on a tour of the premises. In the meantime, a word with you, if I may?"

Harker stalked off into the auditorium, Flemming at his heels. Lily slunk out of her hiding place under the stairs and followed them as soon as Gull's attention was on Mr Holmwood, whose florid cheeks and flamboyant manner were visibly wilting.

"Mr Holmwood, I know you're expecting a discussion of revised rental arrangements as per my solicitor's letter," said Gull, "but that can wait for the time being."

Holmwood perked up a little. "Then how can I be of service, Mr Gull?"

"Ruby Wester. From tonight, she's to receive top billing and fifteen per cent of nightly takings."

Holmwood was halfway to a hearty splutter of laughter before he saw that Gull was serious. "Quite impossible, there's barely a dozen acts in London who'd command that sort of arrangement."

Gull's words had the tired nonchalance of certain victory. "You're aware of the extraordinary stir caused by her last performance?"

". . . Yes. I've heard it was, er, quite something. I missed it, myself, giving Albert Hayes a final warning about his blasted dogs."

Gull grinned. "Highly entertaining, those dancing pooches."

"And their incontinence is costing me dearly."

"So dispense with the dogs and you can afford Ruby Wester."

Holmwood looked Gull up and down. "You her manager now, are you? I've already had to turf my magician out onto the street today, I'm not getting rid of any more turns. That girl's getting above herself."

"Then her performance tonight will be at the Alhambra."

"Is that a threat? Is it? The Alhambra has plenty of draws, they won't want another singer, no matter how good she is. And not at short notice, either."

"Are you sure?" said Gull.

"Yes, matey, if I was any more 'shore' I'd have the sea lapping at my legs. I'll expect her here, tonight, on time, at the usual rate."

"Then she will be at the Alhambra, and she will expect

your apologies first thing tomorrow morning. Now, excuse me, I have pressing business nearby." He crossed the carpeted foyer and stepped out into the heat of the late afternoon.

Back in the empty, unlit auditorium, he was the topic of conversation. "I wish I'd never taken that damn fool into my confidence!" said Harker.

"The fault is mine too," said Flemming. "We both acted for the best."

They sat opposite each other at one of the tables near the stage. Despite the curtains and the lushness of the gallery above them, their voices echoed off the high ceiling. Lily took a seat beside Harker.

"I'm sorry, Miss Murray," he said, "I allow my passions to get the better of me. All too frequently, these days. Are we permitted to learn why you hid from Gull? The man could inspire whole armies to flee, of course, but . . ."

"Let's say, I'd have spoiled his good mood. Thank you for not giving me away." Her smile was weighed down with her growing unease at everything she'd heard in the foyer.

"Recently," said Flemming, "I've been re-thinking a number of topics, Sir Edwin amongst them, but perhaps he's right in one respect. If the vampyr has entered into a truce, then public alarm may be averted?"

Harker shook his head vehemently. "No, Dracul's thirst for blood remains the same, no matter what the circumstances. Whatever goal Gull expects to achieve, he obviously thinks it's worth the daily cost of feeding innocent people to that monster. And I can't believe that the vampyr would simply settle for a convenient supply of blood. There must be more to it than that."

Flemming grew pale and dabbed at the sweat on his cheeks with the back of his hand. "There is the possibility that this bargain encompasses more than Dracul alone, more than one vampyr. What if Sir Edwin is plotting to gather a cohort, as did the Taiping in China?"

"He scoffed at my mention of assassins, I doubt he has military objectives. However, what if the reverse is true? What if Dracul soon demands more and more from Gull, including the sheltering of other vampyrs? If only we knew the host's identity, we'd have a far better idea of what this bargain with Gull entails. The vampyr could have attached itself to any of the hundreds who passed through this area in the hours after it abandoned Herbert Maurice."

Flemming winced at the memory. "I have interviewed all the personnel backstage, including the acts, with the sole exceptions of the magician – I'm afraid his name eludes me – and his assistant, the singer."

"Renfield was given the push this afternoon," said Lily.

"Over the quality of his act?" said Harker.

Lily shrugged. "I d'know, but I got talking to the pianist when I arrived and he said Renfield's been really peculiar the last day or two, like a different person. And today he looked terrible, as if he's very ill."

Harker and Flemming exchanged leaden glances. "Good heavens!" muttered Flemming. "The vampyr was in here all along. It's him."

"That does seem likely," said Harker quietly, one hand in his hair. "Renfield would have been in this building throughout that evening. And the dumping of bodies into the sewers. . . Miss Murray, do you know where he went?"

"No," said Lily, "but Ruby Wester probably does."

"The singer? Can you wait here, to speak to her before tonight's performance? What about your boy?"

"He's with trusted friends at Lambeth," said Lily. "They've got kids his age."

"Then there is yet cause for optimism," said Harker, getting to his feet. "Miss Murray will remain, to speak with Ruby Wester. Arthur, on the assumption that Renfield intends keeping his present occupation, check at every theatre and music hall in the area. I will catch up with Sir Edwin Gull at this new building site of his and quietly follow him until I can identify Dracul's host. With luck, one of us will see results. I believe the net is starting to close."

They parted company. It seemed to Flemming that his friend had suddenly regained the martial bearing of his old army rank.

Lily felt a disturbing mixture of thrill and fear wash over her. Like fingers snatched from boiling water, her mind shrank from the implications of the night Herbert Maurice died. Jacob Renfield had been *in the room next door* to where she, and Jack, and Ruby, were sleeping in bliss-less ignorance!

Captain Harker, meanwhile, strode through the crowds in the direction of Temple Bar, and took up a position in the shadows cast by St Clement Danes. From here he could see right across the broad stretch of open ground, empty for two years since the Board of Works had levelled it, as far as Carey Street and the King's College hospital.

In the few hours since Sir Edwin Gull had pocketed his contract, the whole area had been cleared of the vagrants who made it their home. Gull was at the southern edge of the site, directing a pair of foremen in bowlers who in turn directed shovels and buckets. He stood with his back to the road, and to Harker, but even above the clatter of traffic Harker could make out most of what was being said.

"Yes, sir, test holes down to the water table have been dug," said one of the foremen. "They're a considerable depth, sir. That's all square with what was expected."

"Good," said Gull, "I want the ditches you mentioned finished tonight, to keep trespassers out."

"Tonight, sir? These fifty men couldn't do it in less than two days."

"Then get fifty more. Finished tonight, I said. Apply to Mr Flemming."

"Yes, sir, but even then, we'll be lucky to be done by sunrise."

"Your men are *paid*, with *my* money. Can they not keep their end of the bargain, and *work*?"

Harker, still and silent in the shadows, mulled over whatever-it-was Gull was intending to do, and whatever-it-was might happen when Dracul was located. When Gull finished his inspection and hailed a cab, Harker hopped quietly onto the back plate and sat hunched, holding on tightly as the cab rattled along to wherever-it-was Gull was going.

XXVIII

from the journal of Arthur Flemming, undated final entry

I spent last evening, and much of today, following the magician Renfield's trail like a bloodhound upon the scent! In doing so, I knowingly – indeed <u>wilfully</u> – neglected my professional duties, but I am now <u>firmly resolved</u> to seek new employment. After yesterday's revelation that he is <u>in league</u> with the vampyr Dracul(!!!), I no longer wish to remain in the service of Sir Edwin Gull. I am deeply disappointed by his conduct, by which he has shown himself to be no less than a <u>scoundrel</u>! Naturally, I shall have to remain in his service until such time as I can find new employment, otherwise I will not be able to meet my obligations, but the moment new employment is found, then I will tender my resignation.

When my friend Harker tasked me with locating Renfield, I must admit that I felt more than a little apprehensive. My record in tackling and detaining Dracul is hardly an impressive one. I was about to suggest that I take Harker's place and trail Sir Edwin instead, but it occurred to me that my current status as his employee made this highly impractical. Thus, I rolled up my (metaphorical) sleeves and set forth.

Last evening's initial results were encouraging! At the stage doors of no less than <u>four</u> establishments – one theatre, three music halls – I discovered that Renfield had applied for work within the previous few hours. I explained my interest as that of a concerned relative. Upon asking the reasons for rejecting his applications, I was told (in every case) it was due to the oddness of his manner and the sickliness of his appearance. Half those I spoke to thought him drunk, the other half thought him merely incoherent.

With the hour getting late, and the theatres closing, I returned home. This morning, intent on resuming my search, I was distracted and annoyed by entreaties from one of the foremen at the site of Sir Edwin's Royal Courts of Justice commission.

(I am <u>mystified</u> as to how Sir Edwin secured the contract after such discouraging reports from the Board, and <u>still more</u> mystified as to why foundation work needs to proceed with such expensive and unusual haste, but: I am no longer concerned by these matters!)

This foreman, a garrulous fellow whose knotted neckerchief was almost as foul as his language, demanded a shocking sum in additional wages for his team of labourers who – he informed me at exhaustive length – had worked until { ! } five-and-thirty in the { ! } morning to finish them { ! } ditches. The hour or more I spent visiting the accounting office, arranging the withdrawal, calming the Chief Cashier and paying the foreman was time that would have been better spent elsewhere.

Renfield Is Found

It was almost by chance that I discovered him. I was on my way towards Northumberland House, intending to call at the entertainments in the Haymarket and its environs. I was making slow progress thanks to the wayward traffic and the meandering crush of pedestrians, when I passed one of the numberless side streets close to the railway station. Drawing level, I glanced along it, as is my habit – since keeping an alert eye for footpads is <u>always</u> to be advised – and stopped dead in my tracks in a way which must have looked positively comical.

Renfield was huddled a few paces down this side street, only yards from where I stood, sitting lop-sidedly on a doorstep with a filled sack clutched at his side. I hesitated to approach him, terrified in case the vampyr within him should attack without warning. However, only a few moments' observation of the man was enough to remove any concerns, to show that our supposition about him as vampyr host was entirely wrong. His eyes were wandering, and I could tell he perceived me there, but his pitiable condition was nothing like that of a dangerous predator. I advanced towards him.

How many times, I wonder, have I passed wretches such as he? How many times have I walked by, expending upon them no more thought?

A choking miasma came from a short distance further on, where a back yard was being used to pile up all manner of unspeakably foul refuse. Barefoot urchins scurried over the rubbish, laughing and digging for saleable titbits while old women chided them without so much as looking up from their own scratchings around the mountain's base. The stench kept my hand at my face but Renfield didn't appear to even notice it.

He was already a thin, ageing figure when I had seen him on the stage at Holmwood's, but here he appeared most dreadfully emaciated and decrepit. The lines of his face had deepened into grey, ancient folds and I felt a chill of revulsion as his veined, colourless skin suddenly reminded me of the bodies I'd seen washed up by the river.

Here was no vampyr's host, but its victim. As I drew near, his slow gaze tilted up at me. "Mr Renfield," I said, my voice a-tremor, "what has happened to you?"

He pulled a thin, effortful smile. "The mistress," he said, and I shall never forget the desperate yearning in his enfeebled voice, "she has given me the blessing of death. She has laid her mouth upon me and has drunk but a little, in her kindness, in her wisdom, to show me the path down into Hell itself."

"The vampyr," I whispered. "A woman is host?"

"The mistress. Miss Wester. She needed me no longer. She has new servants. Powerful guardians. I am her vessel, and I glory in her desires. When she said she needed me no longer, I begged for her to drink me whole, that I might sustain her awhile, but she looked kindly upon her old retainer and took only enough to lead me unto the fiery pit. So beautiful, my mistress, so thoughtful."

I was filled with both pity and repugnance. "You have been... weakening?"

He dipped his head slightly. "I walk the path. I am her disciple." His scrawny fingers delved into the sack at his side. Evidently, it contained props and devices from his theatrical persona. He handed me one after another and, not having a sack of my own, I set them down one by one on the grimy pavement beside him. "I have made crowds gasp," he said, "with ghostly illusions, and with tricks of second sight, but, O Destiny, my mistress commands true magic. My mistress is the mystic witch of death. She will cover this place with the blood of the innocent." His eyes gradually closed, and his hands clasped together, as if in prayer.

Broken and discarded, robbed both of mind and flesh, this poor soul was in a state worse even than the madman whom Harker and I had encountered in the Adelphi Arches. Everything this vampyr touches becomes corrupted and insane!

Cold fear plucked at me. "Your mistress," I said. "Ruby Wester?"

His slowly nodding smile was laced with pain. "I am glad to die for her. I see the path. The Hellgates open for me." His head tipped back, but the fact that he was dead entirely failed to enter my mind until, some moments later, I at last saw beyond my own feelings of terror.

And the moment I did so, a dreadful thought presented itself: last night – <u>hours</u> past! – we had left Miss Murray at Holmwood's, waiting not only to interview her friend Ruby Wester, but to interview her on the subject of vampyrs! The monster, knowing it was discovered, might surely have killed her on the spot?

I had visions of the poor girl's corpse floating in the Thames, so it was an immense relief to find her alive and well at our designated meeting point, Harker's rooms off

Ludgate Hill, although it took me some time to get over the palpitations caused by my anxiety, as well as by the exertions of my haste all the way from the Strand! Miss Murray's initial amusement at my flustered state turned increasingly to dismay and thence to horror as I relayed my news.

"I waited all evening but she didn't set foot in Holmwood's," she said. "The place was jammed to the rafters with people wanting to see this new act of hers. Once some other turns came on and they knew she wasn't going to appear, half the audience left. Word went around that she'd gone on at the Alhambra instead."

"By that time, Gull had retired for the night," said Harker. "Since even he wouldn't be stupid enough to allow Dracul into his own home, I returned to Holmwood's on the chance of fresh information."

I gathered from Miss Murray and from Harker, via a somewhat circumlocutory and fragmented discourse, that he and Miss Murray then dined at a nearby night house where Miss Murray (bold as you like!) asked Harker if he did not have a wife waiting for him! Whereupon Harker replied (with a good deal of restraint, in my opinion) that his past life was a little tangled and probably best left off the dinner table. Whereupon Miss Murray said: "Tangled? Mine's tied in knots!"

Harker apparently found this highly entertaining, but I'm not at all sure what to make of the girl. However, I am genuinely <u>pleased</u> to see my old friend's bonhomie resurfacing after such a long period of misfortune and solitary contemplation. This must be due to the positive headway we are now making in our efforts against Dracul.

"With the host known to be Miss Wester, we have less need to shadow Gull, fortunately," said Harker, as he stood by his window overlooking the teeming market and White Hart Street. "I followed him to the Palace of Westminster this morning, but lost his trail because of the many areas to which I couldn't gain admission, even if I'd been on official War Office business."

Miss Murray's eyes, still raw from the terrible news of her friend, were fixed on something distant. "Gents, I've been wondering . . ." she said in a steady voice. "I was badly spooked thinking old Renfield was so close to me and Jack, the night the vampyr got him. But now we know it didn't get him. . . Ruby had every chance to kill us, and she didn't. She could have covered it up, easy, she could have said we'd gone away, anything at all. But she didn't." She rose from Harker's well-worn monk's bench and joined him by the window. "I'm wondering if the vampyr's let her keep some of herself?"

Harker fingers drummed at the window sill. "If that's so, then perhaps Ruby pre-empted Gull in the notion of a pact? Perhaps she submitted to Dracul's possession willingly, and in return was granted a certain freedom?"

"Good God, why should anyone submit in such a manner?" I asked, shuddering with repugnance at the thought.

"A harmonious relationship would probably be less arduous to maintain," said Harker with a shrug.

"Then she wouldn't have attacked me last night either," said Miss Murray. "That gives us an advantage over this vampyr—" (I insert the word 'vampyr' here as a substitute for Miss Murray's more colourful choice of epithet)

"—does it not? If Ruby still sees me as a friend, or at least won't kill me, I can be the one to lure the vampyr—" (and again) "—into a trap. She doesn't know we're aware of the truth. She won't suspect my motives."

Harker pondered for a few moments, then sighed and nodded. "I agree. Lily, you may be the only person alive who *could* fool her."

I felt compelled to intervene. "Oh, this is surely the utmost folly, Miss Murray! To have avoided one situation of extreme peril last night, only to deliberately place yourself into another!"

"What? You think I've not done *that* before?" she said with eyebrows raised.

"Nobody is proposing Lily act alone," said Harker. "You and I will have our fair share of the work, Flemming. However, it appears the vault in Seward Walk may yet have an inmate!"

It was only later, over a simple meal at one of the coffee shops, that Miss Murray's bravado seemed to wax and wane simultaneously. "To seal her up like that. I don't know if I could bear it, not if something of Ruby still survives. You called it a living death." She glanced back and forth between Harker and I. "There is no other way?"

"I'm certain many people, throughout many centuries, have asked themselves the exact same question," said Harker.

"If she did indeed become Dracul's host by choice," I said, "then she must accept the inevitable consequences."

"I've never been one for attachments," Miss Murray muttered, watching her fingers twist around each other.

"Can't afford them, not in this world. But, 'cept my boy, Ruby is the nearest to family I've had for a long time."

"I'll pay our bill," mused Harker, "then we'll prepare an exact plan of entrapment, and then I think we should see this new stage act of Miss Wester's."

A Most Unusual and Un-nerving Experience

By the time we arrived at the music hall, having ascertained that "Ruby Wester, Queen of Song and Sorcery" had <u>returned</u> to Holmwood's for tonight's performance and would not be appearing at the Alhambra, there wasn't a seat to be had anywhere. To compound the irritation, that shameless miser Holmwood had raised the admission by sixpence and the balcony price by <u>another</u> <u>penny</u>! We gradually negotiated our way up to the balcony, through an unpleasantly rumbustious squash of theatre-goers, where we were lucky to obtain standing places several feet back from the balustrade.

(I noted that Sir Edwin's wish to have the balcony cleared of *midinettes* – expressed during his first visit – had at last been partly satisfied, although whether this was as a result of the increased prices or the much-reduced prospect of earnings tonight, I could not say.)

The miser, looking rather the worse for wear, made his customary appearance on the stage to announce that Ruby Wester's would be the only act performing this evening and for the foreseeable future. There was a certain amount of grumbling and disappointment in the crowd, but it soon dissolved.

Before I continue, and even as I write these words, I find I must think carefully.

I have an excellent memory, as a rule, one whetted on the complexities and elaborations of my working duties, but in casting my mind back to that performance, a mere three or four <u>hours</u> ago, I struggle to fix upon accurate recollections.

I find I do not remember Ruby Wester's entry onto the stage at all. I simply became aware of her presence there, dressed in a flamboyant, crimson costume of *risqué* design. I recall the hush that descended, an absolute stillness in which it was possible to imagine that time itself had come to a standstill. I also recall music, a melodious and peculiarly assuasive rolling of notes that seemed to issue from everywhere and nowhere, but certainly not from any musicians since none were present on the stage.

As Harker had counselled, our full awareness of the vampyr's mesmeric nature gave us a certain measure of protection from it, in that a deliberate masking of one's senses would provide at least temporary relief from the finespun 'spell' of the creature. Thus, I took the wise precaution of watching most of the performance from behind or between my fingers. As I think of it now, in hindsight, this must account for my memories of the event being no more than a series of vivid impressions.

Ruby Wester made no sound herself, but moved – or rather flowed? – in concert with the strange music until she, by gradual degrees, began to <u>grow</u> bodily, in proportion, until her head was above the chandeliers and her face was set aglow by the gaslight they emitted! She spread out her arms, which on each side reached almost the entire length of the balcony!

I hid my face and listened only to the appreciative and awe-struck gasps of the audience. I have fleeting recollections of Miss Wester standing (at her normal height!) on the stage while the onlookers peered vertically upward. Also, of giant Gulliver-like hands scooping up one of the tables near the stage, turning it in the manner of a merry-go-round, to the general delight of all.

Then, the vampyr's host was taking her bows and the entire auditorium was cheering loud enough to rouse the dead. While I looked around at their faces, so brightly lit with glee, with their roars for more making the floors shake, I could feel only a nightmare claw of terror at my heart.

Once more, I was drawn back to the horrible spectacle I had witnessed on my return to London, the public hanging, where the mob had gloated in morbid and inappropriate fascination. For here again, it seemed to me, was humanity in its massed and blindly obedient form, as capable of rising to cruelty as to happiness, a force as easily influenced for evil as for good. I'd craved solitude on that earlier occasion, and now did so anew.

Harker, Miss Murray and I retreated to the street. We put aside our trepidations relating to Miss Wester's burgeoning popularity and all it might entail, in favour of a forthright confidence in our scheme of entrapment.

It is set and will be carried out tomorrow – today, rather! I scratch these lines in the early hours.

Harker has argued, quite sensibly in my view, that our plan's best chance of success lies in its timing. The trap must arise as if it were an ordinary and unremarkable event in an ordinary and unremarkable day. The slightest suspicions on Dracul's part would prove disastrous.

We have one, and only one, chance to spring our trap; it depends entirely upon Miss Murray's ability to lure her erstwhile friend without causing her even a hint of alarm.

Should we fail, we likely face death. If not immediately, at Dracul's hands, then (however much it shocks me to admit it) on the orders of Sir Edwin Gull, to protect his disgraceful investment from our continued intervention.

Sadly, I believe he would do it. Dear heaven, that it has come to this! How has the world fallen into such cowardice and folly?

I seem to have been sitting here at my journal half the night! As ever, it has been a restorative for my spirits, but as yet I cannot even contemplate sleep. I hope and pray that simple fatigue will not hamper my efforts in the trial of nerve and skill that lies ahead. A mere few hours.

My aunt in Chiswick is feeling no better. I fear that digestive distress is becoming her *idée fixe*! I cannot make her understand that mutton broth is no substitute for any easily obtainable laxative.

XXIX

Three MPs, who between them represented thousands of acres in Hampshire and Lancashire, made their way abreast along the deadened corridors of the Palace of Westminster. The Honourable Member for the borough of Peterport loped on spindly legs beside the heavily planted steps of the Honourable Member for the borough of Olderdale. Alongside them, Sir Edwin Gull walked with his hands firmly clasped behind his back.

"What I've told you may be relayed to anyone who's with us," he said. "If they doubt my sincerity, I will be happy to furnish them with proof."

"And if what you've told us should get relayed elsewhere. . .?" said Peterport.

"Then I will be happy to furnish them with a different sort of proof. In the short-term. In the long-term, it won't matter. By then, we will have gained a majority and be steering the country back onto a correct course."

"Any end to this turmoil of coalition and radicalism is to be welcomed," grumbled Olderdale.

"We're placing a great deal of faith in this woman, Gull," said Peterport, "are we sure of results?" Gull flopped a go-on-you-tell-him gesture at Olderdale.

"On Gull's advice," said Olderdale, "I sent a man to the Alhambra last evening. He came back with quite the rummiest stories, about the crowd's hats all being levitated off their heads, and this Wester girl doing a trick with a kind of fireball, big as a house. To top it all, the announcement chap said that her act was to be completely different each and every night."

"Exactly as I described to you," said Gull, "a remarkable feat of mesmerism on the girl's part. And an entirely natural faculty. Imagine what that ability will achieve when removed from the sphere of the frivolous party trick and applied to dissenters, or the judiciary, or perhaps even to the sovereign herself."

"If the old bat ever comes out of hiding," muttered Olderdale.

Peterport chuckled and shook his head. "This Wester girl's usefulness isn't in doubt, it's her loyalty that needs to be questioned. Is *she* truly with us? What's to prevent her from running off to Gladstone and securing a better deal? Or worse still Bismarck? Or Johnson in Washington?"

"Believe me," said Gull, "she has no interest in the broader geo-political issues. She is hungry for fame and security and, since her work for us will occupy relatively little of her time and energy, she regards whatever we require of her as easy repayment. We could give her ten times any sum offered by Gladstone, the king of Siam or the Man in the Moon, and still we would draw the greater profit, by a very wide margin."

"Your eye for fiscal prudence never falters, eh Gull?" laughed Peterport.

• • •

"Yes, I think we can safely say that the future looks brighter and rosier than it has done for quite some time."

"I've rung for some brandy, Edwin," said Lady Gull. "It's getting late and it will help you sleep."

"Mm," grunted Gull. The ormolu clock on the sitting room mantelpiece, which had been in Lady Gull's family for almost a century, chimed eleven as the butler entered and placed a tray beside her.

"Do you require anything further, m'lady?"

"Thank you, no."

The clock gently ticked out the minutes, the room's wombful peace and quiet broken only by the trickling of brandy being poured from its decanter and the short glug of Sir Edwin drinking it. When Lady Gull secretly emptied her small blue phial into her husband's glass, it made no sound at all.

"Why, brighter and rosier?" she enquired.

"Mm? I have secured the Royal Courts of Justice contract, the consortium's investment is now safe and will generate handsome returns, the site workers are behaving themselves, and the way is clear to obtain further commissions for additional roads along the Embankment. I, er, don't mind telling you, my dear, that my financial position was looking more than a little precarious, for a while . . ."

"Was it, dear?"

"Fear not, all is smooth sailing upon the calm waters of the Gullic Sea." He tipped back the last of his brandy.

"Even with all your parliamentary critics and combatants?" she said. The compound of arsenic would begin its work quite soon, or so she'd been told when she acquired it.

"*Especially* with all my parliamentary critics and combatants." He gazed into the dancing fireplace, feeling its warmth on his face. "What would you say, my dear, if you were to find, say in two or three years' time, that you were the wife of a prime minister?"

She smiled. "I'd say Mr Disraeli must have shot you and then romanced me with quite astonishing charm."

Gull snorted until his armchair rocked. He reached over and refreshed his glass from the decanter. "Is this the Napoleon? 'S very good."

Lady Gull's fingers tapped idly at her skirts while she considered telling him, before he died, that his infidelity was no longer of any consequence to her, that the ceremonies and sympathies of death would turn others' thoughts in her favour, that she would be the one to write the last chapters of his history.

"London will be full of praise for you, over the coming days," she said. "I know it."

"And I share your confidence, my dear. Then, brighter and rosier it is!" He raised his glass. Once the brandy was gone, it nudged him into a mellower mood and his voice sank close to a whisper. "I'm aware, Frances, that you've had cause to form a low opinion of me recently. That is something I sincerely regret. You understand?"

She leaned over and patted his arm. "I understand you very well, Edwin."

"Mm, I am feeling tired now. I have a slight headache coming on."

They went upstairs to their respective beds, leaving the decanter and glass on the tray, and the sitting room silent but for the ticking of the ormolu clock on the mantelpiece.

• • •

Dawn was breaking when the doctor who regularly attended the Gull household arrived, in odd shoes and yesterday's shirt. Stifling yawns, he tottered and blinked his way to his patient, led by the butler in a dressing gown. Lady Gull sat at Sir Edwin's bedside and the doctor gave her a courteous, carefully executed bow.

Thank you, my lady, no trouble at all. What have been the symptoms? I see, headache, high fever, yes the application of a cold compress to the forehead was perfectly correct, my lady. I see, confusion and delirium, not unexpected with a fever, and severe abdominal seizures. Vomiting, I see, oh dear, quite a lot of blood? And from. . .? Copiously, I see, oh dear. If I may examine him? Indeed, very pale. How long has he been in a swoon? Yes, I see, my lady, it's very clear to me that Sir Edwin has ingested a poison. Is he in the habit of dining out? Favouring spiced dishes? Yes, indeed, a great risk of corrupted seafoods, in too many areas of the city. No, no need for undue alarm, my lady. Yes, medicines and restoratives will settle the stomach and quell fever. Rest a while, my lady, I will attend him, we will see him through the crisis, never fear.

Lady Gull smiled weakly and allowed the doctor to hold her hand. She went to her bedroom, slept for an hour or so, then called her maid and dressed for the day. The butler, after waking up the doctor when Sir Edwin's breathing became shallow and irregular, paced the carpeted landing until the doctor's face appeared around Sir Edwin's door, like a moon in the darkness, and wagged sadly from side to side. He intercepted Lady Gull on her way to the stairs, and haltingly informed her that her husband had passed through the veil.

Sir Edwin's body lay alone for a while. When he knew he was about to die, his mind was filled with Ruby's parting words to him at Simpson's-in-the-Strand, the cold and pitiless weight of the countless dead into whose company he would helplessly fall.

His lifeless eyes bulged and his mouth, streaked red, was open as if caught in mid-cry. The sheet that covered him was smeared and soaked. Soon, it would be impossible to distinguish between this slab of flesh and any other dragged away from rooms and gutters throughout London.

The doctor returned with a cup of tea in his wizened fingers, accompanied by a boy hastily sent from the nearest undertaker's with a bucket and cloth. Once cleaning and certification were completed, the doctor presented himself to the widow in her sitting room.

"His passing was peaceful, in the end, my lady." He turned the brim of his hat in his hands.

"Thank you," said Lady Gull, looking away from the embers in the fireplace. "You may submit your invoice by the end of the week."

The doctor bowed with even greater care than before, his knees clicking. "My very deepest condolences. Even in the midst of life, we are in death."

Lady Gull assembled the staff and told them that her

bereavement would be made public some time in the afternoon, after she'd had more time to gather her thoughts, and that she'd be grateful for their discretion until then. Later, down in the kitchen, they all agreed that she'd showed great courage and great strength of character as she gave orders to prepare the house, and her wardrobe, for mourning.

XXX

Captain Harker and Arthur Flemming took up their pre-arranged positions, close to the vault in the derelict shop at 19, Seward Walk, where less than a fortnight ago Flemming and Sir Edwin Gull had forced open the box from Transylvania.

They waited silently, and in shadow.

At the same moment, Ruby-Dracul was at Holmwood's Music Hall, instructing stage hands on the placement of props for the evening's performance. "In the centre, there, thank you."

"Is this the coffin Renfield used as his mystic cabinet?" laughed Lily.

"It is!" said Ruby-Dracul, with a raised finger. "It's a good, solid one and it gave me an idea. I've taken out the glass screen, and tonight I'm going to pluck someone from the audience, place them inside and present, to my adoring public, my Death Rattle Illusion! They turn into a skeleton, walk around a bit, up and down the aisles, then a billow of fog and they're back to normal. I thought I'd sing a song too, something light and hilarious."

"I saw your act yesterday," said Lily. "It was astounding."

Ruby took her hand. "You really liked it?" she said softly.

"It was like a miracle. My heart skips just thinking of it! You're going to be the most famous person in the whole world!"

"If you were here, why didn't you come to see me afterwards?"

"I followed a bunch of swells out, hooked up with some mutchers to bag them."

"You've no need for that any more, come and work for me. You can be my official assistant."

Lily scoffed. "You'd drive me mad, and you know you would! But, funny you say that, I've come to tell you about my future." She grinned and preened like a child with a new toy.

"What is it?" smiled Ruby-Dracul.

Lily paused as if for a drum roll. "I'm goin' to open a shop!"

Ruby-Dracul stage-blinked at her. "Where's that come from, all of a sudden?"

"It's 'cos of what I got off Gull's wife. Pounds and pounds. I'm so grateful to you for that job."

"She paid up without a fuss?" said Ruby-Dracul. "She's very different to her husband."

"Well," said Lily, lowering her voice, "'tween you and me, I don't think I was a surprise. Too calm about it, she was, even for a toff. I think she was expecting trouble to turn up one day and by good luck she'd greatly overestimated what it'd cost her."

"I'm delighted to hear it!"

"I want to go legit. Well, maybe fence on the side, we've all got to make a living."

"What sort of shop?"

"I've already found a place and I've paid the first month's rent," said Lily. "It was dirt cheap 'cos it's in a mess like you wouldn't believe, but I can tart it up with some of the money and still have enough left to buy stock. For a dressmaker's. You know how handy I am with a needle and thread."

Ruby-Dracul beamed at her. "I'm so pleased for you, Lil. I can't wait to see it."

"You can see it right now! It's only round the corner, Seward Walk."

"I've got to sort out my costume."

"There's nearly an hour yet, we can be there and back in half that time." Lily's every muscle strained with the effort of turning her thumping pulse, and the grind of terror inside her, into a convincingly carefree excitement. "Come on, you hate waiting around for the house to fill, with Holmwood winding everyone up, I bet he's worse now you're a star attraction."

"He is," nodded Ruby-Dracul, grinning. "You're right, let's take a look!"

Lily led the way, chattering brightly about her plans, and about how she hoped to make enough to send Jack to school every week, and about how Ruby shouldn't expect too much because the place really was in a dreadful mess.

They bustled into Seward Walk arm in arm. Ruby-Dracul was dismayed by the run-down appearance of the whole street, but said nothing.

Lily fumbled for the key she'd got from Flemming, one cause of nerves concealing another. She lit the candle left beside the door and held it up in its curling holder to spread the light as far as possible. "Well? I know, it looks dreadful."

Ruby-Dracul paused. "It does need attention," she said, her voice dipping in a frantic search for encouraging words. "But, on the bright side, it will be the toast of every carpenter in the district."

"I'll have shelves along here, for all the bolts of cloth. And I'll sit in the window myself, so I can greet every passer-by as I work."

"Yes," muttered Ruby-Dracul to herself. "I can picture the scene."

"Come through here," said Lily, the light from her candle disappearing down the narrow walkway to the room which contained the vault door. "I'll show you something very unusual. Be careful of that hole in the wall, there's sharp edges where the wood's splintered."

"Unusual?"

"Yes, come and look at this. There's a big storage cupboard!"

Ruby-Dracul followed Lily into the empty back room where the flat, engraved copper door to the vault was set into the wall. "More of a safe or a strongroom," she muttered.

"This was once a jeweller's shop, and a pawnbroker's before that, when the street was built." She put the candle to one side on the floor and swung the door open. Its hinges creaked loudly. "It's like an ordinary room but metal. Look, you can walk right inside it! You could probably fit half a dozen people in there, standing up. I bet you'd get an echo if you shouted loud enough."

Ruby-Dracul stared into the darkness of the vault, one

hand on the narrow edge of the door and the other flat against the peeling wall. "You know its history, then?"

". . . Yes, the landlord told me." Lily stepped silently to one side, putting herself into a position where she could aim a hard shove at the small of Ruby-Dracul's back.

"I thought Gull owned everything around here? Please, you're not renting from one of his trained monkeys, are you? Because—"

Lily's heartbeat threatened to spill over into her voice. "Oh, no, he doesn't own this place. Different landlord." She heard the faintest of clicks from outside the room.

Harker's revolver being cocked.

Ruby-Dracul stood with the cold air from the vault brushing at her face and the meagre light from the candle fluttering around her. She tipped her head back slightly. "Lily," she said, "this money you conned out of Gull . . ."

"Yes? Like I said, a bit of luck."

"Ever since we left Holmwood's a few minutes ago, something's been bothering me. A little itch at the back of my mind. And now I know what it is."

"Itch?" shuddered Lily. She balled her fists, more scared than she'd ever been in her life.

"You haven't asked me if I've had any bother from Gull. Because of your visit, I mean. You know what a spiteful bastard he is, and I know what a compassionate creature you are, and yet you haven't asked me that question."

Lily took a step back. "If you'd had trouble, you'd have said." At fever pitch she told herself to *do it now*!

Push her *now*!

Into the vault! Into her tomb!

"No doubt I would," shrugged Ruby-Dracul. "But you would have asked. And you haven't. Which is most unlike you. And, as well as that, you haven't asked me where Renfield has gone." She turned to face Lily. Shadows shifted across her expression. "*And*, as well as *that*, you said you saw my act last night. But you haven't asked the most Lily-ish question of all."

"What's that, then?" said Lily in a low voice.

"You haven't asked me how I did it." Suddenly, she shot a kick at the vault door, so violent it slammed back on its hinges with a clangorous crash that shook the building. Lily cringed and began to tremble.

"It's almost as if," said Ruby-Dracul with an icy calm, "you already know the answers." Her eyes gleamed with hate, and for the first time Lily glimpsed the snarling presence that lurked inside her friend.

She screamed as Ruby-Dracul pounced at her. The vampyr spun her around with a furious, guttural yell, arms clamping tightly around her.

"Leave her!" shouted Captain Harker, instantly appearing in the doorway, pistol raised. "Leave her or I'll spread your brains across this room!"

Ruby-Dracul, clutching Lily like a shield, slowly smiled at him. "No, you won't. You do that, and I'll have her for a host. You know I will."

Harker's aim didn't falter. "Leave her be, and step into that vault. Flemming! Come in here and stand by, at the vault door!"

Flemming scurried in from the shadows and skirted

the room, keeping an eye on Ruby-Dracul. He held onto the door's edge with shaking hands.

Harker refreshed his grip on the gun. "In! Now!"

Ruby-Dracul slid one hand to Lily's throat, her long fingers pressing deep. "Over the centuries, I've learned when a strategic withdrawal is wise. I've learned to accept the occasional defeat graciously. This is not one of those times. Don't you know I'm protected? In fact, I can't recall a time I've had greater power at my command. Even if you could lock me away, my benefactors would hunt you down, silence you, and free me."

"Sir Edwin Gull is dead."

Ruby-Dracul's composure flickered for no more than the blink of an eye. "Nonsense. Do you weaklings really believe I'd—"

"I-It's true," said Flemming, "it's all over the late editions."

Ruby-Dracul's cackling laugh sent shudders up Lily's spine. Harker's aim was precisely between the vampyr's eyes. "We cannot and will not allow you to leave here!"

"I'll show you how weak you are. I'll give you a choice. I'll give in and enter this vault – after all, I've survived years of imprisonment in the past – on the condition that Lily comes with me. You cage me, you cage her. No tricks or evasions, I'll stick to my word. More than your sort ever do. Well?"

Harker remained motionless, his gaze set firmly on his target, his mouth pressed tight. He dared not catch Lily's eye.

"Harker. . .!" whispered Flemming. "There's something I—"

"Choose!" hissed the vampyr. "Is your victory worth the torture of a human life? Have you the strength to act as you must?"

To Harker, every second was a thousand years. The dim light from the candle guttered and shook. With a sickened twist to his face he pocketed the gun.

Ruby-Dracul was out of the room in an instant, dragging her hostage along with her. Lily bucked and punched, but couldn't release the vampyr's grip on her.

Harker charged after them. Almost out onto the street, the vampyr spun and screamed at him, bent double with the effort, contorted in rage. "Nowhere on this Earth will you be safe!"

In despair, Harker fired two reckless shots after her in quick succession. They flew wide, sending glass from the shop window exploding into the road. Then both vampyr and Lily were gone.

"Harker!" cried Flemming, rushing up behind him. "The monster now has a guarantee of our co-operation!"

Harker's silence was answer enough. He slumped to his knees, exhausted and lost.

Flemming's hand fluttered for a moment, then hesitantly patted Harker's shoulder. "I would have made the same choice, Valentine." He glanced back over his shoulder. "For a different reason. I tried to tell you. . . I think the vampyr's violence with the vault door damaged it. The corner has bent inward a little. Until repairs are made, I. . . don't think the vault will contain the vampyr at all."

Harker's recent return to a modicum of his old self was visibly shifting in intensity, refocussing from past to future. "I'm not only afraid for Lily. I'm terrified at what Dracul might do when it discovers we weren't lying. The protection it thought to rely upon is gone. Its plans, its hopes, are all swept away."

He looked up at Flemming. "It may seek a terrible vengeance."

– THE THIRD HOST –

XXXI

Ruby-Dracul frogmarched Lily through the streets, looking over her shoulder now and again to make sure Harker and Flemming were keeping their distance. Lily's mind flicked through thoughts of escape, but fear kept accelerating them to the point of uselessness.

They approached Holmwood's. The road outside was clogged with cabs and carriages, far more than usual, come to see the marvel of the West End. People swarmed around the entrance, like seagulls massing over an angler's catch, burbling excitement and anticipation. A dozen stallholders had pushed their carts from the Strand to catch some extra business, clashing wheels and hurling evil looks to find a good position, filling the curdled air with the steam of oysters and puddings. A newspaper seller waved copies of the *Examiner* and the *Evening Record* at the edge of the pavement.

PROMINENT PARLIAMENTARIAN DIES

Mr Disraeli &c pay tribute to Sir Edwin Gull –
Much admired for charitable and public works
– Widow grieves sudden demise

Ruby-Dracul stopped dead in her tracks and stared. Lily couldn't see the vampyr's face, but felt Ruby-Dracul's fingers tighten like a vice around her arms. Before she could pluck up the courage to shout for help from the milling crowd, she was pushed around the side of the building to the stage door.

Inside, there was none of the usual pre-performance bustle. As soon as Mr Holmwood had acceded to Gull's demands, and his new star had returned from the Alhambra, he'd done some calculations and sacked the other acts to keep his income aloft. Now the rest of the staff were keeping the lowest possible profile, wary of the same fate.

The muffled drone of tonight's audience steadily assembling filtered through from the auditorium. Ruby-Dracul pulled Lily to a halt again as two tall figures emerged from behind a canvas expanse of painted scenery. Their dress was formal, frock coats and top hats.

"Is one of you Ruby Wester?" said the one with waxed moustaches.

She looked them up and down. "Police?" she said.

"We've been sent by a group of gentlemen with whom you have made a verbal arrangement."

"My only 'arrangement' was with Gull. He's dead."

"Nevertheless, Miss, we're required to take you into custody, for your own safety. You will initially be held at Bow Street. Come along, if you please, Miss, we're supposed to be doing this on the quiet."

Lily felt as if a stream engine was silently hurtling towards her. She wriggled wildly but Ruby-Dracul held tight.

"Piss off," hissed the vampyr, "or I'll pull out your eyes."

"Now then, Miss, there's no need to take that attitude, we're simply—"

Ruby-Dracul punched Lily into unconsciousness with a single blow. In an instant, her hands were digging hard into the policemen's throats.

Their faces suddenly fixed in shock, they scrambled hopelessly at her fingers. She pushed them both backwards, and as they toppled heavily, she leaped and placed a knee against each of their chests. They crashed to the floor with a cracking of ribs and a ripping of flesh.

The vampyr twisted and pulled. Blood began to bubble and spurt from their necks. Ruby-Dracul slapped her yawning mouth onto the one with the waxed moustaches, sucking hard, feeling the heat of his blood run down her throat.

The other policeman, desperately patching his wound with his sleeve, rolled onto his front and crawled for the stage door. His unending screams emerged only as high-pitched squeaks and whistles. The broad smear of red he left behind him kept lengthening until his body lay still.

Ruby-Dracul tore open her meal's clothes and bit into his side to extract a last pint. She stood, breathing heavily, and left the body in a heap of skin and liquid. She picked up Lily's ankles and dragged her away.

Time to clean up and get ready. Her public would be waiting!

She shut her eyes. Calling, calling.

Come to me. Come to me, now. My shield is gone,

my plans betrayed. Come to me. If I cannot have what I want, then together we shall have what we can get! We that are undead! Arise!

Obey me. Obey my call. I am the future. I am the feast of blood.

Come to me.

Close to the river, seventeen vampyrs stirred. Human hosts slunk and scurried from their hiding places like cockroaches.

For days the vampyrs had been gathering in the Dark Arches, sensing Dracul's presence, slowly seeping through the cracks in reality to reach this brand-new feeding ground. In the chambers and tunnels by the river, the ghosts that were not ghosts had made a stinking charnel house where the leftovers of the dead were heaped high in rotting mounds, and the few humans who hadn't fled were penned like cattle for slaughter.

Seventeen hosts crept silently out across the Embankment. Some were armed with knives, to cut and slash their food. Others had clubs, to bludgeon. A few had shovels, to beat and crush.

XXXII

The audience at Holmwood's slowly hushed. Nobody appeared on the stage, and no musicians began to play, but by some unspoken, collective agreement they all settled into a mood of quiet attention. Every seat was filled, every table surrounded, every gap and aisle crammed. Nobody was in the foyer, nobody thrilled to the new diorama.

In the hush, the curtain rose.

At the centre of the stage was the coffin borrowed from Renfield's magic act, lying flat and closed. To one side, where the pianist usually sat, Lily Murray curled in a daze, her hands tied behind her back and her face ripening a bruise.

Out of the silence, faintly at first but getting steadily louder, came a sound that stiffened the hairs on every neck in the audience. A low sound, almost rumbling, slow and rhythmic, like the booming of a gong stretched into infinity, or the beating of a vast and stone-clad heart.

The lid of the coffin raised itself, turned in mid-air and settled gently down close to Lily. Up from the coffin rose Ruby-Dracul, her body straight, like the minute hand of a clock rising towards the hour. Her elaborate, white silk gown fell about her like a burial shroud. Her face, pale and phantom-like in the sputtering limelights, was the most beautiful the audience had ever seen, and the most terrible. From her opulent and vivid eyes came the pain of loss, the loneliness of all life, the bitterness of scorn.

She stepped out of the coffin and moved forward. Her lips parted and the eerie resonance that filled the auditorium finally resolved itself, in an unsettling slide of sound, into her voice. She sang, in unearthly words, a quivering and staccato song of death.

Unbearable sensations of dread breathed through the audience but none of them moved or looked away, transfixed by her unnerving and discordant requiem of despair. They felt nothing but the pitiless and inexorable approach of the grave. They would die, all of them would die, just as every last human being who ever lived had died. Their entire existence would be gone in an atom of passing time, insignificant, unmourned.

As she sang, the expression on Ruby-Dracul's face gradually darkened into an exultant leer. The gas lights around the auditorium grew dim, leaving her bright and glowing in the limelight.

At the back of the crowd on the ground floor, Harker and Flemming slunk in from the foyer, weaving around and behind people, navigating their way to where Lily lay on the stage. Their ears were plugged with wax, and they took turns aiming brief looks at Ruby-Dracul to check they hadn't been seen, but her hypnotic influence over the audience was affecting them far more acutely than they'd expected.

However hard they tried, they couldn't stop the waves

of fear which threatened to engulf them. They couldn't block out the vampyr's baleful song.

You are lice to be crushed underfoot. You are cattle, to be farmed. Be still, be silent, and sup the sour bile of your tiny little lives, for it only makes your blood taste sweeter! I am all that is wise and beautiful and eternal! Be thankful you will feed me, for it is your only value!

Harker had no recollection of reaching the stage, but pulling himself up into the heat and dazzle of one of the limelights was enough to give him a brief period of clarity and self-awareness. He reached back into the crowd and grasped Flemming's clammy hand. Once behind Ruby-Dracul and out of her eyeline, they clambered up and scrambled over to Lily on all fours.

Your blood will gush and flow, your bones will dry. You are lost amid the teeming millions, lost in the ticking clock. You are swarming maggots in the flesh, poison droplets in the foaming oceans. You are a helpless seethe of flies. You are meat and gristle. You are sustenance, and nothing more. Look upon me and know the sorrow of your mortality!

Flemming pressed his hands over his face. "Don't understand . . ." he sobbed, close to Harker's ear. "Why, so hard to resist. . .?"

Harker was working at the cord tying Lily's wrists. He shook his head as if trying to bat away the buzz of wasps. Lily, the flesh over her cheekbone turning purple, was staring in wide-eyed horror, evidently as in thrall to the vampyr as the crowd.

The gas lights went out completely. Most of the auditorium was swallowed in darkness. Flemming looked up, his hands now clapped to the sides of his head, while Ruby-Dracul's mournful lament spun to a crescendo.

"Can't hold it back. . .!" he wailed. "Why. . .?"

"I know why!" In sudden terror, Harker swung to face the audience. "The vampyrs, they're *all* here, they're among us!"

Ruby-Dracul's voice whirled downward in a final, jittering note of agony, her body twisting and drooping like a dying rose. As her song faded, and as the audience still gaped in terror, seventeen vampyrs struck.

Spread throughout the audience, they each attacked whatever human they happened to be near. The crowd had become so fear-striken that it took several seconds for the first victims' screams to crack the hold of Ruby-Dracul's spell. Even then, they hesitated, their senses numbed into submission, made docile for the slaughterhouse, until the shattering noise and the smell of butchery slapped them awake. The vampyr hoard swung their knives and clubs.

Ruby-Dracul stood at the front of the stage, bowing and acknowledging the audience as if the screaming was applause. Solemnly, she clasped her hands to her chest in gratitude. "Thank you, my dear friends! Now the curtain falls at Holmwood's. Your kindness and enthusiasm have made this a special occasion. I thank you with all my heart, and I wish each and every one of you a good night."

The vampyrs attacked with hideous glee, using their weapons and their weight to bring down prey. They tore enough flesh on each victim to ensure wounds would be fatal, but drunk only a mouthful of blood from each before moving on, spiralling themselves up into a feeding frenzy.

The hysteria that quickly seized the tightly packed auditorium made it hard to distinguish friend from foe, human from human-host. In the near-dark, everything was a crush of panicked faces, outstretched hands, crushing bodies, mouths, hair, teeth. Even the dripping coat of red that every vampyr soon wore became a less visible danger sign as more blood leaked and pumped.

One of the seventeen was forced to the floor by a dozen men piling-on. From the host's hand they tore a section of metal pipe bloodied by cracked skulls, and drove it through him. The vampyr inside wrenched itself free in less than a minute and rapidly occupied the tallest and heaviest of the dozen.

Hemmed in close to the stage, people poured and clambered over one another to reach the lowest of the extinguished gas lights and pull themselves up towards the balcony. In the balcony's pitch-dark crush, people clawed for the balustrade, to climb over it and cling precariously out of reach. Desperate to escape, a woman leaped up onto the top of the railing and launched herself at the closest chandelier. She missed it and fell into the crowd below.

In the darkened foyer, the wreckage of Mr Holmwood's diorama blocked the doors out to the street. On top were piled the ripped corpses of Holmwood and most of the music hall's backstage staff. A handful of those fleeing the rear of the auditorium began to drag at the barrier, while many more squirmed to avoid the vampyrs wading through the tightly packed throng behind them, one armed with a meat cleaver and another with a carving knife.

Huddled to one side of the stage, Captain Harker attempted to shield Lily Murray and Arthur Flemming. His revolver shuddered from side to side at arm's length, a useless defence.

Ruby-Dracul watched the hellish chaos unfold around her, smiling triumphantly, her hands crossed over her chest in a semblance of a hug. Choosing her moment, she arched her back forward, and with a nightmare howl she hurled herself into the screaming melee. Her momentum knocked a cowering man off his feet, and she bit deep into the soft flesh around his collar bone before he could cry out.

Harker barely caught a glimpse of his attacker before the man was almost on top of him. The host's face bore the scars of a hundred pub brawls, caked in dirt as well as blood. The weighty shovel he carried as a weapon smacked the pistol out of Harker's hand and it spun across the stage. A second blow put Harker on his back and the man bore down on him, the shovel's handle pressed to Harker's throat.

The host clacked his browned, fractured teeth together, giggling. Harker gripped the handle and pushed. His full strength was no match for his attacker's and he felt his neck pressed ever tighter.

Lily's kick to the side of the host's head was enough to send the man sideways in a daze. Harker, the shovel still in his hands, rolled aside coughing.

"We might be able to get out by the stage door," cried Flemming.

Harker nodded. "Quickly! As soon as others realise there's a route—" The words had hardly passed his lips before the shell-like reflectors protecting the limelights began to be bent and torn off as people swarmed over them.

The floorboards of the auditorium were already littered with bodies and pools of blood. Terror and the darkness were forcing many to scramble helplessly, tripping over the dead and dying, rushing to find help, escape, cover. The vampyrs cut and hammered at whoever crossed their paths, opening veins and gouging skin. The horrible, gulped sounds of their drinking, as they leaped from wound to wound like bees at nectar, mingled with the wailing panic of those still on their feet.

A fat, sweating man, who'd lost track of his wife in the chaos, burrowed his way beneath one of the dining tables where the haphazard flop of corpses formed a concealing curtain. He sat balled inside his den, his eyes screwed up, unaware that he was the source of the whining screech he kept hearing, until fingers dug into his collar and he was dragged out. The sharp blade that slid at his throat kept his howls brief.

A small girl, crouched beside her slain parents, scooped blood from the spreading puddle beside her father and doused herself with it. She lay flat on her face, to appear dead, trying to stop her legs shaking and her breath heaving. A vampyr, its host a spry old crone, snatched her up and hopped away with her screaming over its shoulder.

Lily, familiar with the maze-like arrangements backstage, led Harker and Flemming to the stage door with yells and thudding footsteps clamouring at their heels. One of the dead policemen still lay there, an arm reaching out in vain.

The three of them tumbled into the muddy alley at the side of the building, instantly followed by a rush of escapees. From the street, they could hear the continuing panic inside the building as a distant roar. Through the glass-panelled entrance they saw the makeshift barricade being pulled at and dismantled by a team of hands. A few passers-by were slowing to see what this pandemonium was all about, but most – fearing more riots or radicalist violence – hurried about their business.

The summer sun had dipped from sight in the brick valleys of the streets. Its sinking threw aching lesions of colour across the high, torn clouds. The regular calls and rattles of the evening overpowered the terrible sounds coming from the music hall, but at any moment the reverse would suddenly and inevitably become true.

"We can't stop it," gasped Lily, the back of her hand trembling at her lips.

Harker looked vacantly at the shovel in his hands and at the entrance to Holmwood's which would soon be cleared of the barricade inside. "Only Dracul's incarceration can end this killing. And our one chance to achieve that has gone!"

Flemming hesitated before he spoke. "No, I. . . I think there may be another."

XXXIII

Theatregoers, diners, travellers, revellers, drinkers, mashers, gamblers, pickpockets, prostitutes, swells, toffs, dossers, all moved through the evening clog of vehicles and vendors which stretched from the top of Fleet Street to Trafalgar Square and the Haymarket. The dusty stink of street-filth, horses and sweat swirled in and out of more tempting aromas of cooking and perfumes. The industrial, gnat-soaked air was dyed an amber tint.

Carriages conducting attendees to tonight's Coming Out ball at Norfolk House made passing entertainment for the workers sitting in shop windows, downing their eggs and kidneys. The drivers of overflowing omnibuses called fares and "will a gen'neman go up top t'oblige a lady?" A crocodile line of straw-hatted clerks, pedalling their boneshakers, swerved around a pig being herded along with a stick. Its ragged and increasingly frustrated owner fought a losing battle to stop his prize porker rooting through the vegetable rot and bits of dead animal lining the gutter.

Suddenly, shouts and screams coming from the direction of Holmwood's Music Hall cut across the ambient noise. The screams grew in volume and echoed off nearby buildings. Passers-by, frowning and craning their necks, quickly accumulated on the pavement and spilled out into the road to be shouted at by cab drivers.

The human survivors from Holmwood's, all of them splattered in blood, came cannoning onto the Strand, colliding with the onlookers and knocking them over, running flat into stalls selling whelks and soup. Seeing the blood, others stopped in their tracks or moved away, holding onto whoever was with them, wondering what kind of accident could have caused this panic.

The vampyrs burst from the side street. Fanning out, running, springing, they brought down fresh prey. Their craving for blood, their burning need to split and spill, roared through every fibre of their hosts. Their fingers dug and pulled, their weapons cut, and they gulped a slippery taste of another's life, and another. Outward into the crowded street.

Terror-maddened faces and hurrying feet spread in all directions. Carts and hansoms bowled into each other as traffic began to halt and skew. A confusion of vehicles quickly blocked the road to both east and west. Fleeing people frantically clambered over cabs. Every horse, sensing unearthly danger, began to buck and whinny while their drivers fought in vain to control them.

Nerves froze in those further back, who caught glimpses of the vampyrs through the chaos: a blood-soaked face, tearing hands, a raised blade. More people, more traffic, jammed into the fringes of the thickening bedlam like a river overrunning its banks.

Where the Holmwood escapees had emerged onto the Strand, a horrible scatter of the dead was collecting. Prey was torn, briefly quaffed and thrown aside, the vampyrs' feeding frenzy urging them to keep on killing. Screaming throbbed the air, the shrieks of victims mingling with the dread of the crowd and the high-pitched delight of the vampyrs.

Blood covered ever-larger areas of the road. The few who'd been attacked and were still alive crawled on all fours, gasping for help, watching the holes in their bodies empty between their fingers until they finally succumbed.

The crush of people and vehicles became even tighter at the edges, a growing and hardening blood clot in the artery of the street. The vampyrs fed and the humans were trapped.

Taking cover in a shop doorway, Harker held the shovel to his chest, ready to beat back any host who approached. His two companions huddled at his shoulder.

He shook his head at Flemming. "No, Arthur, whether your idea works or not, you'll very probably end up dead too!"

"I've never taken chances," shuddered Flemming, his eyes darting around the horrors in front of them, "I must cease cowering."

"Meaning no offence," said Harker, "but I'm a good deal faster on my feet than you!"

"No!" said Flemming. "I am firm on this! These terrible events are my fault, and mine alone! And besides . . ."

He leaned into Harker and whispered something to him.

Harker looked at his old friend, profound emotions clouding his face. He nodded grimly. "I understand. Very well, Lily and I will go back into Holmwood's and find what we need."

"The store room should have it," said Lily, "or where they make the scenery. Is Ruby out here?"

Harker pointed across the Strand. Lily spotted her at the edge of the chaos, standing on top of a loaded cart, surveying the massacre.

Harker and Lily Murray hurried away while Flemming picked up a heavily carved walking stick that lay abandoned on the pavement. Brandishing it like a club, and turning anxiously in case of attack from behind, he hopped over a corpse and the pool of blood surrounding it, and ran at Ruby-Dracul in a nervous semi-rush.

Most of the vampyrs were deep into the crowd now, and the bloodstained people who crossed Flemming's path were too intent on escape to take any notice of him. With each fresh eruption in the noise all around him, his grip on his improvised cudgel momentarily slipped. Adding to the screams and yells were the sound of police whistles in the distance and the grinding crash of wheels piling.

He kept his sights on Ruby-Dracul, her white robe flowing in the evening breeze, criss-crossed with broad sprays of darkening red. She stood framed above the battle, the haemorrhage colours of the dying sky behind her, her expression a bloom of hateful pride. To Flemming, she looked like a painting by Delacroix, like Marianne the spirit of France spurring the revolution upon a heap of fallen comrades, but here a figurehead not of liberty but of evil, a herald of massed death and destruction, a silencing of mankind.

Clearing his fear-dried throat, he shouted at the top of his voice. "Ruby! Ruby Wester!"

Her attention snapped onto him. Three other vampyrs did the same, turning their heads in the crowd to see this bold, fresh meat. Ruby-Dracul held up a hand and they returned to their kills.

She grinned down at Flemming, and it seemed to him as if all the torments of the damned were behind her smile and her wide, glistening eyes.

"I-It was I!" he shouted. "It was I who ruined your plans! I killed Sir Edwin Gull!"

XXXIV

Flemming estimated the distance between him and Ruby-Dracul to be roughly the length of three two-seater cabs, around thirty to forty feet. He was taller than her by a dozen inches or so, he reckoned, with a correspondingly longer stride. Her feet were bare beneath her flowing robe, he saw, but whether that would be an advantage or a disadvantage to her, he couldn't tell. Slowly, he took a couple of steps back.

Ruby-Dracul stared at him uncomprehendingly, as if she couldn't quite believe what she was hearing. Her expression darkened into a lividness that Flemming felt as a trembling of his entire body. "*You*. . .?" she breathed. "He was murdered?"

"Y-Yes. I killed him. I stabbed him. With a letter opener. Through the heart. H-His colleagues are covering it up. That's why they came to get you!"

She scuttled down from the cart in sharp, snatching movements, like a beetle or a lizard skittering off a rock. "*You* killed him?"

"You know I was his employee. I-I came to hate him, resent his insults. More than anything, I hated the bargain he struck with you. It would have raised you both to obscene power. I had to end it!"

"And now you are so wracked with guilt you want to die at my hands?"

"I-I'm here to tell you you're finished! Listen, you hear the police whistles? The army will come too! You can't win. No matter how savage you are. Thousands of us, against every one of you!"

Ruby-Dracul moved forward and Flemming moved back, almost stumbling over his own feet. "You think so?" she hissed, fixing him with a baleful glare. "When your frail bodies are no more than a speck in the cosmic eye? You robbed me of my desires, did you? Then I will rob you of yours!"

Flemming yelped like a wounded dog as he dropped the walking stick in terror, spun on his heels and ran. Ruby-Dracul ran after him, relishing his fear, anticipating the taste of his blood.

He headed directly for the side street where Holmwood's stood. No! Wait, was this street the right one? He could barely think straight. Yes, this street! Faster, for God's sake!

Intense fright was all that was keeping him upright and moving. His thin limbs wheeled like a tumbler's on the music hall stage. Gasps of effort and fear pounded through his head.

He flashed a look over his shoulder. The vampyr was barely twenty feet behind him. Ruby-Dracul's face was set in a mask of eager venom. She ran with her robe billowing behind her, her feet splashing through puddles of blood, vaulting over the dead, getting closer and closer to Flemming's coat tails.

He almost fell into the gutter, nearly tripping on the trailing reins of a hansom left driverless and meandering in the middle of the road. Holmwood's was only yards ahead of him now, but the drums of the vampyr's footsteps were as fast as his heartbeat.

His lungs burned and his legs felt like lead. He jumped up the broad, flat steps outside the entrance to the music hall and shot past the open doors.

Nobody was left alive in the cavernous foyer. A scatter of opened bodies lay twisted on the floor and staircase. The air was cooler in here but ripe with the acrid, metallic smell of death. Flemming flew at breakneck speed past the stairs and made for the archway into the auditorium.

He could hear Ruby-Dracul's breath now. Less than ten feet behind him. He let out a long, wailing yell as he plunged into the unlit gloom.

The chairs and benches on which the audience had sat were either overturned or shoved aside, a silent and mocking memorial to terror. Bent and broken, most of the lights at the front of the stage had gone out, but the heat from one still alight, pressed down so that it glowed in a crooked halo, had blistered the boards beneath it and fire was beginning to spread. Where patches of blood hadn't soaked into the floor, they glittered in the light of the flames.

On the stage, exactly as it had been abandoned after Ruby-Dracul's act, was the coffin. Flemming dashed straight for it, shaking fit to collapse, his eyes darting around the darkness. Nearly there! Nearly at the box! Nearly got her to the right spot!

He was an arm's length from the stage when Ruby-Dracul's hands suddenly clamped onto his shoulders. He toppled headlong onto his face, up against the base of the stage's deep apron. Crying out, he squirmed violently to ward off the vampyr.

Ruby-Dracul grabbed the back of his coat and spun him over. He quailed at the sight of her leering down at him, at the shape of her mouth, her dark hair aglow in the burning limelight from directly above them. She descended towards his sweating skin, her jaw working up and down. He mewled helplessly, his lips shuddering.

She lunged but was suddenly hauled back with a sharp jerk. A loop of rope, procured from the backstage storeroom, was around her waist and arms before she had time to react. From behind, Harker pulled her tightly to him. She wriggled madly, emitting a blood-curdling screech. Harker held on, one arm gripped around her while the other played out more rope.

"Flemming! I can't hold her! Hurry, man!"

Flemming had staggered to his feet and now snatched up the free end of the rope. Dashing the moisture from his face with the back of his hand, he threw two more loops around Ruby-Dracul and pulled hard.

"Take her feet!" grunted Harker, straining to keep her still. "Quick!" The seconds ticked like the dolorous ringing of a death knell. If they couldn't get Ruby into the coffin before Dracul could escape her, all would be lost.

Flemming reached down, but Ruby-Dracul's knee

sprung up and hit the underside of his chin with a loud crack. He staggered back with a howl of agony.

Harker shook his head, to clear his mind of the sudden conviction that he was standing on a cliff edge, that he was drowning in the sea, that he was struggling to trap a vampyr. "I see through your defences," he snarled.

He scooped Ruby-Dracul up, his legs and back twisting painfully as he fought to keep his balance. She hissed and thrashed, pulled an arm free and began to claw at his face, drawing blood. He redoubled his grip, stepped up onto a chair with a grunt, then up onto a table and onto the stage. His strength failing, he dumped her down into the coffin. Beside it lay the lid, along with a scenery maker's claw hammer and an old tin full of nails.

Flemming was clambering up onto the stage too, shielding his face from the heat of the growing flames. Lily ran from the wings. "I've locked the stage door," she gasped.

Harker and Flemming were already lifting the coffin lid, but with one sudden movement, Ruby-Dracul sat up, snatched the hammer and hurled it into Harker's face. It cut along his cheekbone and ear, and he reeled.

She was out of the coffin in an instant. The shovel Harker had been wielding lay close to the limelights. She dived for it at the same moment as Flemming and got to it first. Its flat, rusty blade cut the air an inch from Flemming's nose. Harker, dazed, barely dodged a second swing. Ruby-Dracul's expression began to pull into a tortured rictus.

Lily, moving as swiftly and quietly as the streets had taught her, scooped up Harker's pistol from where his earlier grapple with a vampyr had sent it spinning. Her face grim, she strode purposefully across the stage and placed the gun to the side of Ruby-Dracul's head.

The sudden shot reverberated around the auditorium. Blood and tissue flowed along Ruby's shoulder. The shovel dropped from her hands, and the pupils of her large eyes slowly rose until they were out of sight. For a moment there was stillness, then her body dropped off the stage and landed with a heavy thud on the floor.

"We have seconds, at best, before the vampyr reanimates her as it did the bookseller!" cried Harker. "Lily, retrieve that wretched hammer!" Gauging that an inert cadaver would take too long to drag back up to the coffin, and remembering the ancient lore he'd studied, he grabbed the shovel and jumped down beside Ruby's body.

Flemming felt his heart fluttering like a trapped bird. Had he seen. . .? He *had* seen, out of the corner of his eye, something and nothing, an icy impression of a shadow that was not a shadow. He blinked it away. A prickly sensation curled around his ankle, his calf, his knee.

Harker quickly dried his palms on his sleeves and raised the shovel above his head with both hands, blade down. Lily shut her streaming eyes, lips pressed into a straight line and fists held to her chest.

The shovel hacked deep into Ruby's neck with an ugly crunch of bone and sinew. When it came down again, her head detached and rolled to one side. Without hesitating, Harker picked up the head by its hair. It dripped and sagged. He slung it, and the head bumped into the coffin, shedding droplets of blood as it spun. Lily picked up the lid.

"Flemming!" cried Harker, scrambling back onto the stage. "Nails!. . . Flemming?"

Flemming was crouched with his long fingers quivering at the sides of his head, his eyes fit to burst from his skull. He could feel it! Worming, biting! Claiming him for itself!

Harker's voice was a dying sigh. "Dear God, no. Arthur, no."

Slowly, Flemming straightened. "Going to. . .! It's. . .! I can't stop it! *I can't stop it!*"

His features seemed to twist.

He saw the severed head in the coffin and flung himself on top of it with a scream.

Lily slammed the lid down. The split second when her eyes met Harker's was an aeon of helpless anguish.

Nails were hammered rapidly, steadily. Harker never looked up from his work. Flemming-Dracul stirred inside, flexing his new joints and muscles, gaining control, growling.

"He'll force his way out soon," said Harker. "We must go."

Lily placed the shovel on top of the coffin and together they manoeuvred it off the stage. With one of them at each end, they hurried the coffin out of the auditorium, through the foyer and out into the teeming streets.

"The other vampyrs will know?" said Lily.

"We must keep our distance, in case they try to break open the coffin. It depends which is stronger in them, the instinct for self-preservation or the desire to defend one of their own."

They soon had their answer. A weirdly eerie scene of carnage met them on the Strand, dead strewn along the street, blood trickling in the gutters, spattered survivors clasping at the wounded. A tangled obstruction of vehicles snaked east and west almost as far as the eye could see, as if giant hands had bunched and shunted them. Throughout the street and beyond, the screaming that split the air had subsided into a cacophony of angry shouts and cries of pain. Policemen fretted around the edges, directing stretcher bearers, blowing whistles, steadying horses. Dozens of people, hundreds, slunk in corners or sat on the pavements, too shocked and confused to move, while others kept running, aimlessly searching.

The vampyrs' frenzy had ended abruptly, their preternatural senses bristling like the hackles of a hyena, the moment the coffin lid had slammed on the one who'd led them here, the one who'd called them to attack. They stooped and looked up, as if afraid of the rapidly darkening sky, their hands and mouths still dripping blood. They grew silent except for a low, mumbling jitter. Each host, old or young, man or woman, was steeled for instant fight or flight, listening to the fearful tremors shimmering along filaments of the psychic cobweb.

Too frightened to turn away, many in the crowd formed wide empty circles around the vampyrs, jostling and shaking, wary flies surrounding huge, malignant spiders. Police hovered beside them like waxwork studies in uncertainty and fright.

Through the noise and confusion, Harker carried the broader end of the coffin, facing forward to navigate while Lily took three steps to every one of his. She glanced over at the nearest vampyr host. "It seems they're selfish creatures after all," she said.

He followed her gaze but didn't reply. The sight of hosts, suddenly held between attack and retreat, was a torturous reminder of what failure to entomb Dracul would mean, both to the city and to himself. He felt his courage faltering with every step.

The coffin shifted. Flemming-Dracul scratched frantically at the inside of the lid, his voice plaintive and wheedling. "Take pity upon me! My loyal friends, my comrades-in-arms! Fear not, I have forced the fiend to leave my body! I have it here, wrapped tight in my handkerchief! It cannot escape, of that I'm sure!"

Harker screwed up his face. "Shut up!" he barked. He commanded himself to keep walking.

They were passing St Mary's, with the tiered spire of St Clement Danes up ahead. Their way was momentarily blocked by a knot of fleeing people which dispersed just as quickly. In the chaos, nobody questioned the sight of the coffin's jerky progress.

Flemming-Dracul began to kick and batter. "Release me!" he bellowed. "Release me or die!" Fists pounded at the coffin's sides. It almost slipped from Lily's grasp. "I will break free! I will rip out your beating heart, *Captain* Harker! You'll be as dead as your beloved Violet! Dead! Dead!"

The coffin lurched violently with every kick. Suddenly there was a cracking sound. Harker whipped around. "Lily, run ahead! Find what's suitable, as we discussed, fast as you can!"

She nodded, took the shovel, and pushed her way past

an overturned potato stall, its hot coals spilled across the street. Harker took a firm grip on the coffin with one hand and, his other hand held out for balance and his teeth gritted, dragged it at a stooping run.

The bucking motion of the coffin continued, each kick and thump making Harker wince with anxiety. The vampyr roared, louder than the stuttering scrape of the coffin's lower edge against the cobbled road. "Valentine Harker! Your blood shall spill! Your blood will be mine! Your flesh will be spat into the four winds!"

Harker's back was breaking and his knees buckling as he dragged the coffin past the church of St Clement Danes and onto the building site at the top end of the Strand. Neither Gull's workers nor the site's watchmen were anywhere in sight, taking advantage of their boss's absence or scattered by the bedlam further down the street.

The coffin was much harder to drag on loose soil. Harker grunted as he hauled it through the mud, bumping and slipping around tall stacks of timber tied under canvas. Flemming-Dracul's relentless pounding threatened to split the lid at any moment.

Up ahead, Lily signalled from an open patch of ground. Harker redoubled his pace, his limbs straining with effort, his clothes stained with earth and sweat.

Lily stood beside a roughly cut hole in the ground, one of the dozen deep, narrow shafts Gull's men had dug around the site to gauge the level of the water table. "Perfect!" gasped Harker, nodding. "Twenty feet or more. Wide enough. Help me lift it!"

He dropped the wider section of the coffin over the lip of the hole. Together they raised the other end.

"*Harker*! HARKER! Crawl back into your bottle of pain! You will never escape your ghosts!"

As they lifted it level with their shoulders, it began to slide against the lip. With a heave, they pushed it fully upright and it dropped out of sight.

The vampyr shrieked, a blood-freezing howl of rage. The coffin fell, knocking against the uneven sides of the shaft, until it slapped into the soft, soaking mud at the bottom.

Harker was already at work with the shovel, hurriedly flinging spadefuls down the hole. He cut into the soil at an inexorable rate, his head down, his face caustic and reddening, feeling the fierce sting of exertion in his lungs and arms. He dug with anger, savagely and mechanically burying the coffin under a steadily heavier, steadily thicker weight of compacted earth.

Daylight was gone. London's summer night miasma was beginning to suspire darkly, breathing itself over the streets into a gummy ochre blanket.

Harker stamped his worn, grubby boots over the filled hole many times before he threw the shovel aside and sunk back. Lily, sick with fatigue and sadness, gathered him in her arms and he clung tightly to her, trembling.

From where they sat, all the disturbance back past the churches was only visible as a stream of people rushing back and forth along Picket Street, but the sounds of pain and fear were as distinct as ever, reverberating between the buildings. The dominant sound now was the helpless, almost pitiful keening of vampyr hosts. The creatures inside them, the phantoms that were not phantoms, were tearing themselves free, leaving their hosts to die and melting into the ethereal otherness.

The host bodies fell in the street, one by one. Over the low skyline of the city, a column of black smoke began to curl, as Holmwood's Music Hall began to blaze.

XXXV

In the absolute and merciless darkness, Flemming-Dracul begged for death.

Vertical, facing down, his head was pressed hard to one side by the weight of his own body. Every breath and every futile movement felt stifled and leaden. He was slim enough to move his arms with relative freedom, but his knees could rise no more than a few inches before meeting the coffin's lid. His hands hurt from slamming at the sides. They were grazed and tender, and at first he thought they were the source of the sharp smell of blood in his nostrils, until he remembered Ruby Wester's severed head, wedged against his hip. He touched it tentatively. Hair, skin, stickiness.

Claustrophobia suddenly stung him like a scorpion. His mouth gasping, his body trembling, his fingernails scratching, he let out a long, trailing sob of desperation and hopelessness.

No light! Utter black! I have no use for eyes! Can't turn, can't stand, can't walk, can't–

–get out!

The poison of the tomb.

He felt the vampyr squirm and mutter inside him. He

felt it burrow through his mind, felt its hatred. It had recoiled in high dudgeon when the coffin hit the bottom of the shaft, and stayed quiet while every other second brought the rumble of descending earth, but now it reasserted itself and Flemming-Dracul laughed, so loud in the tight space around him that his ears rang.

We shall pass our time together amiably, you and I, sharing memories, and making new ones for my amusement through the waiting.

He sensed the thickness of the wood encasing him, the solidity of it, the tightness – despite all his efforts – of its construction. He sensed the earth. Above, beside, beneath. Compacted. Squeezed. Deep. Down deep. Its heaviness and its moisture.

Oh God, dear God in Heaven, release me from life. I repent my sins, I am humble in your mercy, please, oh please dear God.

Our time together is short, but I will extend it, all I can.

The vampyr steadied his heartbeat and quelled the shaking in his muscles. His fingers journeyed through the soft comfort of Ruby's hair.

He sensed the voices of the undead. Distant and whispering. *Unsafe here*, they shivered, *unsafe, unsafe, the other is trapped, the caller, the promiser. Return, whence.* He sensed the vampyrs worming back into the netherworld, discouraged and alarmed.

Cowardly scum. We are alone now.

Alone, forever. In the grave.

A grave unmarked and lost.

You thought you valued solitude?

He remembered the first time he'd visited the music hall, and the last. He remembered cruel words to an old friend. He held Ruby's head to his chest.

He remembered lives beyond number; days and nights and months and years and centuries; thirst, sustenance, full bellies; the faces of his prey; hunting them, hurting them, consuming them; hiding in the dark and in plain sight; laughing at his victims' disbelief, fooling the stupid and the gullible; always, the flow and gush and spray of blood.

In the pitiless darkness, he experienced every dying scream, every murder, an endless march of death. He remembered how good it felt to kill.

Dracul delighted in each old spill of blood, and in the fresh terrors of a helpless host. Such abundance! The legacy of a purposeful and successful existence.

Flemming lived for many hours, his body sustained by the vampyr, his mind clawing to retain the last pieces of himself and the details of his own fading life. His last conscious thought was for his ailing aunt in Chiswick. She would be wondering where he'd got to.

XXXVI

Lymebeech, Dorset, Summer 1870

Their lives were modest, but happy. They had married in the autumn of 1868 and moved to the coast in early '69. Valentine and Lily Harker tended the smallholding next to their cottage, growing vegetables and keeping chickens; neither of them had the faintest inkling how to farm, but they learned quickly and were soon a fixture at the Lymebeech market.

Lily's young son Jack spent his hours, when not at school, exploring the nearby beaches and studying the ancient life preserved in the limestone cliffs and rockfalls. In fine weather, the three of them would picnic on the cliff tops, looking out at the changing colours of the sea, content in each other's company.

They didn't regret leaving London. A commission of inquiry into events at Holmwood's was set up, but never issued any report. As if to prove Lady Gull's dictum about truth, rumours rattled through the press and through gossipy conversations in fashionable eateries until the dangers of escaped lunatics were at the heart of the firmly established facts. The death of Sir Edwin Gull resulted in parliamentary demands for a tightening of food hygiene standards, and his contract for the Royal Courts of Justice reverted to his rival George Edmund Street. The coffin, unrecorded and undisturbed, was soon built over. Those in the government who'd tried to detain Ruby-Dracul quietly made other plans.

Captain Harker found himself with new professional responsibilities as well as a new family. For a while, he was troubled by what Arthur Flemming had whispered to him amid the noise on the Strand, as disaster had unfolded around them. The words had struck him as chilling, even unfair, until his revived outlook made them clear, and his marriage gave them a focus.

"Your knowledge and experience are too valuable to risk. You are needed. To stand guard, now and in the future. Without you, Dracul's arrival in London would have gone completely undetected. Be glad, I say, for your years of regrets and griefs, for they may save us all! Give proper credit to your past distractions. I am dispensable, but now you are not!"

Harker spent days revisiting the mass of research he'd compiled into vampyrs and similar phenomena. It finally occurred to him that, no matter what his lonely motives had been for assembling all this information, Flemming was right to urge a wider use for it. There might be a dozen similar archives, in other places, to which it could be added. Or there might be fresh data that would make an invaluable addition to his own.

His connections in the army and through the War Office rapidly put him at the centre of an informal, unofficial network. Enquiries led him along chains of correspondents until he was in contact with a variety of academics, local historians, curators, amateur sleuths, students, even a few reporters and minor administrators, between them covering five continents, all of whom had one reason or another to keep open minds on the subject of the supernatural. Although, because of the distances separating them, Harker rarely met with any members of this network, they continuously swapped information and ideas.

They kept a watching brief. Evidence would mount, in time.

Meanwhile, life in Lymebeech plodded in its usual, seasonal rhythm. The Harkers' second summer surrounded by green fields and rocky coastlines was wetter than usual. The town fete in late June was washed out, and the chickens kept sulkily to their coops.

There were thunderstorms in July. Huge black clouds wheeled through the skies, lit from behind by startling flashes, and the sea boiled grey and cool. The crashing foam was hardly audible inside the Harkers' cottage, and drowned completely by the crackle and spit of the fireplace.

Harker sank into his chair, reading books and writing letters, his feet extended in front of the fire to toast away the dampness of the weather. Lily sat beside him, her skill with a needle and thread keeping her fingers busy, and her considerable head for business keeping her thoughts on the future.

Jack had a growing collection of fossils in his room. He was never happier than when scouting along the shore, where the Blue Lias broke cover from the landscape, with a trowel slung from his belt. He liked wet weather because it hastened the fall of any teetering slides in the nearby faces of mudstone. He'd be able to scramble around the broken slabs, gathering whatever he could before the tide took its share.

The Ammonites were his favourite, curling and ridged like strange worms. It constantly filled him with awe to think that these stones, these peculiar and alien creatures, so mysteriously old, were now here, in his care. The largest he'd found was almost a foot across and took pride of place on his shelf, propped up in front of an old issue of *All the Year Round* Mr Valentine had bought him, for the article about Mary Anning. When he grew up, he would be Dorset's second famous fossil hunter!

His memories of London were becoming hazy, the frayed cuffs of a shirt, but the horrors he'd witnessed never left him. Sometimes they'd resurface in his dreams, vividly, as if he'd been dragged back to witness them all over again. He didn't tell anyone about these nightmares, particularly not his mother or Mr Valentine. He was ten years old now, he told himself, and was practically a grown-up. He'd never get to be Dorset's second famous fossil hunter by being a silly crybaby!

But sometimes the dreams were so bad that he'd wake in the middle of the night, convinced that something was coming to get him. Sometimes he thought he could see, deep in the darkness, a shape that was not a shape, and hear the distant muttering of discordant voices.

AUTHOR'S NOTE

This is a story about greed. Where is the dividing line between what's done to survive and what's done merely to take from others? Is self-interest always selfish? Should the needs of the many, to coin a phrase, outweigh the needs of the few?

It's set where it is because, while researching the mid-Victorian period, I became fascinated by accounts of life in the area of London between Trafalgar Square and St Paul's cathedral: Fleet Street, the Strand and all the streets that surrounded them were 24-hour, 7-days-a-week places like no other, jam-packed day and night, home to every cultural, social and commercial activity imaginable. Almost literally, all human life was here. The perfect location, I thought, for a story about avarice in all its forms.

By the way, the Society for the Suppression of Vice, to which Lady Gull belongs, was a real organisation which campaigned against booksellers, like Herbert Maurice, who sold porn as a lucrative sideline. The Adelphi Arches existed too, and must have been an extraordinary sight, although almost nothing of them remains today. Similarly, the site on which the Royal

Courts of Justice now stands was a vagrants' camping ground for years until George Edmund Street began construction, although whether there's something nasty buried underneath it, I really couldn't say.

Milton Keynes UK
Ingram Content Group UK Ltd.
UKHW020315230924
448641UK00005B/142